DEFECTIVE

Kayla Howarth

DEDICATION

For Eli

ACKNOWLEDGMENTS

Sarah. I kinda don't like you anymore. And ... I stole your red pen. Good luck trying to find it.

To all of my betas, thanks for your feedback and advice. Patrick, Michelle B, Michelle L, and Kimberly, Theresa, you're all awesome.

The usual suspects: the many friends and family who have supported me throughout this whole adventure.

To my husband, I know this book pushed our relationship to the limits with how much time I had to put into it. Thank you for understanding and only nagging me a little bit. Okay, maybe you nagged me a lot, but I probably deserved it. Maybe.

PRAISE FOR THE INSTITUE SERIES

Thanks for the great ride. I loved every minute of this series. Looking forward to reading more of this author's work. 5 out of 5 shiny stars!—Michelle Bryan, author of Strain of Resistance and The New Bloods Trilogy.

If you haven't read the series yet, I strongly suggest you start. The author is very talented, and I look forward to her future works—Kimberly Readnour, author of The Mystical Encounters Series.

Allira is a strong, courageous girl that anyone can look up to. I was drawn into the original storyline, realistic characters, and suspenseful plot—Bethany Wicker, author of the Aluna Series.

Love, love, love this series!!! It is so awesome to read about all the different super abilities and how they all work together. Definitely one of my favorite set of books I've ever read!—Amazon Customer.

CHAPTER ONE

A loud thump against the clinic doors reverberates through me. I snap my head up from the reception desk as someone slumps against the left door, blood smearing across the glass. Scrambling to get outside, I grab gloves off the counter on the way out and put them on. The bright sun temporarily blinds me as I swing the right door open and look down at the girl shivering and bleeding on the ground.

"Kenna, I'll need a hand here!" I yell. "I need a gurney, now!"

Kneeling down in front of the girl, I check over her body to pinpoint where the blood is coming from. It's everywhere. Was she dumped here by someone? Or did she make it here on her own?

I find the source of her bleeding, a long gash in her abdomen. Her hand is clutching at her stomach. All of my strength is needed to apply as much pressure as I can to her wound. I glance up at her face and immediately have to look away so my brain doesn't memorise the terrified look in her eyes. I've learnt it's best not to look directly at their faces anymore.

1

She's pale—too pale—her lip is shivering, and her hair is wet with sweat. She's in shock, and her body is shutting down.

Aunt Kenna and a relief nurse from the hospital are ready with the gurney. They help lift the girl while I keep pressure on her stomach.

"Allira! You need to apply more pressure," Aunt Kenna yells at me. She's not being mean; even if it comes out that way, she's just instructing me on how to save this girl's life.

Climbing onto the gurney next to the patient, I push my hands harder into the side of her abdomen, trying to stop any more blood from escaping. Any more pressure and I fear I'll put my hand right through her. Aunt Kenna and the nurse wheel us into the trauma room of the clinic.

Looking down at the scared girl under me but still making sure I avoid eye contact, I wonder if we're doing more damage than good. She's been stabbed—most likely by someone who found out she's Defective. Surely, the hospital wouldn't be able to turn her away and keep her waiting. She's on the verge of bleeding out right in front of me. We aren't exactly equipped here to handle these things. We can, but it's a struggle. I just think the hospital should deal with situations like this.

When Aunt Kenna first pitched the idea of a Defective clinic, we all thought it was a brilliant idea. Yes, Defective people are entitled to get treated at any other clinic or hospital, and yes, they're meant to receive the same level of care as any normal person. The truth is, though, they don't. They're put to the back of the line, the bottom of the list. "Higher priority" injuries or illnesses tend to arrive, pushing the treatment time back further and further. They're given mediocre care—doctors prescribing medications without tests and not following up on results. Aunt Kenna took it upon herself to fix that.

"We'll do everything we can to help you, okay, sweetheart?" I try to sound reassuring. Aunt Kenna said whenever in doubt, just get the patient talking and try to distract them from what's going on around them.

I stopped asking their names about five months ago. It didn't take me long to learn that knowing their names only makes it harder. If I don't put a name to their face, I don't have to relive it when I fill in the paperwork later. It's easier to move on if the outcome is less than ideal. It seems these days there's about a fifty-fifty chance of that happening.

The nurse puts a cannula in the patient's arm as my muscles begin to ache. Sweat drips off my brow, but I remain still, reminding myself I'm doing the most important bit—preventing her from bleeding out.

"Where's Vic?" Aunt Kenna asks as she gloves up and puts her surgical mask on. "We need him!"

Vic is the other doctor who works here. He lives rent-free in the apartment above the clinic, so while he's only scheduled for the four opposing shifts to Kenna, he's on call twenty-four hours a day for situations like this one. It's quite common for him to be here when it's not his shift.

We're going to have to put the patient under. There's no way we could give her a local and stitch her up considering I can feel her insides trying to make their way to the outside. The stab wound is too big.

Aunt Kenna adds monitoring pads to the patient's chest and an oximeter to her finger to monitor her pulse. Vic comes through the door a couple of minutes after the nurse calls for him, gloved up and ready to get to work. He's an older gentleman, about mid-to-late forties, but he looks fit and strong for his age, his muscles apparent through the scrubs he always wears. He's a man of few words, which means he and I get along perfectly. I guess he's learnt that when working with mostly women, it's wise to keep his mouth shut—about everything.

Once the patient is under, Aunt Kenna steps up next to me. "Okay, Lia, try to focus. Can you feel where the blood is coming from?"

I give her a quizzical look. *Feel where the blood is coming from? Is this a trick question?* "I'm guessing from her abdomen is the incorrect answer here?"

Aunt Kenna's mouth is hidden because of her surgical mask, but I know she's smiling, her eyes wrinkling around the edges.

"Is it coming from above her stomach, closer to her lungs and heart? Maybe her liver? Or lower, like the intestines and bowel?"

I look down at my hands. "To be honest, I can't feel where it's coming from. There's just a lot of pressure under my hands trying to get out."

Aunt Kenna's brow furrows. That's not a good sign. I've seen that look before, and it rarely ends well. "Okay, we'll have to move quickly. Nurse, you want to help with this one?" she asks.

Neither of us knows this nurse's name; she's just a fill-in from the hospital. When we're short-staffed, we call on temps to come in and work, and they're usually a different person every time.

"I can do that," the nurse replies, and I'm kind of relieved. I'm more suited to the less traumatic and low-risk cases. I can clean wounds, cast broken bones, draw blood, and even stitch someone up. This is a big step up for a girl who used to feel faint at the sight of a needle. But preventing someone from bleeding out? I feel as if I'm cursed in that department, starting when Chad bled out in my arms eighteen months ago. I've seen many deaths since then, but none has—or even could—hurt as much as his.

The patient's heart rate plummets to an alarmingly slow rate.

"Nurse, she needs two litres of saline. Lia, pull your hands away, now," Aunt Kenna instructs. I remove my hands, move off the gurney as fast as possible, and take a step back. Aunt Kenna and Vic work frantically to find the main source of bleeding. There's nothing for me to do but stand and watch as they begin to lose the fight. "There's too much. There's just too much," Aunt Kenna mutters to herself.

That's when I know. We've lost another one.

* * *

"It's getting worse," I say.

"What is?" Aunt Kenna asks, putting her arm around me.

It's been a few hours since losing the patient, and it's been a relatively quiet afternoon since then. I've been sitting at the reception desk, just thinking about what we're actually accomplishing here.

"The attacks. They're becoming more frequent, more violent. This time it was in broad daylight," I say, my voice low and quiet.

"That's why we're needed now more than ever. What would've happened if that girl was stabbed when we weren't open?"

"The same thing that happened anyway. She died. We didn't help her."

"We tried, Lia," she says in a soft, sympathetic tone. "We can't save everyone. She was already too far gone when she came in here. I don't even think the hospital could've done anything to save her."

"It still feels crummy." Crummy isn't exactly the word I was thinking, but I don't like to curse in front of Aunt Kenna.

"I know," she replies, kissing me on the side of my head. "I know it does."

Excusing myself, I go out the back to the empty treatment room to try to calm myself down.

Vic walks in and stalls as soon as he sees me. I assume my face is all blotchy and red from trying to ward off the tears.

"You couldn't have done anything different," he says sternly.

I know he's trying to help, but I can tell how awkward it is for him to be talking to me at all. "I know. Aunt Kenna just gave me this speech."

"She was practically gone when she got here," he says.

I let out a little laugh between the sniffles. "Yeah. She said that too. I'm okay, Vic. I'll get over it."

"It will get easier," he says, walking over and putting a hand on my shoulder. "You're still relatively new to this, and it may not seem like it now, but it will. It'll get easier." He walks away before I get the chance to respond.

Will it get easier? Do I even want it to? I'm not sure I want to be so desensitised to death that it doesn't affect me anymore. Then again, I'd love to not feel so guilty all the time.

* * *

Entering my apartment building, dazed and exhausted, I really just want to shower and go to bed. Reaching the elevator, I press the button and rest my head against the wall, waiting for that tiny dinging sound to let me know my ride has arrived. I close my eyes for a brief minute, forcing myself to stand up straight when I hear it.

One of the guys from the building security team steps off

when the doors open. I've lived here for six months but I always forget this guy's name. Roger, maybe?

"Hello, Miss Daniels, Mr. James has been asking for you," he says, holding the elevator door open for me.

"Well, when he calls back, can you please tell him that Paxton James is not my keeper?" I force a smile to try to pass it off as if I'm joking, but a part of me is completely serious.

"You can tell him yourself. He arrived home a few hours ago."

"He's home?" My eyes widen. "He wasn't meant to come home until Wednesday." As soon as I say it, I realise. "Oh crap. It's Wednesday, isn't it?"

Roger just smirks, giving me my answer. He removes his arm from the elevator and nods goodbye before walking off. The doors begin to close as I swipe my key and press the "P" button. The elevator starts its ascent to the very top of the building.

When the elevator doors reopen to the living room of my apartment, I find Paxton with a displeased expression across his face. "You forgot, didn't you?" he asks.

"I missed you too! What kind of greeting is that after not seeing me for a week?"

Paxton walks up to me and gives me a brief hug and kiss on the cheek. "Nice try at diverting this, but I know you forgot. I've been trying to call you all day to remind you."

My shoulders slump forwards. "Okay. I admit it. I forgot about tonight, okay? It's been a hectic week at the clinic."

"Hmm?" he asks with no real interest. It's clear he doesn't actually want to hear how my week was.

"I'll be an hour, tops," I say, hurrying to my bedroom to get ready for tonight's political event. *So much for going to bed.*

After a quick, scalding hot shower, I find myself staring at my scars in the mirror. One of them is a white circle on my shoulder that reminds me of the worst day of my life, and the other is a black backwards S shape just on the inner side of my right elbow. I can still feel the pain of the tracker going in, and I can still see the mark as it appeared moments later. It's my reminder that we still aren't truly free.

Tate was right when he said we'd have to face an entirely new set of struggles. When we set ourselves free, our fight had only just begun. We won the right to live on the outside, but that doesn't mean we won the right to be treated fairly.

Paxton bent the rules and found loopholes in the law in order to set us free. Every Defective person now has just as much right to get jobs and work, pay taxes, vote, and be married.

The government, in retaliation, passed new laws. They force us to attend monthly counselling and monitoring sessions at the Institute. I think these are more for the general public's peace of mind—that we're still under control—rather than to actually help us. The use of abilities in public is forbidden, and any offenders are imprisoned in a mainstream prison—the type of prison that makes the Institute look like a nice vacation spot. Then there's the clincher: all-round, twenty-four hour tracking surveillance—and not the cheap Institute agent trackers either but the injectable, scar-inducing trackers.

I often look at the mark on my arm and wonder if the S shape was caused by the insertion of the tracker—like a side effect from the harsh needle used to insert it—or if they purposefully added ink or something to it so it would leave a permanent mark and we'd forever be identifiable. It's a dark bluish black and almost looks like a bruise, but it has a distinct shape and doesn't go away, like a tattoo. There's no significance to the shape. In fact, it almost looks like an incomplete infinity symbol more than an S. Maybe that's what they were going for, letting the world know we're incomplete. Sometimes I want to give the government the benefit of the doubt, but then I berate myself for that kind of naiveté. Of course, they did it so we could be easily targeted.

I force my eyes away from my arm and get started on my makeup, smiling at my reflection when I'm done. Ebb would be proud. Months of these types of events have made me pretty skilful with a makeup brush. I needed Ebb's help the first few times, but I'm a fast learner, and it wasn't long before I could do it myself. Curling and styling my hair, I pin it to one side, letting it fall over my collarbone. Then I add my jewellery—chunky, sparkly earrings and matching bracelet.

Looking at the girl standing before me in the mirror, I barely recognise her as the tomboy farm girl she once was. I try to assure myself she's still in there somewhere, even if right now I'm convinced that girl is long gone.

A package sits on my bed when I come out of the bathroom. Every time I accompany Paxton to one of these benefit things, he buys me a new dress. I always insist that I could wear something he's already given me, but he insists that the girlfriend of a presidential candidate can't be seen in public wearing the same thing twice.

When he says this, I like to remind him that I'm *not* his girlfriend, even if the media thinks differently, and that a repeat outfit would not be the end of the world.

Lifting the lid off the package in front of me, I freeze the moment I see the dress. It's deep emerald green—the dress I was wearing when he proposed to me in my vision eighteen months ago. I jump back from the bed as if the dress was a vicious animal preparing to attack. Standing by my bed in only my underwear, I just stare at the dress as it mocks me.

I've lived with Paxton for just over six months. He and his daughter, Nuka, have one end of the penthouse apartment, and I have the other. There's nothing romantic going on between me and Paxton and there never has been. We're friends, we respect each other, and I definitely do not see him as anything more than that.

After Chad died and we were released from the Institute, I was living with my parents. Things got a little awkward not long after my baby brother came along.

Paxton and I made a deal—I attend these stupid publicity events with him as his date, and I get a place to live rent-free.

My eyes are glued to the dress. When Paxton first offered me a room in his apartment, I almost said no. I was so determined not to let my vision come true, but I didn't have much of a choice. I needed to get away from my parents. Part of me was also hoping that moving in with Paxton would help me forget about Chad. If I fell in love unintentionally, it would make my thoughts of him go away. That was the theory anyway. Of course, it didn't happen that way, and I still think about Chad constantly.

11

Still determined to keep my vision just that—a vision and not reality—I go to my closet. In my messed-up way, I think if I wear a different dress, he won't propose.

Why does he want to propose anyway? Why now? Does he want to take that step into relationship territory? I'm not ready for that. I don't think I'll ever be ready for that—with anyone, not just Paxton. And why marriage? Shouldn't we at least go on a proper date first? I shake my head at the idea. I don't think I'm even ready for *that* yet.

It's been eighteen months since losing Chad, and I have no desire to get my heart broken ever again. Saying I was a mess for the first twelve months would be an understatement. I barely even remember much from that time—just that I was a walking zombie who kept to myself and alienated everyone close to me. I stayed at home every day, ate myself into a walking blob of junk food, and was an all-round bitch.

When Aunt Kenna brought up her plans for the clinic, it was the first time I actually showed an interest in anything. Everyone was shocked when I put my hand up to help her. I not only saw it as a way to give back, but I also saw it as a way to escape my pain.

From there I worked out that if I kept busy, I wouldn't have time to think about Chad, and when I didn't think about him, I could carry myself in an adult and normal manner the majority of the time. Since then, I've mended some of the relationships I crapped all over during my grief, but not all could be righted.

Going to my closet, I pull out a strapless, pale pink tulle ball gown, which was one of the first dresses Paxton ever bought me. Surely, he won't remember a dress from months ago, right? As I step into it, the fabric hugs my skin as I do up the zipper. I pull out my diamanté heels and prepare myself to walk out to the living room where I know Paxton is waiting.

My heels make a loud clacking noise as I walk on the hardwood floors.

With his brown hair styled to perfection and his tailored tux fitting flawlessly, Paxton looks up at me as I make my appearance. He's a handsome man, I'll give him that, but his face immediately falls in disappointment when he glimpses my dress.

"What? What's wrong? I know it's not the new dress but—"

"You're not going to make this easy on me, are you?" he says with a half-smile, rubbing his hand over his head and down his neck.

"Easy on you?"

"I know you had a vision of this. And I hate to disappoint you, but changing your dress won't stop it from happening."

My mouth falls open.

"Please, just come sit down—hear me out."

I must give him a look because he comes over to meet me, grabs my hand, and directs me to the couch, knowing I wasn't going to do it on my own. I try to feel something, anything, when our fingers touch … but there's nothing.

"I—"

"Just listen," Paxton pleads, cutting me off. "Tate told me about the vision a few months ago."

"You've known for months and didn't say anything?" Probably not the issue I should be focussed on, but whatever.

Paxton laughs a little and sits down on the coffee table in front of me. "At first I thought he was joking. We were on one of our campaigning trips, and he asked how living with you was going with innuendo so thick even a child would know what he was implying. When I told him there was nothing going on, he said yeah, not yet anyway. Then he told me about your vision, and I actually laughed."

"I'm so happy that the idea of marrying me is such a joke," I say sarcastically before wondering why I'm getting angry at that. It *is* a joke.

"The funny thing is, after I got over the initial shock, I realised it's actually a pretty brilliant idea."

"Paxton—" I say more whiney than intended.

"Let me finish! This kind of attitude won't fly when we're married," he jokes, and I crack a smile. "All I'm saying is, you've made it perfectly clear that you're never going to date again, I don't want to date again, and if we were to be married, it would show the kind of stability that voters want, and the polls would go in our favour."

"The polls? You want to marry me for a political advantage?" I ask, shocked. I don't know if that's better or worse.

"Gah," he whines. "This is coming out all wrong. I had a whole speech prepared and everything."

"Then by all means," I say, prepared to hear more. I lean back and fold my arms, ready to be entertained.

Paxton sighs, inching forwards off the coffee table and landing on one knee. He pulls out a ring box, and I try to stifle a giggle. By the look of it, so does he. "Okay … So …" he stutters.

"This isn't the best start." I smirk.

He reaches for one of my hands, and I reluctantly give it to him. "I know you only moved in here because you felt you had no other option, but having you here these past few months has made me realise that I want to come home to you every day. I can provide for you, give you anything you want. You want to be a medic? Be a medic. You want to quit your job and go to university to study something? I'll pull some strings. I want to give you the life you deserve, the life you want. And I would love nothing more than to have you by my side when I become president."

I force a smile. "That's a tempting offer, Paxton." Leaning forwards, I put my right hand on his shoulder. "And I have to admit, moving in here was exactly what I needed. I love living here. I love Nuka like a little sister. But you didn't even mention her in your proposition. How would she feel knowing her dad was getting married? To someone not even old enough to be her mother? I mean … I guess fourteen was old enough, but I wasn't that type of girl."

"Allira," Paxton interrupts me. "You're rambling. And Nuka would love to have you join our family."

"I really would." I hear her small voice come from down the hallway.

"Shouldn't you be in bed?" Paxton yells at Nuka, failing to hide his smile.

"I am!"

"I'll be back in a minute," Paxton says, getting up to check that Nuka really is going to bed.

Isn't this what most girls dream about? A rich, handsome, eligible bachelor offering her the world? Could I actually do this?

"She's back in bed," Paxton says, sitting beside me on the couch this time instead of kneeling. He spins the ring box in his hand.

"Are you saying you'd be happy in a loveless marriage?" I ask.

"I love you," he says. It comes out casual and wispy, not at all genuine or passionate.

"I love you too. We've been through a lot together ... but we both know it's not in the way a husband and wife should love each other."

"That sometimes comes after. We could grow to love each other."

I reach for his hand, take it in mine, and then force myself to look at him. His hopeful eyes bore into my sceptical ones. I lean in, knowing I'm about to kiss Paxton, hoping that I will feel something, *anything*. Our lips come together as he lets go of my hand and wraps his arm around me, pulling me closer. The kiss is tender and soft ... but nothing. I just feel nothing. No spark. No butterflies. Pulling away, I see the exact same feeling in his eyes that I have in mine. Not exactly disgust, but not pleasure either.

"Okay, I see your point," he says, looking at the ring box he's fiddling with.

"If we were going to do this, it would literally only be for show, and I don't think the poll numbers would increase enough to be worth it, would they?"

"I guess you're right." Paxton sighs before slumping back onto the couch. "Will you at least think about it?"

"I can do that," I say, not really meaning it.

"I guess we better get to this benefit thing," he says, preparing to stand up.

"Do we have to?" I whine.

"I'd love nothing more than to stay here, curl up on this couch with you, and watch that teenage drama crap you're addicted to, but if I'm going to be president and Tate's going to be vice president, yes, we have to go. Now—go put on the real dress," he orders as he helps me off the couch.

CHAPTER TWO

We pull up in our chauffeured car, our bodyguard getting out of the passenger seat to open the door for Paxton. Paxton then comes around to my side, assisting me out of the car. This is routine for these events. The media is always at the entrance, taking photos of important people arriving. Paxton insists it gives him a gentlemanly quality if he opens the car door for me. I think it makes me look like a spoiled princess, but he's the politician here, not me, so I don't argue.

Paxton escorts me inside the grand foyer of the banquet hall as flashes from cameras go off all around us. With my arm linked in his, a fake smile on my lips, he leads me through the entrance to the elegantly decorated ballroom in colours of gold and white, accessorised with splashes of silver.

The sound of cutlery on plates, the clinking of champagne flutes, and low murmurs surrounds us as we arrive at our table where Tate and my brother are already seated. Shilah stands and hugs me, a little inappropriately for such a formal event. I swear he's seconds away from lifting me off the ground, but he resists. It's been a while since I've seen either of them. Tate stands and kisses me briefly on the cheek before promptly sitting again.

"I'll go get us some drinks," Shilah says.

"I'll come with," Paxton says.

My heart speeds up, knowing I'm being left alone with Tate.

"Nice dress," he comments with a wry smile as I take my seat at the table. It's the first time he's directed a smile at me in a long time. He knows about this dress because he was there when I had my vision. "So where's the rock, then?"

"No rock," I answer curtly.

"Oh, so he hasn't done it yet?" he asks, raising an eyebrow.

"I said no before he could even show me the ring."

Tate sighs. "I figured as much."

"The interesting thing is—he hadn't even contemplated proposing until you told him about my vision. So I can totally blame you for having that happen." My voice is stiff, flat. There's not even a hint of playful banter like there should be.

"You're the one who had the vision. Blame yourself," he retorts.

I purse my lips in thought. That brings up an interesting concept. If I never had the vision, if I never told Tate and Shilah about it, would Paxton still have proposed? Shilah has told us that choices change his visions, could a vision change what wasn't going to happen in the first place? My head hurts just thinking about it.

"So … how's married life?" I ask, trying to change the subject. It comes out more awkwardly than I would've liked. But who am I kidding, it *is* awkward between us. It has been ever since …

"Not any different from non-married life," he replies, interrupting my thoughts.

"Well, that's probably because you guys were practically an old married couple from the beginning." I try to smile, knowing I need to make an effort to be civil.

Just like Paxton's political career, Tate and Shilah's relationship was a whirlwind romance. Everything happened so fast. They moved in together right away, were engaged within a couple of months, and were married a little over six months ago. Their wedding was at about the time I hit rock bottom. It's when I realised I needed to do something to pull me out of my zombified state.

"Have you spoken to your mum recently?"

"Nope," I respond. "And I don't want to talk about her."

'Allira.'

I just glare at him. *Don't. Not here. And not telepathically! Get out of my head.*

Shilah and Paxton return at that moment, and I take the opportunity to drag Paxton away to mingle. Even though I *hate* mingling, it's better than sitting at that table for any longer.

As I walk away, I hear Shilah scold Tate. "What did you say to her?"

"Nothing," Tate snaps back.

Paxton pulls me aside. "Are you okay?"

"Yeah, I'm fine." I try to shrug it off. "Just Tate being Tate."

"You used to be inseparable when you were at the Institute. I just don't—"

"Please, can we not talk about this," I plead, my voice a little louder than I mean it to come out.

Paxton looks around and notices what I do—a lot of prying eyes, trying to work out what type of heated discussion is going on between a presidential candidate and his date. He gently grabs my hand, leading me to the dance floor, pulling me in to him for a slow dance.

"I don't understand what happened between you two," he says in my ear, making it look as if he's whispering sweet nothings to me. No wonder the media believes we're an item.

"It's just been difficult. It shouldn't be a surprise we grew apart after losing the most important person in both our lives. It happens."

"There's got to be more to it than that," Paxton pries.

"You know how hard it was for me after Chad died. Being around Tate just reminded me of everything that happened, and I just couldn't handle it. I wish we could go back to how we used to be, but the longer we've spent ignoring the issue, the harder it is to try."

He lifts my chin with one of his fingers so I'm looking in his eyes. A bright flash goes off beside us, and we turn to see a photographer taking a photo of our intimate moment.

"You did that on purpose didn't you?" I ask Paxton, my face wrinkling in anger.

"Anything for the perfect shot," he says, smiling. He twirls me on the dance floor, and I try to squash my annoyance. "How about you forget about him, have some drinks, and try to enjoy yourself."

I lay my head on his shoulder as he pulls me in close. "Fine. I'll try."

* * *

Once I blocked Tate out of my head and focussed on the food, the drinks, and catching up with Shilah, I actually had a good night last night. With Shilah being away campaigning with Tate and Paxton a lot, I don't get to see him as much as I'd like. Being an election year, the campaign is full on right now. They're leaving again tomorrow for *more* appearances, junkets, and whatever else is on their agenda. If I had said yes last night, most likely I'd be going with them. Another reason for me to say no, I suppose. The four of us—plus the ridiculous entourage that follows—on a road trip to tell people why they should elect Paxton, a known Defective advocate, and Tate, a Defective himself, to run the country? Yeah, no thanks. I've seen the protests on the news and the rallies at campaigning events. They don't look fun.

It's my day off today. The clinic closes at six a.m. on Thursdays and won't reopen until tomorrow. Aunt Kenna goes to the Institute on Thursdays to help them out. It's a bit of a trade-off—they give the clinic some funding, and Aunt Kenna gives them some of her time. Without a doctor at the clinic, we have to close. We have Vic, but between him and Aunt Kenna already doing fifty-to-sixty-hour weeks, there are still gaps where there is no one to look after the place. Ebb and I are only employed as medic interns, so along with crappy pay, we aren't qualified to run it ourselves yet.

Ebb continued her training with Aunt Kenna from when she was with the Resistance, and I'm trying to play catch up. I'm on my way to becoming a fully qualified paramedic, but Ebb wants to do more. She wants to become a doctor.

She has to do it the long way though. Not many, actually no Defectives I know of, have been accepted to university, so we have to do on-the-job training with assessments via correspondence and practical work. I still don't think Ebb will get a fully qualified doctor's license this way—there's no correspondence course for such an important position—but she's determined to do as many health and medical courses as she can, so when she can finally go to university, she'll be prepared and already know a lot. She's so hopeful that one day soon they'll start accepting us to university that I almost feel bad for her. I don't have the heart to tell her I don't think it'll happen. Maybe in ten or twenty years, but not anytime soon. Everyone's still getting used to us being integrated back into society.

Paxton's spending the day with Nuka today, so I've arranged to meet Ebb at the twenty-four-hour café that's a few stores down from the clinic. We meet here occasionally, usually before our shifts, to study, or just to catch up if we're on different schedules for a while.

After ordering my coffee, I take a seat at a table outside in the fresh air. The clinic isn't in the best neighbourhood, but I've never felt threatened in any capacity. It's one of the poorer areas of the city, but that just means there's more of us here. Paxton gets annoyed that I walk to and from work—he claims it's not safe—but with the six am, six pm starts and finishes, I'm usually walking home in daylight, so I tell him not to worry.

"Here you go, Allira," Campbell, the waitress says, handing me my coffee before swiftly walking back inside. Being a regular here, they all know my name and I know theirs.

Breathing in the scent of fresh ground coffee beans with a hint of vanilla, I lose myself in a state of euphoria, if only for a moment. That sudden feeling of being watched is creeping up on me yet again. The hairs on my neck stick up, and my arms flush with goose bumps. I look around, but of course, I don't see anyone obvious. My eyes quickly drop to my arm, checking that the sleeve of my top is still covering my mark. It's an instinctive reflex to check that first. Revealing my Defective mark in the political world is one thing, because they all know that I'm Defective, but on the streets, by myself, I always make sure I'm covered up.

I get this being watched feeling often, but I haven't for the last month or so, and I thought maybe I was finally over my paranoia. I keep telling myself if I *were* being watched, it would most likely be the media following me to get a story on Paxton. It wouldn't be the first time. But there's a part of me that always wonders *What if it's him? What if Brookfield has come back?*

"Hey," Ebbodine says, taking the seat in front of me, causing me to jump from fright.

"Hey," I stammer.

"Whoa, what's up with you? You're so jumpy."

"Nothing. It's just been a long twenty-four hours," I reply, taking another sip of my coffee.

"You can tell me all about it after I get my latte," she says, walking into the café to order.

"Get me another one?" I call after her.

Watching her as she saunters inside in her strapless sundress, I can't help feeling a little envious. She has no qualms about showing off her Defective mark. I admire her confidence but wonder how she doesn't feel like she's constantly on display. I don't like answering the questions you get when people think it's okay to stop you on the street and ask you the nature of your ability. They look at you as if you're a zoo animal— with fascination but always that element of fear of what would happen if we stopped following the rules.

"So, long day, hey? Must be hard, partying it up with all of those politicians," Ebb says, sitting down, coffee in hand.

"How did you—"

Ebb throws a newspaper down in front of me, with a raised eyebrow and cheeky look on her face. There, on the political page, is a photo of Paxton and me dancing, our faces so close we look like we're about to kiss. The headline reads "Love for Candidate James?" I can't help rolling my eyes. At this point, it seems as if they're just recycling articles and updating the photo. At least they spelled my name right this time. I've seen many versions: Allyra, Alirya, and Aleera. I even saw an Illyra once.

"You know, you're never going to meet someone if the world thinks you're taken," Ebb remarks. I ignore her, taking another sip of coffee. "Allira …" She sighs when she sees the look in my eyes. "It's almost been two years."

"Not even two years. It has *only* been eighteen months. I'm not ready. He was the love—"

"Ugh. If you tell me he was the love of your life, one more time …" she looks at me as my eyes start to fill, and she sighs again. "I'm sorry, okay. But you're barely twenty years old. You're too young to have had the love of your life. You're life has barely started. Chad was a great guy, though you weren't exactly suited to each other—"

"What do you mean, we weren't suited?"

"You fought *all* the time. You can't deny that."

"Only because we are so much alike … Were. *Were* alike."

"Yeah. Stubborn as hell," Ebb mumbles. "Look, it's a tragedy what happened to Chad, it should never have happened, but you can't go on the way you are—hiding behind Paxton and your phoney relationship, closing yourself off to new possibilities. It just needs to stop, okay?"

"What, have you been talking to Tate or something? You sound just like him," I spit out.

"Are you going to shut me out, too, like you did him? Like you did your parents? Have you even seen your parents lately? Your brother?"

"I was with Shilah last night!"

"Not *that* brother—Liam, what is he now, like six, seven months old?"

"Somewhere around that. It still creeps me out to know that Mum and Dad are even still doing *it* at their age, let alone having new babies," I say. "And I've seen plenty of him. Dad too," I lie. They've become casualties of Mum's and my fall out.

"But not your mother?" she asks. I don't answer her. "What even happened between you two? It's been a while, can you even remember what you're fighting about?"

"I do remember." *That's the problem. I still remember Chad, and she could've helped me fix that. All she had to do was use her ability and erase him from my memory.*

"Fine. We don't have to talk about her," Ebb concedes after quite a lengthy silence. "But you *do* have to start moving on, start dating."

"Hey! Of the two of us, who is the one who got proposed to last night?" I say, hoping that my near engagement will be enough to keep her off my back about this whole dating thing for a while.

"Paxton proposed?" She screws up her face. "I don't see a ring, so I'm assuming I don't have to kick your ass for saying yes?"

"I didn't say yes."

A look of relief crosses her face.

"Although, the more I think about it, the less crazy it sounds."

"No, it's just plain crazy. Tell me you're not seriously considering marrying Paxton?"

I smirk. "I'm not. I just wanted to see your face looking like that." I raise my palm, gesturing to her freaked-out expression.

"Damn. I was looking forward to delivering you a swift ass kicking," she smiles, taking a sip of her coffee.

"I'd like to see you try."

"So," she says changing the subject, "dating then?"

"You're one to talk. You're not dating. You haven't had a steady boyfriend since Hall."

Ebb broke up with Hall not long after we were freed. She's admitted she was only ever interested in him because he was a piece of home. Once she was able to go back to Eminent Falls, she didn't need him anymore. Ebb and her mum moved to the city soon after she returned home, though. Small towns like Eminent Falls aren't the most welcoming to our kind—

even for people like Ebb who grew up there.

"That's by choice, and at least I'm putting myself out there. I'm not saying you have to get a boyfriend—just have some fun."

"Ugh. Dating is *not* fun. Granted I don't have much experience in that department, but getting tongue-tied, trying to keep your heart from leaping out of your chest, getting so nervous you can't even think straight? Really not my definition of fun."

"That's the best part!"

"You're weird," I say, cracking a smile.

"You are," she replies, matching my smile.

It feels good to be normal with someone for once. Ebb's words may hurt when she steps over the line—which happens more often than not—but at least I can rely on her to always be herself around me.

"Got plans for this afternoon?" I ask, trying to steer the conversation in a new direction.

"I've got a few assignments due soon. I was thinking I should, you know, start them."

"Start them?"

"So I'm a bit behind, I'll make it up," she says.

It annoys me how Ebb can leave everything to the last minute, get the assignment done, and ace it. I find myself studying any spare chance I get, and I'm still struggling to get anything higher than a pass.

"Want to come over, and I can help you?" I ask, hoping she doesn't see through my charade.

"Now, if I were to do that, just who would end up helping whom?" She smiles.

"Okay, fine. I'll admit it. I need help. Will you come?"

"Sure. But you know, I don't even know why you're bothering with this course."

I raise my eyebrows at her.

"What I mean is, you're studying something you don't even like," she clarifies.

"I like it," I say noncommittally.

"You *hate* working at the clinic," she states. I want to dispute her, but we both know neither of us would believe me. I do hate it there, but it's something I have to do.

"What is this? 'Pick on Allira's life choices' day?"

"Yes. And before you ask, it will be the same tomorrow, and the next day, and the next day. Until you do something about it … or until I get bored of ripping on you."

I sigh. I think I'll be dating again before Ebb gets bored of lecturing me. My stomach churns at the thought. *Dating? Really?* Ugh.

* * *

"Can I talk to you for a minute?" I ask Paxton when I get home. He and Nuka are sitting at the dining table eating lunch.

"Sure. What's up?" One look at my face and he knows this needs to be a private discussion. "Uh, in your room?"

"I think that would be best," I say with a smile, trying not to alarm Nuka. We try to hide as much of the ugliness as we can from her—she's only six ... no, almost seven, as she reminds me constantly.

"You keep eating, sweetheart," Paxton says to Nuka, excusing himself from the table.

We walk to my bedroom, and I close the door behind us. "It's nothing alarming or crazy or anything," I start. I notice Paxton let out a breath he must've been holding in. "I'm just wondering if there's been any developments regarding ... Brookfield?" I struggle to say his name.

"Brookfield?" Paxton asks, taken aback. "I haven't heard that name for a long time."

For the first few months after Brookfield escaped, there were reported sightings of him almost daily. None of the tips seemed to check out. After the buzz and media died down, so did the anonymous tips and alleged sightings. He hasn't shown his face once, has never made a move to try to kill me again, and everyone believes he's dead or in a remote location, hiding. I don't know what to believe. I hope that if he's still out there, he has no desire to come looking for me to finish what he started, but it's Brookfield. I don't know if giving up is really his thing. Then again, it has been a year and a half, maybe he really is dead? I like that thought a little more than I should.

"What makes you ask?" Paxton inquires.

"Just that feeling again," I say. "I know it's probably nothing. I'm just being paranoid. I was just wondering if you'd heard something."

"The being watched feeling again?" he asks, and I nod. "I can tell you with almost certainty it wouldn't be Brookfield."

"How do you know?"

"I just know, okay?"

"What, did you kill him or something?" I joke.

"You know me—I don't like getting my hands dirty. I hired someone to do it."

I stare at him blankly. The words came out so naturally and breezy, I can't tell if he's joking or not, but then he smiles.

"I haven't heard anything about him, but maybe it's not nothing," he says. "You want me to leave a few extra bodyguards here this weekend while I'm away?" he asks.

"No, no. I'm sure it's nothing. You'll need them more than me."

"It's really no trouble," he insists.

"No. It's okay." I emphasise my words with a smile to let him know it really is okay. "I'd just feel a lot better if we knew where he was. I'm sure I'm just reading into it, like always. It was probably some stupid journalist wanting to know about our relationship."

"There was a journalist? You didn't say anything, did you?"

I sigh. "I didn't say there was definitely a journalist. I said that there was probably one, and that's why I thought someone was watching me. Calm down—geez, you'd think I haven't been in a fake relationship with you for a little over six months now."

"And what would you say to a journalist if they did approach you and ask about me?" he says in a teasing yet condescending manner. Part of me thinks he's actually quizzing me, making sure I still know the one and only rule about "dating" him.

"No comment," I say slowly with an almost sarcastic tone.

"Good girl," he says, stepping forward and giving me a kiss on my forehead. I roll my eyes, and he exits my bedroom.

Grabbing a change of clothes, I head for my bathroom and have a shower before Ebb comes over to study. That way I can just go straight to bed when we're done.

I avoid going into the living room after my shower to save intruding on Paxton and Nuka. I sometimes feel guilty when I impose on their time together. Being away a lot, he doesn't exactly get a lot of time to see her. He sometimes takes her with him, if it's a really long stint, but mostly she's being raised by her nanny.

I get a jumpstart on studying, and before I know it, it's night time and Ebb still hasn't turned up yet. Paxton knocks at my door. "Hey, Ebbodine called. She wants to study at the café instead of here. I told her I'll drop you off if she could bring you home. Are you ready to go? I've given Linds the night off so we'll need to take Nuka with us, and I'll need to get her back before her bedtime or she'll never go to sleep."

I look down at my grey sweatpants and black singlet top before shrugging. "I guess so. It's not like I'm out to impress anyone," I say before grabbing my books off the bed and my backpack from the corner of my room. I grab my hoodie from the couch so I can cover up my mark while I'm out. It's in dire need of a wash, but I can't be bothered finding something else.

Arriving at the café, I sit down at the same table I was at just a few hours earlier. Ebb hasn't arrived yet. Reaching into my bag, I start getting my books out when I sense someone standing over me. I lift my head to see some random guy with black hair, wearing red skinny jeans and a white polo shirt, looking down at me with a weird smile on his face.

"Are you Allira?" he asks.

"That depends," I respond, wary of what this guy wants. "What newspaper are you from?"

"Huh?"

"I'm assuming you're a journalist?"

"No, not a journalist," he says, shaking his head. "Ebbodine didn't tell you I was coming, did she?"

I raise my eyebrow. "No. Who are you?"

He smiles, taking the seat opposite me. "I'm Dex. I'm your date."

CHAPTER THREE

"I could kill her," I mutter, hanging my head.

"Sorry. I thought this was a mutual setup. I didn't know she was keeping me as a surprise," Dex says. "I can go if you'd like?" He starts to get up out of his seat.

"No, that's okay. I'm just caught a little off guard. I wasn't expecting … I mean … I'm not exactly dressed for a date," I say, looking down at my raggedy, dirty clothes. He sits back down, and I almost kick myself for saying it's okay. I should just send him away.

Dex shrugs. "I think you look cute. Fashion sense isn't exactly on my list of criteria for a date. In fact, clothes aren't even needed at all."

I'd blush if I wasn't so stunned by his innuendo. "What?" Did I hear him correctly?

He gives a half-smile. "I just mean, what you're wearing isn't a factor to me. You could probably wear garbage and still look adorable."

This time, I do blush. He's confident and suave, and I guess he's not too unattractive. His teeth are straight—that's something. And if going on this date means I'll get Ebb off my back for a while, I think I can endure a few hours with this guy.

"So, dinner?" I ask him.

"Sure," he replies, grabbing the menu off the table to have a look, stealing the occasional glance at me with a smile.

While Dex goes into the café and orders our food, I repeatedly tell myself to resist the urge to flee while he's not looking.

Dex comes back and takes his seat opposite me. We hold each other's gaze for a moment before he looks down at his hand, playing with his napkin.

"So why did you think I was a journalist? Are you famous or something?"

I let out an involuntary huff noise. "Hardly. It's just that I'm roommates with someone who is."

"Who?" His eyes light up like a star-struck groupie.

"Paxton James," I reply.

He tilts his head to the side, confusion marring his face. "Who?" he asks again.

"I'm guessing you don't follow politics?"

"Nah. Not really."

"Fair enough," I say, trying to hide my disapproval.

I don't understand those who don't care about politics, about the people who are leading our country. Maybe it's because of what the previous governments have done to us, or because I live with a politician, but I take pride in the fact that I get to say who I want running our country.

"You seem disappointed at that."

"No," I say quickly. "Everyone has a right to their opinion."

"It's not that I don't like politics, I just don't think my say would really have any impact. I rarely even tick a box—any box—when I vote. I don't see the point."

"Do you not care at all about who make choices for us as a country? You'd rather throw your vote away and then complain when someone you don't like gets in?"

"It doesn't matter who gets in, they're all the same to me. My life doesn't change either way," he says with a casual shrug.

I tell myself to bite my tongue. "That must be nice," I mutter hastily. *So much for biting my tongue.*

Campbell comes out and puts our food on our table. "Still here, Allira?" she asks, a smile on her face.

I smile back. "Nah. I went home, but what can I say, I just can't stay away from this place."

"It seems that neither can I," she jokes before eyeing Dex in an almost confused manner—like she's thinking *Allira, with a date? It must be the end of the world!* "Can I get you guys anything else?"

"Nah. We're all good, thanks," Dex says with a flirtatious smile. Campbell walks back in, and I can't help but notice Dex's eyes follow her, scanning her body up and down. I know I should be annoyed, but I'm not. He looks back at me and sees that I was watching him but doesn't comment—just starts digging into his food.

I shrug and follow suit.

"So. Guy roommate?" he asks with a mouth full of pasta.

"Yup," I answer between bites.

"That's … unusual?" he says, his voice heavy with meaning.

My brow furrows. "I'm surprised Ebbodine hasn't filled you in on that situation."

"Situation?"

"Just how well do you know Ebb?" I ask, changing the subject from Paxton's and my unconventional relationship.

"Not very well. Why do you ask?"

"Oh, just curious."

"I work at the hospital—the real one. Not that pissy excuse of a clinic she works at. I've seen her around when she's had to do her practical assessments."

I almost choke on my food. "I'm guessing she didn't tell you what I do for a living."

"No. Why?"

"My aunt is the founder of that 'pissy excuse' of a clinic. I'm

39

doing the same course as Ebb; she's just more advanced than me. I haven't started my prac-work yet."

"Oh," he says, and that's it. Just *oh*. No apology, nothing. This date is going about as well as I expected it to.

"I just don't know how you do it," he finally says.

"Do what?"

"Work with all those Defective people," he says, screwing up his face. I shove more food in my mouth just hoping that I can contain myself. "I mean, I know Ebbodine's Defective, and she seems normal, but I'm guessing not all of them are like her. It would be a hard job to deal with."

"It's really not hard at all," I state confidently.

He looks up at me from his plate. "Ah crap. You're Defective too, aren't you?"

My silence is answer enough.

"I'm sorry," he says. I'm a little surprised by his apology after him not giving one earlier. "I'm just nervous. I ramble crap when I'm nervous. I'm really not good at this blind dating stuff. I think I'm going to need my foot surgically removed from my mouth by the end of tonight."

"Well, I am training to be a medic. I could probably help with that." I give him a smile even though I don't believe he deserves one. He's lucky he doesn't need my foot surgically removed from his ass.

While we finish our dinner, I try really hard to come up with an excuse to leave right away. I should be able to come up with a good lie. I was a double agent not that long ago. But my brain has obviously turned to mush since then because when Dex offers to walk me home, I accept.

We casually stroll the few blocks to my apartment with awkward chitchat about things we like and don't like. The farther we get, the more apparent it becomes that we have absolutely nothing in common. He likes sport, and I don't—although, he doesn't exactly look like the sporty kind. I loved it when we had our own farm and I got to work on it; he has never been outside of the city—he doesn't even know what a real cow looks like. I try to talk about the hospital under the impression we have similar jobs, but it turns out he works in the laundry room of the hospital, not in the medicine side of things.

I sense him trying to move closer to me with each step, and I find myself stepping farther away. If he keeps it up, I'm going to be walking up against the buildings soon. His fingers brush against mine for a second, and I fight my instincts to pull away—that would just make it more awkward, right? Two of his fingers intertwine with my ring and pinkie fingers, and I can't help but hang my head, look at the ground, and refuse to lift my eyes to his.

We reach the entrance to my apartment building, and I almost want to keep walking around with him, just to put off the awkward goodbye that I know is coming.

"This is me," I say, forcing myself to stop outside my door.

Dex lets go of my hand and looks down at his feet. "Well, thanks for not bailing on me," he says, bringing his eyes up to meet mine. "When I realised you weren't told you were going on a date, I thought you were going to blow me off."

I half-smile. "To be honest, the thought did cross my mind."

He matches my smile and takes a step forwards, his hands finding my hips. I suck in a breath as he brings his lips next to my ear. "So are you glad you stayed?" he whispers.

How can I say no? I really want to, but this whole dating thing is new to me. Surely, he doesn't think this date has gone well, does he? Before I have a chance to respond, his lips are on mine, his tongue trying to assault my mouth. He pulls me closer to him so my body is up against his. I don't know why I'm letting this happen. Maybe a part of me is curious to find out if I can feel anything again, for anyone. I don't, other than the overwhelming urge to wash my mouth out with detergent.

'I've never been with a Defective before. This is going to be so good,' I hear him think.

Shit, Tate must be near and I'm borrowing his ability subconsciously.

I pull away from Dex with a strong desire to punch him. I'm glad that when I take a step away from him, Tate's standing by the door. He doesn't look as pleased to see me though.

"Uh, hi, Tate." I stumble for words.

"Who's this guy?" Dex asks in a possessive tone that he has no right to use.

Please help me, I ask Tate telepathically.

"I'm her ex," Tate says to Dex before turning to me. "I came to tell you … that … I'm still in love with you, and I want you back." He says it with so little meaning behind it, I expect Dex to see right through it.

"Well, that's not going to happen," Dex says. Okay, I was wrong. But *really?* He goes on one date with me and thinks he can say stuff like that?

"Actually," I say, stepping in front of Dex, closer to Tate. "That's exactly what's going to happen." I start walking towards Tate, pretending as if I'm in some sort of hypnotic love trance. Tate puts his arm around me as I turn to face Dex. "I'm sorry, Dex, but I never really got over my ex. Ebbodine keeps trying to force me to move on, but I just can't." *Not a complete lie.*

'You're so telling me how Ebb talked you into this when we get upstairs,' I hear Tate think.

Dex shakes his head and begins to walk off. "Whatever. *Defectives, pfft*," he mutters.

Tate keeps his arm around me until we see Dex round the corner. I let out a sigh of relief as he pulls away and goes to open the door. "Shall we?" he asks with a smile on his face.

"Thank you," I say to him as I walk into the lobby. "I'm so going to kill Ebb tomorrow."

"I still can't believe she convinced you to go on a date. Although, I have to say, it's about time."

I ignore his second remark, because I don't want to get into that again—with him or Ebbodine. "She didn't even convince me. She ambushed me. We were meant to be meeting up to study, and *he* turned up instead."

"Ah. So that explains why you look like a hobo," Tate says, pressing the button for the elevator. "I thought you were trying your hardest to turn him off." I look over to him to see him grinning from ear to ear. "Lucky you didn't dress up. He might have tried to eat the rest of your face." He's laughing now.

"Yeah, well, he was only interested in one thing."

"That was pretty obvious from the thoughts he had while kissing you. What a dick."

The elevator dings and we get on. "So what are you doing here anyway? Are you in love with Paxton or something? You don't see him enough with all this campaigning? Should I be telling Shilah to watch out?"

"And if I was? You going to fight me for him?" he jokes back.

"He's not mine to fight for!" I exclaim.

"I'm here because Paxton is flipping out over these upcoming appearances. I've come to talk some sense into him. And we'll see about you and Paxton. I still think it'll happen between you two."

"You don't really think we'll end up together, do you?"

Before he can answer, the elevator reaches our floor, and we enter to find Paxton in the living room, still wearing his suit and tie, minus his jacket. He's sprawled out on the couch watching the TV.

'You deserve to be happy,' Tate tells me so Paxton can't hear.

Well, how can I resist that? I reply, gesturing to Paxton, slobbed out on the couch.

We both laugh, and before I can think better of it, I lean over and give him a hug. "Thank you for rescuing me. I'm going to go wash my mouth out now—twice."

Paxton sits up. "What did he rescue you from, and why do you need to wash your mouth out?" he asks. I didn't even realise he could hear me.

"Bad date," I say, not caring to elaborate.

"You went on a date?" Paxton asks, standing.

"It was Ebb's idea," I reply.

"I don't care whose idea it was! You can't do stuff like that, Allira. What if a reporter saw you? We need to show stability, remember?"

"Paxton," I say slowly, "I know you're stressed right now, so I know this outburst isn't all about the fact that I went on a date, but you're out of line. We aren't actually together. We've never gone public to say that we are, and you can't hold me to what the media thinks is going on between us."

"That's not the point. They think we're together, and the last thing I need is a scandal in my campaign. It's already scandalous enough that we're a Defective party. Our struggles are already big enough without adding fuel to the fire." He pauses to take a breath. "Just please promise me you won't date anyone. At least until the campaign is over," he says a little calmer.

I shrug. "That's fine by me. I didn't want to go in the first place." A lengthy silence ensues before I finally throw my hands up in defeat. "I'll let you guys talk," I say, stalking off to my room.

CHAPTER FOUR

"All right, where is she?" I ask as I arrive for my Friday night shift at the clinic.

Aunt Kenna looks up from the reception desk, a confused expression on her face. "Where's who?" she asks.

"Ebbodine," I say through gritted teeth.

"Oh, she's back on hospital rounds for the next week or so. Sorry, I probably should've told you I'm going to need you a bit more this week."

"More?" I ask. "I'm already doing five twelve-hour shifts. How many more do you need me to do?" I try to dull my whine down to slight annoyance, but Aunt Kenna just looks at me as if I'm a tantrum-throwing toddler.

That's the annoying thing about being an employee on a salary—I have to do as many hours as they ask of me, but I don't get paid any more.

"It's only one extra shift. I'll sort something out for the other ones," she says, her eyes looking too tired to fight me. It's only then that I notice how visibly upset she is. Her eyes are red and her cheeks blotchy.

"I'm sorry. I can do more."

"I appreciate that, Lia." The small smile falls from her face as she looks back down at whatever she's looking at on the reception desk.

"What's wrong?" I ask.

"Oh, it's nothing," she says, waving her hand as if to shoo me away.

"It's clearly not nothing if you're worrying about it."

"It's the clinic," she stutters as tears start to fill her eyes. "We can't afford to keep going the way we are. We're understaffed and overworked. We only get so much funding from the government and the rest we rely on donations, and as you can imagine, that's not bringing in much funds—if any. I don't know how long we can continue to stay operating like this."

I go behind the reception desk and put my arm around her. "I had no idea. I'm so sorry. I know with Dr. What's-his-face leaving suddenly, we've had to alter opening times, but when we replace him, we can reopen twenty-four-seven."

"We can't afford to replace him," she mumbles. Aunt Kenna wipes her eyes and lifts her chin. "We'll work something out. It's all okay. You've just caught me at a weak moment. You don't need to worry about a thing." She walks into the treatment room in the back, leaving me to tend to the reception desk.

It's easy for her to say that, but how can I not worry about it? This is her baby, and as much as I don't enjoy working here, I don't want to see it fail. We're doing something good here. At least, we're trying to.

I'm relieved to see that not much has been going on for the day, just general practitioner things, mainly. No stabbings. That's a good start. I don't say this aloud, though. Everyone knows it's a jinx if you say anything like that aloud. It's just like saying "Gee, we're quiet today." If anyone ever says that, it's a guarantee that your day is about to get exhaustingly busy.

"I might go grab myself a coffee while we're quiet," Aunt Kenna says.

"I know you did not just say that!" I exclaim.

"Oh, you'll be fine. I'll be two doors away, and Vic is here if you really need him," she says, leaving the clinic.

I prepare myself for an onslaught of patients fighting over who arrived first, who's in a more critical condition. But it doesn't come.

Another thing that'll always get people to come through the doors is to think that it's so quiet, I may as well get my books out to study while I have some downtime. It's Friday night and that's usually our busiest, along with Saturdays. Drunken bar fights, and people letting loose over the weekend doing stupid stuff. Tonight seems to be different so far, but it's still early.

Just as I reach into my bag on the ground for one of my textbooks, I hear it. The swinging of the doors whooshing open, the urgent footsteps heading towards the reception counter. I almost fall over myself as I stand.

It's *him*, I see Chad. Ash-blond hair that's naturally blonder at the tips, and strong muscled arms wrapped around a woman's limp body.

I shake my head and really focus, noticing that the man in front of me is—of course—not Chad. This guy is tall, well over six feet, and the more I look at him, the more I realise he looks nothing like Chad apart from the two similarities I seemed to pointedly notice first.

This tends to happen a lot. I see someone with similar hair, eye colour, or build, and I immediately think of Chad. I secretly come up with crazy theories that the person I'm looking at is really Chad and that he somehow had to fake his own death and get reconstructive surgery to look vastly different. Deep down I know these theories are just painful fantasies, brought on by my never-ending grief over the loss of him. I saw his body. I know he's gone. He's dead, and he's not coming back. This still doesn't stop me from thinking crazy things about him, though. I see him in almost everyone I know and even strangers on the street.

"A little help, please?" the guy says to me, bringing me out of my daze.

"Sorry, of course. Bring her this way," I say, gesturing towards the treatment room.

By the looks of her, she's in bad shape. Not as bad as the girl from the other night, but she's been beaten pretty badly. I begin to wonder if the guy carrying her did this to her.

Gesturing to the closest bed in the treatment room, he sets her down in a gentle and caring manner. Maybe he's not responsible after all. She lets out a groan of pain as she holds on to her right side.

"I'm going to need you to step back into the waiting room, please, sir," I say, following him out and grabbing registration forms off the desk. "If you could fill these out while I start treatment on your girlfriend, that would be great. Thanks."

"I … uh … She's not—"

"I promise we'll take good care of her. Just take a seat, and I'll come let you know when you can see her," I say before walking back into the treatment room.

Approaching the girl, I try to focus on anything other than her face, but it's her face that has the most damage. Her right eye is so swollen it's closed shut. There's a bump on the left side of her forehead that's red and easily going to be bruised in a few hours. She has a patch of skin missing from the left side of her chin; I can only guess it was caused by a fall on cement or bitumen of some kind.

"Hi there," I say in a calming tone. "My name is Allira and I'll be fixing you up tonight." The girl just looks at me, her eyes wide … well *eye*—the one that isn't closed shut. I'm not sure if she fears what I'm going to do to her or if she's reliving what's already been done. "Can you tell me what happened?" I ask, knowing full well she probably won't tell me.

She tries to shake her head but winces in pain and grips her side a little tighter.

"I'm going to examine the rest of you, is that okay?"

"Yes," she manages to get out.

Lifting up her shirt reveals a huge, red, bruising mark on her ribs about the length of a foot. I think it's pretty safe to say that at least one of her ribs is broken. Pulling her shirt back down, I look at her with furrowed brows.

"What I'll do first is get all of your stats, take you for an x-ray, fix up that open wound on your face, and we'll get a cold compress for your eye. Is that okay with you?"

"Yes," she says, again struggling to get the word out.

"Is there anything else we should know? Anywhere else that hurts?"

"Just my ribs," she says breathlessly.

"We'll get you x-rayed as soon as we can, okay?" I tell her. She nods in response as I start getting the things I need to fix her up.

I check her stats to find she has slightly raised blood pressure, which is understandable in the state she's in, her temperature is fine, and her pupil reacts when I shine a light in her good eye, which is all good news. After grabbing an ice pack for her eye, I'm about to take her to get an x-ray when Aunt Kenna comes back in.

She must've had dinner, too, as she was gone for at least half an hour. "Sorry, I didn't even see anyone come in. I was trying to keep an eye out. What do we have?" she asks, approaching us and standing at the foot of the patient's bed.

"She's going to need an x-ray on her ribs. She has a wound on her chin, which needs to be cleaned and patched up. Her right eye is swollen and is currently being iced to try to bring the swelling down."

"Great work, Lia. I'll take it from here, I need you back out on reception if that's okay."

"Sure."

I make my way back out into the reception area to find the guy who brought the patient in sitting in the waiting room, still looking at the forms. He gets up when he sees me and makes his way to the desk.

Again, I'm flooded with memories of Chad. This guy even walks like Chad. I shake my head. *Stop thinking about him.*

"Got them all filled out?" I ask, grabbing for the forms.

"Uh, not quite. I filled out what I could," he says sheepishly, handing them to me.

He's only filled out her first name and address. *Wow. What a catch this guy must be.*

"You don't even know her last name?" I try to hide the condescension in my voice.

He slowly shakes his head while he looks at his shoes.

"Well, she might be here for a few hours yet. You're welcome to go home, and we can call you when she's ready to be picked up."

"I don't mind waiting."

"Suit yourself," I say, sitting down at my desk with the barely filled-out form. I can't even put this information into our computer yet. I'll have to give it to the patient later to fill in.

He remains standing at the desk, leaning on the bench with his elbows, looking down at me with a weird smile on his face.

"Can I help you with something else?" I ask.

"Yeah. I've just been wondering about this place. I didn't even know it existed. Tina told me to bring her here."

I glance down at the form to confirm Tina is the patient.

"We're still relatively new. We've only be open a few months," I inform him.

"And it's a clinic solely for the Defective?"

"Well, we'll treat anyone. We just don't get many non-Defective here. Any actually. They all go to the hospital."

"Why can't the Defective go to the hospital?" he asks, confused.

"They can, but we feel that we'll give them a higher level of care here," I say as diplomatically as possible.

"Oh, okay," he replies, but he still seems a little confused.

I resist the urge to look at his right arm. It's pretty clear he's not Defective, and I don't want to be one of *those* people. I hate when people do it to me, so I don't want to do it to others.

"Was that all?" I ask, still in a professional manner even though his lingering is making me self-conscious.

"I was just wondering. Umm … what time do you finish tonight?"

"Well, we're open twenty-four hours a day over the weekend. We close on Monday mornings from six a.m., and reopen at six a.m. on Tuesday until Thursday at six a.m. when we close, and open again at six a.m. on Friday and go through to Monday morning." It took me a long time to memorise that confusing timetable.

"Oh. I didn't mean …" He looks at me with an analytical stare before continuing. "Why the odd and different opening times?"

"We had a doctor leave, meaning we only have my aunt and another doctor, Vic, to run the place. We're understaffed, but there's no budget to hire new staff. We really need volunteers, but there's not many of them around these days who will work with blood, pee, and spew for free."

He gives a slight laugh at that. "Fair enough. It's a shame though—there must be high demand for a place like this."

"There is. This is actually quiet for a Friday night." As the words fall out of my mouth I curse myself, and just as I do, the door opens with another patient entering.

Tina's boyfriend guy, man, person—whoever he is—smiles down at me. "Looks like you might have spoken too soon." He taps the desk with his hand before going back to the seat he was sitting in earlier, leaving me to attend to the next patient.

* * *

I jinxed myself. I've been run off my feet all friggin' night. Typical. It's 5:30 a.m., and I'm finally back at the empty reception desk, getting ready for my shift to end. In the waiting room, the guy is still here. He's fallen asleep in one of the chairs—quite a common occurrence when waiting for someone to be treated. His girlfriend is asleep in the treatment room. She has two cracked ribs, and Aunt Kenna wanted to observe her overnight. In the mad rush of things, I managed to get a chance to tell him that Tina was going to be here all night and that he should go home, but he said he was fine to wait. I guess he has that going for him; he's loyal, even if he doesn't know her last name. Maybe they haven't been together all that long.

I don't even know why I'm thinking about this. It's their business, not mine.

I find myself watching him sleep. *Nope, not creepy at all.* He doesn't snore. A half-smile finds my face. That's one thing I don't miss about Chad. His snoring could've woken a whole neighbourhood. But I'd put up with it every night if it meant he was here.

The guy startles awake, confused for a moment before he remembers where he is. He sits up and tilts his head from side to side, cracking his neck. He runs his hand over his hair and down his neck as he yawns, and I mentally beg him not to do that. Yet another reminder of Chad. I know I should stop comparing, but it's too difficult not to with this guy.

He stands and comes over to the reception desk where I'm sitting. Looking up at him, I notice his eyes for the first time, like really notice them. They're sky blue and incredibly intense. I don't know why this puts an involuntary smile on my face, but it does. Maybe because it *doesn't* remind me of *him*.

"You're still here," he says, his lips turning up slightly in the corner.

"Yep, sure am. I'm about to go home though," I say, looking at the time. I can't wait to get to bed.

"Can I buy you breakfast?" he asks.

This throws me. Did he really just ask me out when his girlfriend is asleep in the other room recovering from a beating? What kind of person does that?

"I don't think that's a good idea."

"No? You got a boyfriend?" he asks.

"No." *Hmm, Paxton.* "Not really."

"'Not really' as in there's no one, but you want me to think there is, so I don't ask you out? Or 'not really' as in you do, but you're thinking of going out with me anyway?" His charming arrogance actually makes my lip quiver, as I contemplate whether to smile at that or not.

"I can't go out with you," I say, trying to be confident and totally failing.

"Because? Oh, let me guess. Because … you're joining a nunnery?"

I shake my head with a smile.

"Because … you have six months left to live?"

I shake my head, my smile falling from my face slightly.

"Because you have six kids to five different baby daddies, and you aren't looking for a new one?"

I let out a laugh. "No. But there are many reasons why I'm not going out with you, the main one being your girlfriend lying in the next room."

"Girlfriend?" he asks. "You think she's my girlfriend? She's my neighbour. I don't even know her all that well. I found her on the stoop of our apartment block and brought her here. I thought you would've gathered that I didn't know her when I didn't know any of her information." He looks at me with sudden realisation, his shoulders slumping forward. "You just assumed I didn't care to know my girlfriend's last name?"

"I'm sorry. I shouldn't have assumed. I just figured because you brought her here and stayed all night." I try to hide my embarrassment.

"Well, now that's out of the way, breakfast?" he asks, smoothly.

"Sorry. Still no."

He steps back from the desk, hand to his chest and shaking his head. "You're breaking this poor guy's heart."

I reluctantly smile. "I'm sure you'll get over it. Now if you'll excuse me, I'm going home to go to bed."

"Whoa, hey, that's moving a little too fast for me, but if you insist …"

"Your neighbour should be able to be released after she wakes up. It'd be great for her if you could take her home," I say, switching back to professional mode, although the smile still lingers.

"I plan to," he says seriously. "And thanks for taking care of her."

"You're welcome."

His voice follows me as I grab my bag and head for the exit. "Oh, Allira?" I turn to face him. "My name's Jayce. It was nice meeting you."

I don't reply. I just walk out. He knows my name? I don't wear a nametag; how did he know my name? Did he ask someone about me? My cheeks flush as a grin finds my face. As I start walking towards my apartment, I kick myself for not saying what I should have said, what I wanted to say.

It was nice meeting you too, Jayce.

CHAPTER FIVE

Making my way down the street, I prepare myself for a Sunday night shift. I'm covering Ebb's usual shift so she can do more prac-work at the hospital.

It's been a week since I met the guy with the neighbour, and for the last week, I've found myself wanting him to walk back through the clinic doors. Then I think to myself that that might mean I'm wishing for his neighbour to be beaten again, and that seems extreme. I tell myself it's because he reminds me of Chad, that's why I want to see him. But if that was true, why do I keep thinking about his insane blue eyes and the confident smirk he flashed when he asked me out? Neither of those are traits of Chad's.

The reception desk is dead quiet when I arrive. Stashing my bag under the desk, I hear Aunt Kenna yell from the treatment room. "Lia, can you come out here for a minute?" Sunday is usually her day off—what is she doing here?

I wander into the back room and almost trip over myself when I see *him* standing there with Aunt Kenna. He is wearing jeans and a yellow T-shirt, and his biceps bulge as he crosses his arms casually.

Be careful what you wish for.

He looks at me, and I can't bring myself to keep his gaze. I tuck my hair behind my ear nervously, watching my feet as they start walking in their direction.

"What are you doing here?" I direct at Aunt Kenna. "I thought it was your day off?"

"The hospital couldn't spare a relief doctor tonight, and Vic is off, so I'm it," she replies.

As I glance over at Jayce, our eyes lock for a brief second before I avert my gaze back to Aunt Kenna. "You needed me?"

"Yes. Lia, this is Jayce. You'll be working with him tonight, showing him the ropes."

"The ropes?" I ask, looking back and forth between Aunt Kenna and him so fast it looks like I'm watching a tennis match.

"He's our new volunteer, so I need you to teach him what you do here. He'll be doing administrative stuff mainly, but I'll get you to show him all aspects of the clinic so he knows how we operate. Sound good? Great. I'll check in with you guys later. I'll be in my office if you need me."

Aunt Kenna walks off without giving me a chance to respond, and just like that, I'm left alone with the first guy to give me butterflies in a long time.

He wasn't meant to come back. Last Friday night was good; it gave me hope that maybe one day I could be open to dating again. Part of me wanted to say yes to his offer for breakfast last week, but I don't need this right now—I don't need him … here.

Keeping my eyes on the floor, I have to force myself to look up and make eye contact with him. He has his hands in his pockets and is looking right at me.

"Hey, I just want to say that I didn't know," he says.

"Didn't know what?"

"I didn't know who you were. I never would've asked you out if I knew you were Paxton James' girlfriend."

"So you're not just volunteering to ask me out again?" I ask in a flirty manner, startling myself. *Where the hell did that come from?*

"No hidden agenda here," he says, holding up his hands before putting them back in his pockets. "I just thought that with everything you said about being understaffed and needing volunteers that I should do something productive with my spare time. I think what you guys are doing here is incredible." He must see me instinctively look at his right arm. I hate to do it, but I have to know. "I'm not Defective. I just want to help." He smiles. "And I promise I won't ask you out again."

"I guess we better get started then," I say, walking off. I get to the hallway before I realise he isn't behind me. "You're meant to be following me," I order. He hurries to catch up.

I take him to our laundry room to find him some scrubs to change into, but something nags at me in the back of my mind.

"How did you know about Paxton?" I ask him.

"Sorry, what?"

"Paxton. How did you—"

"Oh. Newspaper. I thought you looked familiar. It wasn't until I read the paper at home a few days ago that I realised where from."

"Oh" is all I can seem to reply. "I was in the paper again?" I ask rhetorically and more to myself than to Jayce.

"It was an older issue. I live with my sister. She … uh, has a lot of newspapers. For her job."

"What is she, a journalist or something?"

He nods, and I freeze. A journalist? Is that why he's really here?

"How long have you two been together?" he asks, adding to my suspicion. Is he asking for himself or for his sister?

There's a part of me that wants to tell him the truth—that Paxton and I aren't together—but I know I shouldn't. Especially now I know he lives with a journalist. So I lie.

"About six months, but I've known him for two years. I was there when he took over the Institute." I have to choose my words carefully.

The general public doesn't know what really happened at the Institute when Paxton took over. All they know is Brookfield was a corrupt man, and Paxton was the courageous hero who overthrew him and exposed him for what he truly was.

No one knows about the slaughter of eight innocent people or the hostile moves we took to secure the Institute for ourselves. No one knows that I played a big part in the whole thing, apart from the Defective population, of course. Paxton, Drew, and I are well known in the Defective community for what we did. Paxton's political team has been vigilant in keeping that hidden from non-Defectives.

Most are grateful for what the three of us achieved. Some— like those who decided to stay with the Resistance and continue to live out there—think we've endangered our kind even more by setting us free. Some days, especially after losing a patient, I tend to agree with them.

"What ever happened to that Brookfield guy anyway?" Jayce asks.

I get a chill at the sound of his name. "Dunno. They never found him," I reply as calmly as I can manage.

Handing Jayce some scrubs, I show him where he can get dressed. When he comes back out, I get started showing him around the clinic, explaining what will be expected of him.

I don't know if it's because Brookfield's name was mentioned or if I'm just on edge because Jayce is here, but that uneasy feeling creeps over me once again. My skin tingles with goose bumps, and I shiver. As we make our way past the front windows of the clinic, my heart stops. Out of the corner of my eye, I see a figure standing just on the other side of the glass. I can't make out any features in the dark, and by the time I turn to face them, they're no longer there. *Was it just my imagination?*

"Did you see that?" I ask Jayce.

"See what?"

I shake my head. "Never mind."

Jayce spends the night shadowing me. As much as I'm happy that we'll have more help around here—free help, too—I hate that it has to be Jayce. Every time he brushes past me, I find myself holding my breath for no reason. And when our fingers accidently touched earlier when I was handing him something, I actually flinched, and not in a bad way, although I'm sure he probably thought it was. I haven't been this self-conscious since … well, actually, I don't think I've ever been this self-conscious.

It's nearing the end of our shift, and the thought of going home, getting into bed, and wrapping myself up in my blanket like I'm in a cocoon brings a smile to my face. Then I remember that it's the last Monday of the month. It's Institute day. I let out a sigh at the realisation.

I'm still going to go home for at least a nap before heading out west for my monthly "counselling" session. It'll make me late, but they're not going to send out a search party if I'm an hour or two overdue.

Just as I make my way out of the clinic, I see Ebb's car and remember that she's going today as well and we'd arranged to go together. She usually goes on Thursdays, but she called me last night at the clinic to say she has to be at the hospital on

Thursday, so she's coming with me today. I'd already forgotten.

"Hey," I say, climbing into the passenger seat of her car. I throw my head back on my seat and close my eyes.

There's a tap on the window, and I open my eyes to see Jayce outside the car. Putting the window down, I give him a forced and tired smile.

"Hey. I just wanted to thank you for showing me around last night."

"No problem. This is Ebb, by the way—she works at the clinic, too, so you'll be working with her a lot as well," I introduce them.

"Nice to meet you," he says in a friendly, casual tone. "I'll see you tomorrow then," he adds before walking off.

"Yes, you will," Ebb says seductively once he's out of ear shot. *Uh-oh.* "Long night?" she asks me. I notice a similar look of weariness in her eyes that I must have in mine from the all-nighter we pulled last night—hers at the hospital, mine at the clinic.

"The usual."

"How about you nap on the way there, and then you can drive home, and I'll nap on the way back. After you tell me everything you know about the new guy."

"I'll tell you about him later. I'm too tired right now." I slump back into my seat, preparing for sleep, which I know will come easily.

It seems like we get to the Institute in record time, probably because I slept most of the way.

As we pull into the parking lot, I get a crippling shiver down my back—the one I get every time I come back here.

We enter the building unescorted. There are no guards, no locked doors, and no security codes to get in and out. We make our way to a freshly renovated room that now operates as a reception area.

We're greeted by two staff who wear the old Institute uniforms, although the stripes on their shoulders no longer hold significance to a ranking system.

"Name?" the one in front of me asks without even bothering to look up. Ebb starts the same process with the second lady.

"Allira Daniels."

She looks up at me, startled. "Of course, Miss Daniels. Sorry."

Everyone knows me here, and I kind of hate it. She inputs it into her computer, and an all-too-familiar two-tone warning alarm springs from her speakers.

"Ah. The director has requested a meeting with you," she says.

"Of course, he has." I mutter.

Ebb looks over to me. "He just misses you, you know."

I ignore her and begin walking in the direction of the offices.

Making my way down the hallway, I suck in a breath and

count to three before opening the door to his office. I need to prepare myself mentally to come face to face with the person who has taken on so many different roles in my life.

He started out as the boy I saved from a car crash, but he quickly became my boyfriend. Then he revealed himself as an agent of the Institute, sent to me with one purpose—to gather enough intel to arrest me. After my arrest and the months of bickering between us that followed, he was assigned as my partner when I reluctantly became an Institute agent myself. During our partnership, we were able to at least be civil, sometimes even nice to one another. He slowly moved on to be a confidant of mine, and then he became the person who saved my life. He shot dead the woman who killed Chad and attempted to kill me. He became my saviour.

We've had our ups and downs. We've both lied to each other, we've both sabotaged one another in different ways, and yet we've both saved each other too. Through it all, we've managed to find neutral ground, a balance of what we shared. We've managed to find friendship.

"Mr. Director," I tease in a posh accent while curtseying. "I believe you sent for me," I say, keeping up with the charade.

Drew puts the paperwork he was reading down on his desk, and I'm in his arms within what feels like impossible time. He picks me up and spins me, making me dizzy and feel silly.

"Put me down," I scold, hitting him in the shoulder.

"Sorry. Had to," he replies, putting my feet back on the floor. "It's been too long. You do know you don't *only* have to come when it's mandatory, right?"

"Excuse me, but I'm pretty sure the last time I was here, it was *you* who was too busy to see *me*."

"That's true. Sorry about that. Some days it's just chaos here." He gestures for me to take a seat as he walks around his desk and sits back in his big boss chair. I can't help giggling at the image. It gets me every time.

Drew took over the Institute when Paxton announced his run for presidency. It's a little surprising to see him doing so well. I guess there's always going to be that tiny part of me that doesn't trust him. It kind of sucks because he's done nothing but prove himself time and time again. Maybe when someone hurts you that badly, you can never rebuild full trust again.

Not that I don't trust him at all. I'd definitely trust him with my life, but I'd never be able to trust him with my heart. Not again.

"So, how have you been?" he asks in a professional manner.

"Oh, is this my counselling session?" I ask with feigned excitement.

"Just getting formalities out of the way."

"Well, in that case: I'm doing well, I haven't used my abilities in any capacity, I'm working, paying taxes, and being an all-round stand-up citizen."

"Works for me. But really—how are you doing?" he asks seriously.

"I'm doing *fine*."

"Yeah, it's my experience that when a woman says she's *fine*, she's not *fine*. Not to mention I can read you." *Stupid Empath ability*. "Has it got to do with your mum?" he asks quietly.

"Not you, too? Why does everyone ask me that? No, I haven't spoken to her, and no I don't intend to anytime soon."

"Okay, okay," he says, holding up his hands in surrender. "I'm just trying to get to the bottom of the black cloud of emotion that you're giving me. I want to know why you're upset."

Taking a deep breath, I prepare myself to let it all out. "There's a lot of things making me feel this way. Right now, my main reason is lack of sleep. I've been doing night shifts the last three nights; I'm running on about two hours' sleep that I took in the car on the way here. I'm tired, I'm overworked, and when I'm home, I have to put on the confident girlfriend act for Paxton's campaign. Plus I have studying to catch up on, and to top it off, it feels as if Ebb is trying to pimp me out to anyone who agrees to go out with me!"

"What?" Drew asks.

I hang my head. "I went on a date last week," I admit.

"Oh?"

"It was a complete disaster. Ebb forced me into it. She told me she was going to meet me and had this guy turn up instead." Which reminds me—I was so tired this morning I didn't even remember to scold her about it. She's lucky she's been working at the hospital and has been able to avoid me until today.

He laughs. "Sorry, but that's pretty funny."

"It was horrible! Is this what I'm going to have to deal with when I'm finally ready to date? Guys who only want one thing, sticking their tongues so far down my throat they can practically taste my stomach?"

Drew screws up his face. "Ugh. There's a visual I don't want in my head."

"Sorry," I say quickly. I realise we haven't really spoken about dating or relationships with each other. I've probably crossed some sort of line between us.

"No one can tell you when you'll be ready to start dating again. You have to decide for yourself. Ignore Ebb, as hard as that may be. We all know what she's like."

I smile, but it's a sad smile. "Thanks."

"Besides, aren't you all shacked up with Paxton? I heard he proposed," he says, one eyebrow raised.

"Not for real though. He wants me to be his trophy wife. He wants his poll ratings to go higher. Real romantic, right?"

"I did always think it was weird—you and him, together. It just didn't seem right. Not like you and Ch—" He stops himself before he says Chad's name.

"You can say his name," I reassure him. "I think I'm finally at a point where I'm not going to break down every time I talk about him."

"Well, that's progress, right?"

"Yeah, I guess so."

We're interrupted by a man coming into the office. He's probably in his fifties with dark hair that's beginning to grey and green eyes that have wrinkles around the edges. He's wearing overalls, so I assume he's the janitor. "Oh, sorry, I didn't realise you had someone in here."

"That's okay, Dad. This is Allira," Drew says.

"Dad?" I blurt out accidently.

"*The* Allira?" the janitor asks.

"Yes, and yes," Drew answers both of us.

Drew's dad wipes his hand on his overalls before extending his hand for me to shake. "I'm so glad to finally meet you," he says warmly. "I've heard so much about you."

I wish I could say the same about you, I think as I shake his hand. I didn't even realise Drew was in touch with his parents. They sent him to live here at the Institute when he was fifteen, and he has never talked much about them before.

Ebb comes through the door without even bothering to knock. Then again, I did the same thing when I came in, and so did Drew's dad, so I guess I can't judge her.

"Ready to go?" she asks me.

"Sure," I say, getting up from my chair. "It was nice to meet you," I say to Drew's dad. He nods in return.

"Already? It feels like you just got here," Drew complains. "Can't you hang out for a while? Come look at all the things

I'm trying to accomplish here? So much has changed since you were last here for a proper visit. It seems these days you're in and out within five minutes."

"I want to stay," I lie. "But Ebb's my ride home."

Drew gets up, coming around his desk to hug me again. "Please come back and see me when you can. I don't want it to be another month before we talk, okay?"

"Okay," I say, knowing full well that's not going to happen. "And if you ever have time off, come to the city—we'll catch up."

"Okay," he replies in the same empty-gesture tone that I just used. "Nice to see you, too, Ebb," he says over my shoulder.

Ebb bows exaggeratedly. "The honour is all mine, Director, sir."

I can't help but laugh.

"Get out of here, you two," he says, trying to be serious but not pulling it off.

Ebb and I start walking back down the hallway towards the entrance of the building, when I reach over and punch her hard in the arm.

"Ow! What the hell was that for?" she exclaims.

"Belated punishment for setting me up with that Dex guy."

"Oh. I was hoping you'd forgotten about that," she says sheepishly. "I thought because you hadn't mentioned it, that maybe—"

"Maybe I'd forgotten you ambushed me into a horrible date that I didn't want to go on in the first place?"

"I was hoping anyway. I saw him at the hospital a few nights ago, so I figured it didn't end well when he saw me and ran the other way as fast as he could."

"You have to promise me you won't do that again."

"I don't know if I can do that," she says. "How else will I get you to start dating again?"

I sigh in frustration. "We've already been over this. I don't want to date."

She sighs in louder frustration. "Fine." She looks around as we reach the parking lot. I don't know what she's looking for, but she tosses me the keys to her car. "You take the car. Come to my place and drop it off, and then I'll take you home."

"You're not coming with me?"

"Nope." She teleports out of the parking lot, leaving me to a two-hour car ride by myself. I don't know if I'm annoyed or grateful.

I'm annoyed that she's using her ability—especially in the parking lot of the place that polices those sorts of violations. I guess she assumes being friends with Drew will be beneficial if she ever got caught.

Driving back to the city with nothing to distract me from my thoughts is a dangerous thing. Drew was right. There's a black cloud of emotions swirling around me, and I want it to stop. I want to be normal like everybody else. But where am I meant to start?

CHAPTER SIX

Jayce seems to be a natural at medical stuff, just like Ebb. He's technically only an administrative volunteer as he has no medical training, but he does have previous first aid training, so he's been able to assist with easy tasks. The few times I've had him help me, it seems he knows more than me.

I know I've only been doing this a few months, but I'm really beginning to wonder why I struggle with it so much. It's not that I think I'm too dumb; it just doesn't come easily. I have to force it.

Jayce hasn't offered up too much information about himself apart from the fact he goes to university, is studying psychology, and lives with his sister. He'll be starting shifts on his own in a few short weeks, so we've managed to stick to mostly medical talk, which is fine by me. The more I learn about him, the more I reluctantly like him.

He's out back dealing with the laundry when the door swings

open, and I look up from the reception desk to find Ebbodine strolling in to take over for the day shift. We haven't spoken since she ditched me at the Institute on Monday. I returned her car, put her keys in her mail slot, and walked home. I was fearful that if she saw me, I'd have to endure yet another conversation about dating, or my mum, or anything else she likes to lecture me on.

"Hey," she says in a calm, almost sympathetic tone.

"Hey." My tone is curt compared to hers.

"I'm sorry about what I did."

"Ambushing me into a horrible date or ditching me with your car?"

She looks down at her feet. "Both?" She eventually meets my stern eyes and then rolls hers. "Fine. I promise I will never set you up on a date again"—she pauses—"until you want me to."

"No! No 'want to.' I don't want to date anyone. Why can't you understand that? Stop pushing me into something I'm not ready for." Why is this such a preposterous request to her?

"Laundry's done." Jayce's voice comes from behind us. We turn to look at him, and I wonder how much he heard. He's staring at me, his arms crossed and his expression neutral.

The urge to explain myself brings words to the tip of my tongue, but I can't get them out. Luckily, Ebb breaks the silence.

"Hi," she says with a flirtatious smile. "I'm Ebbodine. We met the other day," she says, reaching forwards and shaking his hand.

"Hey," he replies, taking her hand in his before crossing his arms again.

"So how are you settling in?"

He shrugs. "Fine, I guess."

"If Allira hasn't been all that welcoming, I understand. She can be a bit crabby." She smiles as if she's joking, but I know she's telling the truth. Even I'll admit that I'm crabby a lot of the time. I don't mean to be—it just comes out of me.

He looks back at me and smiles. "She's actually been pretty great."

My heart does an involuntary jump.

Ebb looks at me with narrowed eyes and then back at Jayce with a smile. "Well, how about I take you out for a proper welcome? Say, dinner and drinks? Tonight?" she asks before side-glancing at me. I stiffen in my seat reflexively, but I hope she doesn't notice. Did she really just ask him out? And so casually as well. I could never pull something like that off.

Jayce awkwardly glances at me for a moment before answering Ebb. "I actually have plans with my brother tonight."

"Bring him along. Allira can come with us, too. The clinic is closed tomorrow, so we'll all have the day off to … recover."

Did she actually just wink? Ugh. The last thing I want to do is go to dinner and watch Ebb fawning all over Jayce.

She turns to me. "You're up for that, right?"

"Aunt Kenna said something about me working tonight. Relief nurse can't make it or something." Ebb just stares at me, knowing that I'm lying. "Ebb," I say in a warning voice that says she's crossing that line again.

She grunts, and her shoulders slump forwards as she grabs my arm and drags me out into the treatment room.

"You have to," she states as soon as we're out of earshot of Jayce.

"No, I don't," I counter. "You literally just promised no more dates, and now you want me to go on a double date? Are you freaking kidding me right now?"

"It's not a double date. It's just friends hanging out. It's a chance to get to know the new guy, and a chance for you to have normal twenty-year-old experiences as opposed to thirty-year-old political ones."

"I don't want to be ditched with Jayce's brother while you two … you know."

She rolls her eyes, offended that I'd think she'd do something like that—even though she's done similar plenty of times. "I promise. Just dinner and drinks, and I'll even come home with you and stay the night—girls' night. Paxton's still away, yeah?"

"Yeah, but Nuka and her nanny are home, so we'll have to be quiet."

"Deal. So you'll come?" she asks, hopefulness filling her eyes.

"Ugh, I guess."

She briefly hugs me before rushing back out to Jayce to work out the details. *Why did I just say yes?*

* * *

I told Ebb I'll meet her, but she arrives on my doorstep anyway, pursing her lips as she eyes me up and down. I'm wearing jeans and a hooded jacket, my hair pulled back in a plain ponytail.

"I knew you were going to need my help," she says, entering the apartment. She's carrying six or seven coat hangers full of clothes, and she makes her way into my room, throwing them on the bed. "Okay. Here are your options."

"You didn't say anything about dressing up."

"This isn't dressing up, it's looking nice. There's a difference."

"I don't look nice?" I ask, only mildly offended.

"No. Are you even wearing makeup?"

"Yes, but I wanted it to be subtle, not like I was going to a benefit or political appearance."

"Go finish your face, I'll pick your outfit."

I don't bother arguing—it's Ebb, there's no point—and after I've done what I'm told, I come back out of the bathroom to find a short black dress with tiny floral print all over it.

"No." I flat out refuse. "It's too short, and it doesn't cover my arm."

Ebb slumps her head to the side. "You can pick leggings or your elbow-length denim jacket to go with it."

"Both," I say defiantly.

"No. You have to pick only one."

"Fine. Jacket."

As I walk past her, she quickly turns and pulls my hair tie out, letting my hair fall past my shoulders.

"Perfect," she says.

After getting dressed, we walk down the street towards some restaurant I've never been to. I complain about the shortness of my dress the whole way. I should've fought harder to get the leggings.

"My dress is even shorter, so you can't complain," Ebb says. She's right, too. Where my dress is flowing and loose fitting—but short—hers is figure hugging and a lot shorter than mine. But she's always showing off her skin. She has no reservations when it comes to showing off her mark, her legs, and her boobs. I do.

We arrive at the restaurant to find the guys already seated in a booth up against the window. Jayce stands when he sees us and moves over to the other side so he's sitting with his brother. I'm grateful for the move. I didn't want to be stuck next to Jayce's brother.

"Hi," Ebb singsongs as she sits, sliding into the booth across from the brother. I'm surprised by her move considering she's here to hit on Jayce.

"Hey," I say casually, sitting down and looking at Jayce.

He smiles and nods hello to me. "This is Jamie," he says, gesturing to his brother. "This is Ebb and Allira."

Jamie reaches across the table and shakes my hand and then Ebb's. I notice he has the same intense blue eyes as Jayce, but his hair is a darker blond, almost light brown, and he's a lot shorter than Jayce, but he looks older by a couple of years.

"So where's Paxton tonight?" Jayce asks me. The question throws me a bit. I don't know why he's asking it. He hasn't brought Paxton up since he first found out about him. I'm worried he's trying to catch me out in my lie after overhearing Ebb and me earlier this morning.

"He's out campaigning. Has been for the last few days," I reply.

"Who's Paxton?" Jamie asks.

"Uh ..." I stutter. How in the world am I going to answer this with Ebb here?

"Allira's boyfriend," Jayce responds, a slight smile on his lips.

Ebb practically chokes on the water she started sipping. "Boyfriend?" she exclaims. I glare at her, begging her not to expose me. Although by the look on Jayce's face, he already knows, and Ebb's just confirmed his suspicions.

"Campaigning? You mean Paxton James is your boyfriend?" Jamie asks.

"Uh. Let's not talk politics tonight," I say.

"So, what are we drinking?" Jayce changes the subject, letting the issue slide.

"Something strong," I mumble, making the table laugh.

A few rounds and some food later, I actually find that I'm enjoying myself. The conversation is flowing as easily as the drinks. I thought it was going to feel weird, like Jamie and I were the third and fourth wheels on a date, but surprisingly enough, we've all interacted equally.

"So Jayce was telling me about this clinic you all work at," Jamie says. "I'll have to come by sometime and have a look."

"You really should do that," Ebb says in a flirtatious tone.

Taking a purposeful sideways glance at Jayce to see his reaction, I discover he isn't paying attention to Ebb and Jamie at all. He's looking at me, making me blush. I make a point to blame the alcohol for my warm cheeks.

"I have to go to the bathroom," I say, excusing myself from the table. I lost count of the amount of drinks I've had. I'm not drunk, but I certainly need to pee.

"I'll come with you!" Ebbodine exclaims a little louder than necessary. I can't say the same for her about not being drunk. She's had about twice as many as me.

She follows me into the bathroom and immediately says the words I've been dreading to hear. "I know I promised I wouldn't do this … but …"

"No," I say before she can finish. "You cannot leave me alone with a complete stranger."

"Jayce isn't a stranger," she says, surprising me.

"Wait … what?"

"I want some alone time with Jamie," she whispers.

"Really?" I feel my face light up even though I tell it not to.

"Yeah. Is that okay?"

"That's fine by me. I can walk home by myself—it's only a couple of blocks." *Really fine by me.* I try to hide my smile.

We get back to the table to find Jayce standing. "Hey, thanks for the evening, ladies, but I should be getting home. I actually have classes tomorrow."

"Oh, would you be able to walk Allira home? She's suddenly not feeling so well, and I worry about her walking by herself." Ebb's concerned manner is convincing, even though I know she's faking it. She was all too happy to have me walk home by myself two minutes ago.

He smiles. "Yeah, no problem."

"Call me tomorrow," I tell her.

As I go to walk away, Jayce briefly puts his hand on the small of my back, sending shivers up and down my spine.

"So, not feeling well?" he asks me as we start walking down the street.

"Classes tomorrow?" I retort.

"You were told to get lost, too?"

"Yup. I'm pretty sure your brother just stole your date," I say with a laugh.

"How do you know it wasn't the other way around?" he asks with a wry smile. "I wouldn't have come if I thought it was a date with Ebb."

Silence fills the air, the type of silence that can get awkward quickly if you don't change the subject or make a joke. Luckily, he continues talking, because I have no idea how to respond to that.

"Can I ask you something? And keep in mind, it's completely okay if you don't want to answer. I just don't want to be lied to."

"I think I know what's coming," I say with a sigh. "You want to know about Paxton."

He nods.

"I didn't technically lie."

"Is he your boyfriend or not?" he asks flat out.

"Not. But it's not as easy as that. Paxton and I have been through so much together. He has a six-year-old daughter—he doesn't have time to go out and meet eligible women between spending time with Nuka and campaigning, and I … well, I don't date—like ever—so he offered me a room in his apartment on the condition I'd be his partner to these benefits and campaign appearances. So while we aren't technically together, the media thinks we are, and he doesn't want me dating because if they were to find out, it'd show 'instability' or something. I don't understand what that means, but basically, I can't date until the election is over, and even then, I probably won't want to. So when you saw that article and assumed what everyone else assumes, I ran with it because it would've saved me from having to have this conversation."

He just nods his head, a smile playing on his lips. "You could've just told me that from the beginning."

"I could've, but you understand that you can't tell your sister about it, right? I really shouldn't have told you … I don't actually know why I told you."

"I promise I won't say anything to Jenna. And seeing as I now know the real reason why you won't go out with me, how about we go get a drink at the bar up here—just as friends. It's still early, and after my shift last night and sleeping most of the day, I'm not even tired."

I know I should say no. I need to say no. I'm going to say no.

"Sure." *Damn it.*

We walk to the nearby bar, order some drinks, and go to a booth in the back where the music isn't so loud.

"So, I think I remember you telling me you live with your sister?" I ask.

"Yeah. I'm a uni student, so I don't exactly have a lot of

money. She's only been in her job a few years, so she's just starting to make decent money now. We didn't have much of a choice about living together. It was either be roommates or live at home with Mum and Dad."

"You don't get along with your parents?"

"No, I do. They're really great, but … living with them drove me crazy."

"I understand what that's like. I was living with my parents before moving in with Paxton. It was my main reason for accepting Paxton's offer to be his crazy 'only for show' girlfriend."

"Well, just so you know, I'll be counting down to Election Day when you no longer have to be his girlfriend, and I'll be on your doorstep asking you out again."

I turn away to allow myself to blush in private. I'm met with an arrogant smirk when I face him again.

"Just don't get your hopes up. I haven't dated anyone in eighteen months, and I don't plan to anytime soon—even after the election."

"I don't suppose you want to tell me why that is?"

I don't, but for some reason I find myself saying the words anyway. "Because of my ex … Hmm, I don't know if I can even call him that. If he were still alive, I'm sure we'd still be together. Ex seems to imply a break up. We didn't break up, he didn't choose to leave me."

"Yup. That would explain it," he says in realisation. "What happened to him?"

"Ah, now *that* I'm not so comfortable talking about." Mainly because I can't tell him the truth. I could tell him Chad was shot, I could tell him I was there, but I couldn't tell him who did it or under what circumstances.

"No worries, I understand. It sucks you had to go through that—especially so young. Or was he older, like Paxton?"

"Paxton's only thirty. That's not *old*. Certainly not old enough to accept death anyway."

"Sorry. I didn't realise he was that young. And that's true about the death thing." He sighs. "I guess that was just my poor way of bringing up the fact that Paxton's too old for you anyway." There's that smirk again.

"You sound just like Ebb. Paxton may seem old, but it's only because he's had to take care of his daughter, Nuka, since his ex-wife abandoned them. And now that he's in politics, he's had to grow up really fast. Thirty is not old, no matter what you or Ebb say."

Jayce scoffs. "It's funny that Ebb thinks thirty's old."

"Why?"

"Because Jamie's twenty-nine." He laughs.

"Whoa. He doesn't look it."

"Yeah, he doesn't act it either."

"How old are you and Jenna?"

"Twenty-one. Did I forget to mention we're twins?"

"Yeah, you did."

"Oh. Well, Mum and Dad had pretty much given up on having any more kids after Jamie. They tried for years—and they like to bring it up and tell us all about it which makes us all cringe," he says, screwing up his face. "They turned to IVF, and they had one last chance. The result being Jenna and me."

"And you're studying psychology, right? That's what you said the other day at the clinic?" I fake struggling to remember what he's studying.

"Full of questions tonight, aren't you?"

"It feels good to talk about something other than me, the clinic, or Paxton for once." Not to mention how easy the conversation flows between us. He definitely has the charisma psychologists need. He makes me want to open up to him. It's scary how much I want to … or maybe that's the alcohol talking.

"I've always been fascinated by people's actions. The difference between instinctual actions and learnt behaviours. I figure why not make a career out of something I'm interested in."

"That does sound interesting. More interesting than medicine, anyway."

"You don't like medicine? Why do you do it?"

"Why do you think? Aunt Kenna needed someone, so I stepped up. Plus, I want to give something back to the Defective community. I sometimes feel responsible for what it's like now. All the violence, the killings … it's all my fault." *Stop talking!* I yell at myself. *Damn my loose lips.*

Maybe I shouldn't drink any more. Just because I want to open up to Jayce doesn't mean it's a good idea. If I'm not careful, I'm going to say something I shouldn't. And as much as he says he won't tell his sister anything, I can't risk that. I have no reason to trust this guy. *You have no reason not to trust him.* I grunt and tell my inner voice to shut up.

"How is it your fault? I don't understand."

I shake my head and smile. "Don't mind me, I'm talking gibberish. I think I've had too much to drink." I try to play it off. It's obvious he doesn't buy it, but he doesn't push the issue either.

"So why do you continue to do it—work at the clinic? I know plenty of students at university who are studying nursing who'd gladly take over your spot. Have you guys advertised for staff or volunteers around campus?"

I shake my head. "To be honest, we never imagined getting non-Defective volunteers in. We didn't think anyone would want to do it."

"You'll be surprised. Not all of us normal folk are scared of you." He says it lightly, but it just cuts that much deeper that it's the truth. A lot of people out there are afraid of us. "And you don't owe anyone anything. Staying in a job that you don't even like because you feel guilty over something that couldn't possibly be your fault is no way to live."

If only he knew the truth. "I know," I say, looking down at my drink. "Maybe you're right."

* * *

After a few more drinks, he walks me to my door like the gentleman that he is. He doesn't try to ram his tongue down my throat. He doesn't even hug me goodbye. He stands at the entrance to the building, his hands in his pockets, just waiting until I'm safely inside.

"I'll see you at work on Friday," he says before leaving.

Walking through the lobby of my building, I feel light and almost—dare I say it—happy. I'm just about to get to the elevator when one of the security guys behind the security desk yells after me.

"Miss Daniels. I have something for you," he says.

Confused, I walk over to him, and he hands me a yellow envelope. There's no address, just my name.

"Where did it come from?" I ask.

"It was dropped off via courier about an hour ago," he replies.

I look at the clock above his desk noting that it's 1:06 a.m. "Midnight is a bit late for a delivery, isn't it?"

The security man just shrugs. "You'll be surprised at what gets delivered here at all sorts of hours." His voice drips with innuendo, and I don't think I want to know any more.

Taking it in my hands, I head upstairs. I stare at the envelope, wondering what it could be.

When the elevator reaches my apartment, I open the envelope, pulling out a photograph and a typed note.

The photograph is of Jayce and me walking the street tonight on our way to the bar. We're smiling and looking at each other, and the moment looks intimate even though we aren't even touching. My blood freezes when I read the note.

Looks like Paxton isn't the only one with secrets.

CHAPTER SEVEN

I drop the papers to the floor. I can't breathe. What does this mean? Who would do something like this? What am I supposed to do with this?

"Pax—" I almost call out to Paxton, not caring that it's the middle of the night, but then I realise he's still away. He won't be back until tomorrow.

My heart hammers fast in my chest, my breathing quick and shallow, as I stand in the entryway. I bend down and pick the papers off the floor, taking them and the envelope into my room.

Sitting down on the edge of my bed, I rack my brain trying to figure out who could've sent me this. What could it mean? Shocked, I run my hand over the photo of Jayce and me. This was literally only taken a few hours ago; now, here it is, in printed form, dropped off at my doorstep.

My first thought is that it must be Brookfield, but I shake my head at the thought. If Brookfield was alive, and he came back, he'd just kill me. He'd shoot me on the street, not take a photo of me. As much as Brookfield was evil, he wasn't about playing games. If he wanted something, he took measured steps to get it as quickly as he could. He didn't play with his prey first. And why come back now? What's changed?

Which leaves the only other thing I can think of—a journalist. What do they want?

The note. I grab it off my bed and look at it again.

Looks like Paxton isn't the only one with secrets. Isn't the only one. Are they implying that I have secrets, too? That Paxton and I are hiding the fact our relationship isn't real? Are they saying that Paxton is keeping something from me, just like I'm hiding Jayce from him? Or is it saying that Jayce has secrets? He's in the photo, too—it's not just me.

I promised Paxton I wouldn't date, and I'm not. But I did have every intention of keeping Paxton in the dark about Jayce. Not that that will be an option now. I know it'll make him angry and jump to the wrong conclusions.

I rub my neck where it's all tense from worry. Flopping backwards on the bed, I wiggle my way up to my pillow. Whether it's the booze, the strange envelope, or the fact that I'm so tired and exhausted, all I want to do is switch off.

Sleep isn't accepting my open invitation. My mind is in that middle area—not yet asleep but not quite awake either. I'm conscious of my surroundings, but I'm also confused when I hear a baby cry at the foot of my bed, and I look up to see a talking piece of pizza in my room. Clearly, I'm dreaming, but

I'm oddly aware that I'm not really there. *This is why I shouldn't drink.*

I wake at nine a.m., still in my clothes from the night before, still with the mysterious envelope on the bed next to me.

My plan was to spend the day in bed, but I know I won't be able to get any actual rest. I make my way into the kitchen to cook a good hearty breakfast to squash the queasy feeling left over from last night's drinks.

There's a note on the kitchen counter.

Allira,

Mr. James called. He's staying away a few more days. He's asked me to bring Nuka out to him. We will be back on Sunday morning.

Linds.

Crap! Now what am I going to do? I don't have anyone to talk to about this envelope and what it means. Tate and Shilah are away with Paxton. Ebb is so not the person to take this to—she's almost as anti-Paxton as the Collective for Normals' Advocacy Group. I *could* take it to Drew; he'd know how to handle something like this. But going back to the Institute when I was only there a few days ago? My hatred for that place is just as strong as it ever was, even if it is different now. Too much happened there. I'm not going back there unless I truly have to. Talking to my mother about it is a possibility, but I shut that idea down as quickly as it comes. I can't confide in Jayce either—I don't want to bring him into this.

I have no one.

* * *

Sitting at the kitchen bench, my right leg bouncing rapidly, I keep going to chew my nails, only to force myself to stop. I stayed inside the apartment all day yesterday, not daring to venture out, not even daring to stand by a window in case someone was watching. The thought of going to work tonight is churning my stomach. I have no idea what to do.

I go over my theory again. *A journalist sent the photo. They're trying to get me to open up. They'll be approaching me soon. There's not much I can do about it now.* This is what I've been repeatedly telling myself for the last twenty-four hours, hoping I'll finally convince myself that my words are true.

Arriving at the clinic for my usual Friday night shift, I find Ebb puttering around, preparing to end her day shift.

"You didn't answer when I called yesterday," she says.

"I know. Sorry. I was in a Chad mood, and I know you hate it when I'm in one of those," I lie. "Chad mood" is what Ebb calls it when I'm wallowing in grief. As bad as it makes me, I'm finding that excuse works better than PMS when I want to get out of things. *Yup, I'm probably going to hell.*

"You probably didn't want to hear what I had to say then," she says.

"Oh? What's that?"

"That Jamie is … I don't know what he is. He's like the most amazing person I've ever met."

"Whoa," I say. Coming from Ebb, that's massive. "But you've spent one night with him. How do you know …" Her face flushes as she looks down at her feet. "You spent yesterday with him, too, didn't you?"

She nods slowly. "I don't think you understand. I don't want to be away from him. He—"

"No, no. I do. I understand completely," I say, smiling.

I wonder how long it'll take before Ebb gets sick of Jamie. It always happens. Fall fast and hard, get bored, and break up a month or so later.

"So what happened with you and Jayce when he walked you home?" she asks with hope in her eyes.

"Nothing," I snap, thinking of the photo.

For a brief moment, I get the crazy notion that she sent the envelope. But no, she was out with us, and it would've been impossible for her to leave the restaurant, take the photo, print it plus the note, and have it delivered to my apartment. More importantly, she's Ebb—she's my oldest friend. I'm clearly too strung out over this—now I'm thinking like a crazy woman.

"Nothing?" she asks, raising her eyebrows.

"We went for a few more drinks, but that's it. We're friends."

"I know you want more," Ebb says. "I realised it the minute I asked him out."

"And you went out with him anyway?"

She rolls her eyes. "After dragging you out with us. It wasn't my original plan to fall for Jamie, but it definitely was my plan to leave you and Jayce alone," she says with a conspiratorial smile.

Before I get the chance to yell at her *and* mock her for saying she's fallen for Jamie after two days, the doors to the clinic open, and Jayce and Jamie walk in.

Damn, Jayce looks good in scrubs. No! Stop it!

Ebb's around the counter and in Jamie's arms within seconds, her legs wrapping around his waist, their mouths coming together for a deep, passionate kiss.

Jayce walks around the back of the reception desk and puts his backpack down underneath it. "Well, it looks like their date went well," he says.

"Maybe you picked the wrong girl after all," I joke.

"I picked the right girl, I'm just waiting for her to pick me," he whispers in my ear as he brushes past me. It puts a smile on my face.

Aunt Kenna comes through the doors next. "Oh, please, Ebbodine, this is a sterile environment."

We all laugh as Ebb peels herself away from Jamie.

"Go get your things and we'll get going," Jamie says, slapping her on the butt as she walks back to the desk to grab her bag.

"I did not need to see that," Jayce says.

"It's Ebbodine. You'll have to get used to stuff like that," I say as she walks by me.

"Ha. Ha. I'll see you guys on the weekend," Ebb says, leaving with Jamie.

"Ready for another fun-filled night at the clinic?" Aunt Kenna says, overly excited.

"Why are you so chipper tonight?" I ask.

"Did you see the paper this morning?"

"No?" My heart starts racing. *Am I in the paper again? Has Paxton and my relationship been exposed? Is it the photo of Jayce and me?*

Aunt Kenna grabs the paper out of her bag, handing it to me. The headline reads: "Clinic for the Defective in Need of Funds."

Quickly skimming the article, it advertises the concept of the clinic, praises Aunt Kenna for her innovation, and then it mentions our struggle to survive on funding from the Institute alone, making a public appeal for donations and volunteers.

"How … who …"

Aunt Kenna directs her gaze behind me to Jayce. I turn to see him looking a little sheepish and nervous. "I may have spoken to my sister about this place," he says, running his hand over the back of his neck nervously.

Reading the article again, I find the byline. "By Jenna Harrison."

I throw my arms around Jayce without even thinking. "Thank you," I whisper in his ear. His hands wrap around my back and I realise I'm probably holding on for just that little too long. He holds me tighter when I try to pull away.

"I would've done it sooner if I knew I'd get this kind of reaction out of you," he whispers before letting me go. I feel the fresh blush on my cheeks but I don't even try to hide it.

"Oh good," Aunt Kenna interrupts, making me break eye contact with Jayce. "I was worried I was going to have to give you two the sterile environment talk, too. Jayce, thank you so much. We've been struggling and … just … well, thank you," she finishes, getting a bit teary.

"It was nothing. Really. You two deserve to have this place work out," he replies. "Word just needs to spread around about it. I didn't even know it existed until two weeks ago."

"Well, thanks to you, we're already on our way to doing that. We've already had donations coming in." I can't remember seeing Aunt Kenna this excited, not since the clinic's been open anyway. "Now, you two, get to work. I suspect we're going to be a lot busier now."

* * *

While Jayce is out back sterilising some equipment, I have a moment to myself. I don't know what possessed me to bring it, but I reach into my bag and pull out the envelope, making my way into the walk-in supply closet to be alone. I've already spent the last twenty-four hours looking at this, but I keep thinking that I'm missing something, and my mind keeps going back to it every chance it gets.

I'm concentrating so hard on the photo that I don't register the almost silent footsteps behind me. Not until there's a hand on my shoulder. Instinct takes over, and my self-defence training that Chad taught me kicks in. I elbow the person in the ribs, turn, and punch whoever it is in the face.

Oh, holy shit. I just punched Jayce in the face.

"Ahh, what the hell?" he says, his voice muffled from holding his nose.

My hand goes up to my mouth in shock. "Oh my God, I'm sorry, I'm sorry, I'm so sorry."

Jayce's gaze falls to the floor, noticing the papers I dropped during the kafuffle. "Is that …" he says, his head tilting to the side. He bends down and picks up the photo with his right hand while his left still holds his nose. "Why do you have a photo of us? And where did you learn to hit like that … ow! And why did you break my nose?"

"There's a lot you don't know about me, Jayce."

"Then tell me," he says, as if it's as simple as that. *Maybe it is that simple?*

"At least let me fix your nose while I do it," I say, grabbing his hand and leading him out to the treatment room.

"What happened here?" Aunt Kenna asks, rushing over to us.

"Oh, you know, just your butt-kicking niece thinking I was a punching bag," Jayce says, laughing and then wincing in pain.

Aunt Kenna looks at me. "There's the girl we've been waiting to see again." She comes over to hug me.

Jayce, shocked, looks at Aunt Kenna. "You're happy that she punched me?"

"You have to understand, Jayce, this side of Allira hasn't been seen for a long time. After losing ..." she looks at me suddenly, afraid she's about to cross a line.

"He knows about Chad," I mumble.

Her eyes widen in surprise, but a smile crosses her lips. She turns back to Jayce. "When Chad died, it was like a part of her died with him. It was almost like"—she hesitates—"as if he took all of her strength and determination with him. Like he was the reason she was so confident, so brave, so strong. I haven't seen her like that in a long time."

I wipe the few tears that have escaped me as she wraps her arm around me again. "You never told me you felt that way."

"I didn't think you had the strength to hear it," she says, holding me tighter.

"You do now?" I ask.

"By the look of his nose—yes."

"So you used to beat up guys a lot?" Jayce asks.

"Please," Aunt Kenna scoffs. "She knocked one of her boyfriends out cold once. You should thank your lucky stars you're still conscious." Aunt Kenna walks out, leaving me to explain everything to Jayce.

But where the hell do I start?

Jayce sits on the edge of one of the treatment beds as I start cleaning up his nose.

"So what did you want to know first?" I ask, stepping forwards between his legs and examining his face. Our bodies are so close, his thighs brushing up against my hips, and I find it hard to concentrate.

"How about we start with the photo."

My eyes scrunch as I start wiping away some blood from his face. "I'm really sorry about your nose," I say, stalling.

"I'm starting to think you just wanted to mess up my face so no other girls will ask me out. It's a pretty vicious way to mark your territory."

"Please, if anything, I've made you look better. Girls like tough guys."

His eyebrows go up in surprise before he winces in pain again. "So is that what I have to do to get you to go out with me? Go punch someone out?"

I laugh. "You're persistent, I'll give you that. But—and please don't take this the wrong way—I don't exactly see you as the 'punching someone out' type."

His eyebrows pull together in a small scowl.

"Don't get me wrong, physically you could pull it off, but from what I've learnt about you, you'd be more of a 'talk it out' rather than 'fight it out' kind of person."

"Am I that transparent?"

"Well, you didn't even try to stop me when I attacked you."

"You were too bloody quick," he retorts. "But you're right, I guess. I've never been in a fight, nor do I intend to ever get in one. I just don't see how violence could solve anything."

I take my hands away from his face and stare down into his eyes. "Once upon a time, I would've agreed with you."

"But not now?"

I just shake my head. "Enough about that—you wanted to know about the photo."

"Right, the photo. We should probably talk about that."

"It was dropped off at security in my apartment building. I don't know who it's from or what they want," I say while continuing to fix up his nose.

"When?" he asks.

"When, what?"

"When was it dropped off?"

"That night."

Jayce's eyes narrow. "They went to all that trouble in one night? Was there anything with the photo?"

"A note. 'Looks like Paxton isn't the only one with secrets.'"

"That's what the note said? *Isn't the only one* with secrets?"

"I thought the wording was weird, too. The only logical explanation to me is that some journalist found out about Paxton and me and is going to out us."

"Then why send the photo? Why not write the article and expose you?"

I hadn't really thought of that. "I don't know."

"I can ask my sister to look into it if you want, but—"

"No. Please don't. I don't want her writing an article about it or Paxton."

"She wouldn't do that."

"I just don't know what I'm going to do about it, and I think the less people that know, the better. At least for now."

"Okay. But have you at least told Paxton?"

"He hasn't been home," I say, finishing up with his nose and reluctantly taking a step back. "There you go, it doesn't even need a bandage. I actually didn't really do much damage at all. I must have lost my touch."

"Have you told anyone about the note?"

"I've told you."

"Only because I caught you looking at it, and now I'm paying the price," he says, rubbing his nose. "Were you going to tell anyone?"

"I was thinking about it."

Jayce sighs, giving up on that part of the conversation. "Okay, so next thing I want to know is where you learnt how to be some kind of karate kung fu master?"

"It's krav maga, and that's a pretty long story. A really long story actually."

Jayce continues to stare at me, waiting for me to continue.

"The short version is that Chad taught me when he was alive." I take another step away from him at the mention of Chad's name. It feels weird being close to Jayce while talking about Chad. "There's just so much you don't know. I don't exactly know where to start."

Jayce grabs my hands and gently pulls me towards him. "Then don't," he says.

"What?" I ask.

"I want to know everything about you, but it doesn't have to be all at once. It's obvious you've been through a lot, and I don't want to push you. You can tell me whenever you're ready. I don't mind waiting."

I can't help narrowing my eyes. I'm so confused. "Okay, but you have to tell me something."

"Anything," he says.

"What is wrong with you?"

"Wrong with me?" He quirks an eyebrow.

"Nobody is as perfect as you seem to be. Something has to be wrong. Like you're a serial killer, or you have pent-up mummy issues and I remind you of her, or you're an undercover cop just waiting for me to use my ability so you can arrest me and throw me in a jail cell." *Wouldn't be the first time that's happened.* "There's something wrong with you—there has to be. Especially if you're willing to wait around for a girl like me who has more baggage than a train station."

Jayce tries not to laugh. "Well, I can tell you for certain that I'm not a serial killer, I have no mummy issues that I'm aware of, and just so you know—you remind me nothing of her— and if I was an undercover cop, don't you think I would've asked you about your ability by now? I have no idea what your ability is, and it hasn't even really occurred to me to ask. I hope that one day you'll tell me, but right now, I actually don't care what it is. You're not going to scare me off with your baggage. I like your baggage. It made you into the person you are, and while I've only known you a couple of weeks, I can undoubtedly say that I like you."

Well, that makes one of us.

"I'll be ready to listen when you're ready to talk," Jayce says, letting go of my hands that I'd forgotten he was still holding. He stands up and walks out of the treatment room, leaving me wanting him to come back.

CHAPTER EIGHT

There has been a shift in me this morning. Instead of dreading going to work tonight, I'm actually looking forward to it—on a Saturday, no less! I try to kid myself that I'm simply enjoying the job more, but deep down, I know it's because of Jayce. I'm just not going to admit that to anyone—ever. I already feel guilty enough just thinking it, as if I'm cheating on Chad or something. I know it's ridiculous to feel that way, but I can't just turn it off so easily.

By the time evening rolls around, I'm a jumbled mess of excited nerves but in a good way. I walk into the clinic, and my smile immediately falls when I see him. His eyes have dark circles under them. If I didn't know what happened to him, I'd guess he'd not slept for days, but I know better. It's bruising from my punch yesterday.

I approach him cautiously. "Hey," I say casually, trying to feel out his mood. He was relatively fine with it when it happened yesterday, but now that he's probably seen his face, he might not be so okay about it.

"Hey," he says warmly. "How was your day, did you get much sleep?"

"Uh … it was fine. I slept good actually, probably the best I have in a while." He seems more than okay, but I feel the need to apologise again. "I really am sorry about your face."

He laughs. "Consider it a lesson learnt. I'll definitely know not to sneak up on you again—ever. I still maintain you were just marking your territory."

"So it's been a week of nights, how are you holding up?" I ask, changing the subject ever so expertly, like I try to every time he makes a joke about us.

"Will you judge me if I tell you that I'm exhausted?"

I give him a sympathetic stare. "No. I'd welcome you to the club. We're all tired."

"Kenna said that since the article there's been some interest in more volunteers. That'll mean you can have a break soon, yeah?" he asks.

"Hopefully. She has a few interviews lined up for next week, but then she'll probably need me to train the newbies too. Ebb would be better at it, but she's a little busy with her assignments and prac-work at the moment. Although she should be back to normal shifts here in a few days."

"From what Jamie's been telling me, she's not getting a lot of studying done during her time off," he says.

I shake my head. "I really hope Jamie doesn't get his heart broken."

"Why do you say that? I'd be more worried about Ebb being heartbroken."

"Ebb's not the 'girlfriend' type. She's a 'leave before you develop feelings for them' type."

Jayce gives a slight nod. "Jamie's the same. Maybe they *are* perfect for each other."

"Maybe."

"So what type are you?"

I look at him confused. "Type?"

"Yeah, are you 'girlfriend' material? Or more of a 'hit it and quit it' kind of girl?"

I laugh before answering seriously. "I hate dating."

"I wouldn't have guessed with the whole 'I don't date' thing you've got going on."

"What I mean is, I hate going on dates. With Chad ..." I hesitate. Do I really want to talk about him to Jayce? I worry I bring him up way too much.

"You can talk about him," he encourages.

"Well, we never went on a date. We were friends one day and together the next, and it just felt natural, easy. Like it was meant to be," I say, wistfully.

"Dating can be fun. You just need to do it with the right

person," he says with a slight arrogance.

"Let me guess, *you* would be said 'right person'?"

"You'll never know until you say yes," he says, smirking at me. I just give him a look. "I know, I know. I have to wait until Election Day."

I continue to stare at him.

"And even then, the answer will probably still be no," he says in a dejected tone.

"The answer will definitely be no if Paxton wins the election. I'll probably have to marry him if that happens."

"Paxton James, you just lost yourself a vote," Jayce jokes before looking at me, realising I'm being serious. "Wait ... what?"

"He's already asked, but I—"

"That's taking the charade a bit too far, isn't it?"

I'm a little surprised by the sternness to his voice. "Maybe." I shrug. "But how would he expect the voters to trust that he can run a country if he can't even keep his girlfriend on a tight leash?"

"Is this about the photo again? It's not like we were doing anything—we were just walking along the street. Have you spoken to him about it yet?"

"He doesn't get in until tomorrow. I'll talk to him then. Maybe."

"No maybe. You need to tell him."

"And if he tells me that I can never see you again?"

"He could try to keep me away, but I'm like lice. Once you've got me, there's no getting rid of me."

"Except with an industrial-strength solvent?"

"Exactly." He smiles before turning serious. "Would he actually ask you to do that?"

"There's no asking with Paxton. There's telling," I say and immediately regret it. I cut him off before he starts to protest. "I don't mean that the way it sounded. I know Paxton only wants what's best for him and me and this country, so usually when he suggests something, I do it no questions asked."

"Maybe that's what the note meant? Maybe you shouldn't be so quick to jump at everything Paxton says. It says he has secrets—what is he hiding?"

"You don't know Paxton. It's not going to be that," I say, even though I've thought that very same thing. What could Paxton be hiding apart from our fake relationship?

"But—"

"Can we just not talk about this anymore?"

Jayce nods. "Okay," he says, walking off into the treatment room.

* * *

I'm organising the supply closet … okay, I'm hiding. It's five-thirty in the morning, and Jayce is on the floor and at reception, so I have some time to do the extra jobs I don't get around to. Yup, that excuse sounds legit. I'm actually on an avoidance mission—avoiding talking to Jayce about Paxton again.

The door clicks open, and footsteps come towards me.

"I'm not sneaking up on you," Jayce says in a slow and clear voice. "It's only me, you don't need to attack," he says mockingly.

I turn around to face him. "Thanks for the heads-up."

"About earlier," he starts.

I shake my head. "Don't—"

"I just want to say I was out of line. You're right, I don't know Paxton. I just got the impression that he tells you what to do, and it just took me by surprise that you let him. I'm pretty sure the girl who punched me yesterday wouldn't let anyone tell her what to do."

I hang my head, almost shameful at the truth to his words. "But like my aunt told you, I haven't been her in a really long time."

He takes a step forwards, closing the gap between us. I reflexively take a small step back when he reaches me, my back pushing up against the shelf.

"You should find a way to bring her back"—he leans in—"because as much as my nose friggin' hurts, that girl is someone I could easily fall for."

My heart hammers in my chest at his proximity. As I look up into his eyes, his mouth curls into a smile on one side. Am I blushing? I'm pretty sure I'm blushing.

"Here you two are!" Vic's voice booms from behind Jayce, making us both jump. We turn to look at him, and I can't help noticing the smirk on his face. "They're in here, Kenna— making out in the supply closet."

Aunt Kenna rushes in.

"We were not making out!" I exclaim. Jayce just laughs.

"If you say so, Lia," Aunt Kenna says.

"Did you need me for something?" I ask, ignoring her blatant mocking attitude.

"Oh. It was nothing important. I'll let you get back to … what you were doing." She leaves, but Vic's not so quick to move. He's still standing there, staring at us. Aunt Kenna reaches in, dragging Vic out by the shirt.

"Well, I'm never going to hear the end of that," I say, managing a smile.

"Aww, there are worse things than making out with me in a closet, aren't there?" he asks.

"Hmm … yeah, like going to a dentist, maybe," I say. Jayce laughs. "What?"

"My brother's a dentist," he says, laughing harder.

"Damn. And just when I thought things might work between him and Ebb. She's going to have to break up with him now."

"Uh … why?"

"Because, dentists are weird. No normal person wants to look inside people's mouths all day."

"You look at people's bodily fluids all day. How is that any different?"

"Hmm … I'm not going to talk to you anymore if you're going to be all logical," I say before walking around him and towards the door. I stop before I reach the door and turn back around, thinking he'd still be standing where he was; instead, I smack my face right into his chest. *Damn, he's tall.* "Ow!" I say, rubbing my nose. "This is why there are personal space boundaries."

"You're the one who stopped walking," he says with a laugh. He puts his hands on either side of my face. "Let me have a look." He bends down so we're at eye level, and I find it hard to breathe. I totally forget the reason I stopped walking in the first place. "Oh, you're fine," he says, waving dismissively. "You're not even going to bruise," he says, pointing to his eyes.

I wince. He's right. I shouldn't complain. "Sorry, again." Yet another thing I'm probably never going to live down.

"Hey, why don't you get out of here a bit early? I've got things under control here," Jayce suggests. "Go home and get a good sleep in before you have to face Paxton."

"Yeah … I've been thinking," I say shyly.

"You have to tell someone, and it involves Paxton. He should know."

"Maybe. I'll think about it some more," I say. Jayce just sighs in return. "I will head home though, since you're offering."

"I'll see you tomorrow night? Oh. I guess it's technically tonight."

I shake my head. "Sunday is my day off. The only reason I was here last week was because Ebb was away. She's back for her shift tonight."

"Oh. So Tuesday night then?"

I shake my head again. "I'll be on day shift. Finally. It feels as if I've been on nights for a month."

"Well, I will see you sometime during the week then."

I nod before gathering my things and heading for the door. The cool morning air hits my face as I begin my walk home. The sun is almost ready to rise, making the streets a dull grey. At this time of morning, the street seems deserted, peaceful.

I walk the three blocks to my apartment without even seeing anyone, but before I reach my door, I get that feeling again. Someone's out there, and they're watching me.

Discreetly looking around, I try to scope out where they are. I try to get just a glimpse of them to see who they are. But as usual, there's nothing.

Can I really just put this down to paranoia? I have a photo that proves I'm being followed. Shaking my head, I try to squash my anger. Turning to look out to the street, I put my finger up my nose. *That'll give them a good money shot,* I think before walking into the building. Paxton will probably get angry if that gets printed; I probably shouldn't have done that. It has to be a journalist, it just has to be, but at six a.m.?

When I reach my apartment, I take my clothes off, throwing them on the floor. I don't bother showering, because I'm too exhausted. I collapse on the bed in my underwear, wrapping myself in my sheet. It feels as if I've only been asleep for ten minutes when I hear voices coming from the front door. My bedside clock tells me I've actually been asleep for almost five hours. It's nearly eleven.

"Nuka, you need to be quiet," I hear Paxton say. Funnily enough, I heard his voice first.

"I'm awake," I yell out to them.

"Lia!" Nuka yells, barging into my room and jumping on top of me.

"I missed you too, kid," I say, sitting up and hugging her.

"Nuka." Paxton's voice comes through the door. He stands in the doorway in casual clothes, leaning up against the doorframe. "It's not polite to barge into Allira's room."

"What, you're worried you might find someone in here?" I say jokingly.

He looks at me a little angry, but then his eyes go wide, and he averts his gaze.

I quickly grab the sheet and pull it up over me, suddenly remembering I'm half naked. "Sorry. I couldn't be bothered to find pyjamas when I dragged myself home from the clinic this morning."

Paxton shakes his head, looking straight ahead at the wall of my bedroom and not at me. "Our fault. We shouldn't be in here. Come on, Nuka."

"But I want to tell her about my trip," Nuka complains.

"And I want to hear all about your trip, but maybe I should have a shower and get some clothes on first. I smell like the yucky clinic," I say to her, scrunching up my nose.

"I'll go make you some breakfast!" she exclaims, running past Paxton and out of the room.

"Translation? 'Daddy will make you breakfast, and I'll watch.'" Paxton sighs.

I half-smile. "Thanks. I'm glad you're back. I have something to talk to you about though. Something happened while you were away."

"Oh?" he asks.

"After breakfast," I say, looking down at my almost naked form.

"Right," he says, walking away.

I spend my entire shower going over what I'm going to say. How do I even broach the subject? "Oh yeah, you know how you told me not to date? Well, I kinda did but not on purpose. It wasn't even technically a date. Anyway, it got photographed, and now I'm being blackmailed … or not blackmailed—I don't know what they want." *Yeah, that'll go down well.*

A stack of pancakes awaits me when I reach the dining room.

"Thanks, Nuka. These look great," I say, sitting at the table. Paxton clears his throat from the kitchen, still flipping more pancakes on the stove. "Thank you too, Paxton," I say with a smile.

He brings another stack of pancakes to the table, sits down, and we start to dig in.

"So what's been going on?"

"Nothing. Not a lot. The usual. Not much at all," I say, repeating myself.

"So nothing then? You're being a little unclear."

"We have a new volunteer at the clinic. Aunt Kenna is interviewing more this upcoming week. I may even be available for more political appearances coming up," I say with a mock shocked look on my face.

Paxton looks down at his plate, avoiding my eyes. "We'll talk after breakfast."

Ugh, what now?

Nuka proceeds to tell me about all the places she got to see, which basically means hearing a list of all the hotels she stayed at and what the differences between them were. One of them had the hard soap, but she preferred the liquid soap; one of them had a fountain in the foyer, so, of course, that was her favourite.

I nod along and ask all the right questions to get her to keep talking, successfully stalling the conversation that's about to happen between Paxton and me.

"I think it's bath time, little one. You skipped it last night," Paxton says to Nuka.

"All right." She hangs her head disappointedly before getting up and going down the hall to the bathroom.

Once the water's running, Paxton turns to me. "So what really happened?"

"I'll be right back," I say, getting up and going to my room to collect the envelope. Picking it up, I surprise myself by ditching the photo under my pillow and heading back out to Paxton with only the note. It was as if instinct took over my body, telling me I shouldn't tell Paxton about Jayce. Not until he's seen the note anyway.

Walking back out into the dining room, I hand him the note and envelope. "This came for me, here. It was delivered to security on Wednesday night. I don't know what it means, and I can't for the life of me think of who sent it."

"No reply address?" Paxton says without even looking at it properly.

"Do you really think I'm not smart enough to look for a reply address?"

"Sorry," he says, finally turning his attention to the note. His eyes go wide before his brow furrows together, almost causing a monobrow.

"Monobrow!" I shout.

"What?" Paxton looks up at me.

"Where's Zac these days?"

Zac was an employee of the Institute and an avid Brookfield supporter. I always called him Monobrow because that was all I could focus on when looking at his face. He was at every one of my interrogations, every one of my "tests" that the Institute forced me to endure while I was imprisoned there.

He was arrested for helping Brookfield escape. According to Paxton, he was the one who found out where Brookfield was being held and found a way to smuggle him out without anyone noticing. Paxton also says Zac's the one who tried to kill me while I was in the hospital by slipping something in my central line, but this couldn't be proven, and he got away with attempted murder. Last I heard, he got a few months of jail time for Brookfield's escape, and that was it. He'd definitely be out by now.

"When he was released, he moved up north, as far away from here as possible. That's what I've heard anyway," Paxton answers me.

"Could it be him? I don't know why or what he'd want, but … I don't know. I'm grasping at straws. My first thought was Brookfield."

"What makes you think it could be either of them? What if it's just a journalist trying to get to me, through you?"

"We thought of that, but why wouldn't they just write the article?"

"Blackmail? Trying to get an exclusive? Trying to get the whole story before they can go to print? There's many reasons why they'd do something like this first. What I want to know is, what have you been doing while I've been away to warrant this, what do you mean by '*we* thought of that,' and why does this piece of paper say that you're keeping secrets from me?" Paxton's tone has escalated to downright livid.

"If you read it, it says *you're* the one keeping secrets," I reply defensively.

"I'm not the only one, apparently!" he yells.

"I'm not keeping anything from you!" *Liar.*

"Allira, I don't have the time or patience to deal with this. This is nothing. It's some reporter trying to get a story. Just ignore it and it'll go away," he says in a more rational tone.

"Okay," I say, a little relieved. He thinks it's a journalist, too.

"When do you think your aunt will have the new staff trained by?"

"Why do you want to know that?"

"We're at a pivotal point in the campaign." He sighs. "I hate to ask this, but I'm going to need you by my side more than ever. I'm going to need you to come with us on the campaign trail."

My heart sinks. "Come with you?" I stutter. "That was never part of the deal, Paxton."

"Well, it needs to be," he practically orders.

"Okay, just say I go with you to do all of your campaigning, and then come Election Day, you win—what's going to happen then? What happens to me? Will you ever tell everyone the truth?"

"You want to end our arrangement?" he asks, slinking back

into his chair in surprise.

"I'm not saying that. I just don't know how long I can keep it up. We can't do this forever. I'm not going to become your wife. I'm just wondering if stopping it now will be better in the long run. Wouldn't it be worse to have a public break-up when you're president than now, when we haven't even confirmed we're together?"

"I was hoping you'd stick by me through it all."

"And in turn, prevent me from living the kind of life I want? What if I wanted to date someone? I wouldn't be able to."

Paxton stands up out of his chair, his face full of rage. "You've met someone, haven't you?"

"No!" *Yes!* "But I've decided that eventually I will want to date again. Do you just expect me to put my life on hold, for you?"

"It wouldn't be just for me. It'd be for every single Defective person out there. It'd be for Nuka, Shilah, Tate. It would be for Chad."

Tears fill my eyes in an instant. "It's unfair of you to put that on me. I've already done enough damage to the Defective community. I don't want any more responsibility to them," I whisper.

"Isn't that why you're working at the clinic? Because you feel guilty for what you've done?"

"What *we've* done," I correct him. "You, me, and Drew. It's our fault that people are out there getting killed."

"At least they're free! They get to live their lives the way they want. They're not under the Institute's reign. They're not confined to that building! You really think we were wrong?"

I shake my head. "Sometimes I'm not sure."

He walks over to me, lifts me out of my chair, and hugs me to him. When I pull away, his hands find my shoulders.

"I need you more than ever right now. Please don't back out now. I'll do anything. I *need* you, Allira."

I nod silently and he wipes away a tear on my cheek with his finger.

"Good girl. You can put your notice in tomorrow," he says, kissing my head and walking away.

Did I really just agree to leave the clinic?

CHAPTER NINE

"Hey, Aunt Kenna," I say, arriving for my Tuesday shift. "Can I talk to you in your office for a moment?" My voice is shaky.

"Sure." She turns her head towards the treatment room. "Ebb, can you come up front?" she yells.

"Coming." Ebb's voice comes from the back.

We start walking towards her office, and I'm fidgeting already. *Why am I doing this?*

As she leads me into the room and closes the door behind her, she sees the struggle in my eyes. "What's wrong?" she asks with true concern.

"I have to give you my notice," I mumble, though I try not to.

"What? Why?"

"Paxton thinks it's best if I go join him on the road with Tate and Shilah. He needs me."

"Lia, I need you, too."

"I know, and I don't want to let you down, but what other choice do I have? I made a deal with Paxton. You're getting more volunteers, and with my full-time salary gone, you may even be able to hire another doctor to do your two days off."

"That's not the only reason I need you, Lia. I love that I get to spend time with you here. I love watching you learn, and I know you don't exactly enjoy it here, but … I don't know. I guess I just love that this is our little thing that we get to do together."

"Well, maybe I can come back and volunteer sometimes," I say, forcing a smile. I mean, that's not exactly what I'd want—it's hard enough getting me to come here when I'm being paid, but what Aunt Kenna is saying is true. I love that we have something that's just ours that has nothing do with the rest of the family.

"I'd love that," Kenna says with a small, sad smile.

* * *

I make it through my Tuesday shift with only a little bit of complaint from Ebb. Okay, a lot of complaint. She's pissed I'm going campaigning with Paxton, but I know she'll get over it eventually.

Today's Wednesday though. Jayce will be coming in to work tonight to take over from my day shift, and I'm going to have to tell him. Part of me wants to skip out early like I did last night to avoid him, but if I do that again, I'll have to tell him on Saturday where we have a whole shift together. At least today, I can tell him and then leave, giving him a few days to get over it before I see him again.

It's getting close to the time he's due to come in, and my nerves have been slowly building over the last six hours to a point where I think I'm about to throw up. *Why am I getting so worked up over this?*

The door opens, and he walks in with a scowl on his face. He already looks as if he's in a bad mood. Maybe I should just tell him on Saturday. He walks behind the reception desk, dumps his bag, and keeps walking until he reaches me. Without stopping, he grabs my wrist and drags me into the supply closet.

"Is it true?" he asks, once we're inside and the door is shut.

"Is what—"

"You're leaving?"

"Who told—"

"Jamie."

How did he …? Oh, right, Ebb. "It's true. It's not something I

126

want to do. It's something I have to do," I try to explain.

"Is this because of the photo?"

I shake my head. "I didn't even show him the photo, just the note. But he'd already made up his mind before I even gave him that. He needs me on the road with him."

"No, he doesn't, not as much as your aunt needs you here. Not as much as I want you here," he says before he shakes his head in confusion. "Why didn't you show him the photo? I mean—there's nothing going on between us, so it wouldn't have mattered, right?" His lips turn up into a half-smile.

I avoid eye contact with him, glancing down at my feet. "I don't know why I didn't show him. It was a last-second thing where I shoved it under my pillow instead."

"You sleep with a photo of me under your pillow? Damn, you must have it bad for me." He laughs.

I swallow hard, not really knowing how to respond to that. "It doesn't matter how I feel about you because nothing could ever happen. Not until I'm free of Paxton … which at this rate, might be never."

"I think that's the closest you've come to actually admitting that you like me."

"I do," I whisper, as if I'm ashamed. "But—"

I'm cut off by Jayce's soft lips on mine and his strong arms around me. His kiss is reserved at first, unsure if this is okay or not. When my mouth opens, accepting his, he pulls me in tighter, and his kiss becomes more urgent. My body reflexively reacts to his, moulding to him. I've never felt this kind of spark—this jolt of need—with anyone, not even Chad.

This thought sobers me. I come to my senses and will myself to break the connection, as hard as it is to do. I'm breathless, hot, and I'm certain I'm bright red. "What are you doing to me?" I complain. He's certainly not making this easy on me.

"Just showing you what you could have if you stay," he whispers, not removing his hands from around my back. Our faces are still only centimetres away from each other.

Running my hands up his arms and across to his chest, I whisper, "I can't stay. And this can't happen again." I manage to sound slightly convincing as I say it. It's even more convincing when I push myself away from him and walk out of the room.

I grab my bag and quickly head for the exit. Jayce leans on the doorframe to the supply closet, watching me leave.

As I walk the few blocks home, I think about his lips on mine, and I suddenly don't care where it happened, when it happened, or how it happened. I just want it to happen again.

I wince at my thoughts. *No, it can't happen again.*

* * *

Ebbodine stands in front of the reception desk, holding out a coffee for me as I arrive for my Saturday night shift at the clinic. She has a suspicious smile on her face, and my nerves kick in immediately. What has she done now?

"I have a surprise for you," she says with a cheeky smile.

"Why does that fill me with dread?" I ask, taking a sip of my coffee.

"Ugh." She slouches. "Come on."

She grabs my arm and starts dragging me, my coffee spilling all over my hand. I place it on the reception desk as she continues to drag me to the bathroom, where I find a mini-skirt and black top hanging from the windowsill.

"What is this?" I ask.

"You have the night off," she says matter-of-factly.

"No, I don't."

"Yes, you do." She grabs my hand and drags me back out of the bathroom, past reception, and into the treatment area. With how fast she's moving and how erratic she is, I wonder just how much coffee she's had tonight. "See," she says, pointing at Aunt Kenna who's showing around two people in scrubs whom I've never seen before.

"Aunt Kenna gave you and Jayce the night off. Since that article, we've had heaps of interest in volunteering here. The two girls over there are nursing students."

"Why didn't you call me sooner? I could've stayed in bed."

"No. You have a Saturday night off, you're not going to spend it in bed. Allira, it's *Saturday* night. When do we ever get a Saturday off?"

"Uh, never?"

"Exactly!" she exclaims.

"Why don't you take the night off then if you want it so badly?"

"Ah, because it turns out your Aunt Kenna is as cunning and manipulative as me," she replies with a proud smile.

"What?"

She grabs my hand, and *again* with the dragging. We get back to the reception desk where Jayce is standing in jeans and a tight-fitting button-down shirt with the sleeves rolled up. His hair is messed, as if it was purposefully done that way, and he looks amazing.

"She'll be right with you," Ebb says to Jayce, continuing to drag me back to the bathroom. He gives me a sympathetic stare as I go by. "Now. Get dressed," she orders.

"Ebb," I start to protest.

"Nope. You can't blame me for this one. This is all your aunt's doing. I'm just here to enforce what she wants." Ebb's face is almost giddy.

I find myself about to smile, but I push it away. Forcing a sigh as if I'm disappointed, I reach for the clothes. I don't want her to know that I actually want this, even though I shouldn't be doing it.

"Good girl. Now hurry up so I can do your makeup."

"Makeup? Really? You brought your makeup here? He's already seen me without it. He'll think I'm making an effort."

"Good."

We exit the bathroom after Ebb "beautifies" me and walk in to the end of Aunt Kenna telling Jayce that we deserve the night off with how much work we've been doing.

"You two should go out and have fun," Aunt Kenna says to me.

Grabbing my coffee off the desk, I down the entire thing in one gulp—perfect drinking temperature.

"I'm ready," I say as we make our way out of the clinic. When I turn to say goodbye to Ebb and Aunt Kenna, they both have suspicious conspirator's smiles plastered across their faces.

"I just want to say that this wasn't my idea," Jayce says as soon as we're outside.

"Hmm, that smile of yours says otherwise."

"Well, I didn't say I think it's a *bad* idea." His smile disappears when he sees the hesitation in me. "We don't have to do this if you don't want to. To be honest, I wasn't even sure if I should've come after …" He looks down at his feet briefly before meeting my eyes. "This doesn't have to be like a date. I can take you to the least romantic place possible if you want? Some uni friends are going to the bar on campus if you want to go there. Nothing says unromantic like drunken students."

"I guess that sounds safe."

"Safe? You worried I'm going to attack you? Because I'm pretty sure you can handle yourself," he says, pointing to his face that's completely healed now, but the memory remains.

My hand goes up to my mouth to hide my smile. "I really am sorry."

"You've apologised enough. And it'd be more convincing if you weren't laughing."

"Sorry," I say again, trying to stifle my laugh.

"So what did you mean by 'safe'? Really?" he asks.

"Safe as in very unromantic like you said."

"Ah. Scared you'll fall victim to my charm if I romance you?"

I shake my head. "Let's just go already." *I think I'm already falling for his charm.*

"My car is over here," he says, leading the way.

We pull up to the bar fifteen minutes later. The outside looks dingy and dirty, and the air smells of stale beer and that cleaning stuff we have at the clinic that soaks up vomit. *Charming.*

"So this is your world," I say. "I didn't think it would smell so bad."

Jayce laughs. "Yeah, I used to spend many nights here before the clinic. You get used to the smell." He grabs my hand and starts leading me in. "It's not as bad inside."

He lets go of my hand once we're inside, my disappointment embarrassingly obvious. The inside of the bar is not much better than the outside. Smell-wise it's an improvement, but it feels like my retinas are being burned by neon lighting. Where in the world do you even get neon lighting from these days? That's so last century.

The music is dim and on the quiet side which is a welcome surprise for a uni bar. The atmosphere is relaxed, and it seems like a casual place to hang out. I can see why Jayce would spend a lot of time here.

He leads me over to a table with four people already seated. One of the guys stands up, giving Jayce a man-hug. He's shorter than Jayce, but nearly everyone is.

"Dude! I thought you were working at that *Defective* place tonight?" he says.

"Managed to get the night off," Jayce says, not bothering to pull him up on the condescending tone. "Robbie, this is Allira, Allira—Robbie."

"Nice to meet you," Robbie says politely, reaching out and shaking my hand.

Jayce grabs two chairs from another table, bringing them over for us to sit.

"Beer?" Robbie offers.

"No thanks, I'm driving," Jayce replies.

"Allira?"

"No thanks. I'm good for now."

I don't feel like drinking tonight. All I see around me is inebriated people everywhere and others trying to catch up to the same state of drunkenness.

Jayce introduces me to the others at the table, two girls, Whit and Max, although I don't know which one's which, and the other guy, Ryan.

"So how do you and Jayce know each other?" the blonde girl asks with Ebb-like peppiness. The other—the brunette girl—looks at me with less than friendly eyes. "Is this like a date?"

Jayce and I look at each other with the same smile. "No," we say in unison.

"I work at the clinic, too," I say.

"Oh," the blonde girl says, surprised. "What's it like working with … *them?*" She's way too excited. I can tell already that she's going to be one of *those* people. The kind of person who likes to pretend she's all-knowing, she's all pro-Defective, but actually knows nothing and frequently says offensive things, even though she doesn't mean to. Their hearts are generally in the right place, but they've just never been around us enough to know what's acceptable and what's not.

The brunette has her face screwed up, disgusted at the thought of working with people like me. It's pretty obvious Jayce hasn't told his friends about me. Not that he would've had reason to, and we didn't know we were coming until half an hour ago, so he didn't have time to warn them.

"It's not any different than working at the hospital or any other clinic," I reply.

"I still can't believe you work there, Jayce," Robbie says, sitting back down after getting beer from the bar. "They should all go back to the Institute where they belong."

Oh yeah, tonight is going to be real fun.

"Uh, guys," Jayce starts, but I grab his arm, slowly shaking my head.

"They don't belong in society," Robbie continues. "They're coming out of the woodwork now they're free. They seem to be everywhere. They're stealing our jobs, government housing, and funding. Next they'll be taking our spots at university." He looks at Jayce and me. "I know you guys work with them so you have to defend them, but I just don't know why they can't go back. Keep them away from us. I wouldn't mind being given everything I need, not having to work. I don't know why they complain so much."

"Wow. You sound like the Collective. Maybe you should go to the Institute if you think it's so great." My tone is still relatively calm. I've met with this sort of ignorance before—random strangers around the clinic and well-educated political people at some of Paxton's events—and I worked out quickly that getting angry just makes them think they're right about us.

"I don't understand how you can work with them when they could use their magic on you, kill you on the spot," Robbie says.

I have to laugh at that. "Magic? Really? You think Defective people sit around, conjuring spells like witches? Do you believe in Bigfoot, too?"

"Magic, abilities, same thing. They can still kill you."

"What's the difference between someone taking a gun and shooting you and someone using their ability to kill you? In the clinic, we see more shootings, stabbings, and beatings than ability injuries. And, by the way, I'm yet to come across an ability that *could* kill you. I did meet this kid once who could give an electric shock through his fingertips, but even at his strongest, I don't think he could kill you."

"You don't know what you're talking about. What about the kid who destroyed half the country?" Robbie says, going straight for the number one excuse used for why we should be banished from society; the boy who blew up the country more than *forty* years ago.

"So because of one kid four decades ago, we should all be punished for his actions? Which could've been totally preventable had the government embraced or nurtured us instead of treating us like we're less than human."

"*Us?*" Robbie asks, his head cocked to the side.

I roll up my sleeve, showing my mark.

The table goes silent. Jayce's mouth opens in awe.

"You're one of them?" Blondie asks, almost giddy with excitement. It seems no one else shares her feelings, though.

"I am," I say, leaning back in my chair.

"You were at the Institute?" she asks.

Jayce glares at her. "Whit," he says in a warning tone.

"No, it's okay," I say. "I'm open to answering questions. I get it a lot," I say, shrugging it off. "I was at the Institute."

"For how long?" Ryan speaks for the first time since meeting me.

"I was pretty lucky. I was a late bloomer. I didn't get my ability until I was eighteen. I was only in custody for six months before Brookfield was kicked out."

"Was that photo real?" Whit asks. "The one with the guy in the cell? He's running for vice president now, isn't he? Is that what it was really like there?"

The photo of Tate in his cell in the last few days before the Institute was liberated was everywhere after Paxton televised it to prove the mistreatment of Defectives there. It seemed to be that anywhere you looked—TV or newspapers—that photo would appear.

"It was real. The guy in that photo is actually my brother-in-law."

Whit's face lights up as if she just got the best piece of gossip ever. "Were you treated like that?"

"I—"

"Allira," Jayce says quietly, touching my arm, "You don't have to do this."

"I know I don't have to. But people need to know the truth, and if people are willing to listen, then they deserve to know." I turn to face Whit. "When I was arrested, I didn't know I was Defective. I didn't have an ability. So when I couldn't tell them what I could do, they beat me. When that didn't work, they put me in a room with bright, blinding light and an alarm so loud that the sound didn't leave me for days after the ringing stopped. Next thing they did to try to get me to reveal my ability was put me through electroshock therapy to see if it could trigger it within me. All it did was make me lose consciousness. They told me that they were simply 'running tests' to try to bring my ability out of me somehow. I was lucky. I only had to endure days of it. Others I know endured weeks."

"Why did they stop?" Whit asks.

"Only after a freak accident—through no fault of my own or theirs—revealed my ability."

"What *is* your ability?" Ryan asks.

"Dude! You can't just ask people that," Jayce says.

"Why not?" Whit asks.

I politely smile at her as best I can. "It's kind of like asking someone what sexual position they prefer," I say as an analogy. "You know what it is, but you don't exactly want everyone else to know."

"I don't think there's anything wrong with *that* question either," Ryan says. The table manages to laugh, even given the seriousness of our conversation.

"Also, it seems to be that once you tell someone what your ability is, some people want to see it in action. They don't really seem to care that it can send you to prison."

Robbie and the brunette have been remarkably quiet since I revealed my secret.

"Don't worry, Robbie, you don't have to be scared of little ol' me," I tease.

He doesn't seem to appreciate the banter.

"I can't use my ability unless I'm near another Defective person."

"Why not?" Whit asks.

"I can borrow other abilities, but I have to be in range," I say.

"That's what you can do?" Jayce asks, leaning forwards and taking my hand. My skin warms to his touch.

I nod, telling myself I can fill him in on the whole "double ability" debacle another day … or not.

"Hey, is it also true that they were training you all up like ninjas, like some sort of super army?" Ryan asks.

The ninja comment makes me laugh, but I give the response Paxton has always said I should give when asked this. "You can't believe *all* of the conspiracy theories," I say with a convincing smile but notice a look of realisation cross Jayce's face.

Robbie gets up from the table without a word, heading back to the bar again. Jayce stands up to follow him. "I'll be right back," he says. Ryan also gets up to go after them, leaving me with the girls.

"So are you sure you and Jayce aren't, like, together?" Whit asks.

"I'm sure. Why do you ask?"

"Oh, no reason. You just seem … close," she says, glancing at the other girl, Max. I get the feeling I may be stepping on Max's toes.

"We're just friends," I say.

"But you like him," she states.

I feel my face flush. There's silence between the three of us for what seems like an excruciatingly long time. I don't really know how to respond to her, and now too much time has gone by to say anything.

"Excuse me," I say, getting up to go find Jayce and the others.

The three of them are standing, facing the bar with their backs to me. "Why would you bring her here?" Robbie asks. "You're not seriously on a date with her, are you?"

"I don't understand why you're being like this," Jayce says.

"I don't understand why you're here, either," Ryan says. "I've heard Defectives are firecrackers in the sack. You should be in bed," he says with a laugh.

Where did that rumour start? My bad date, Dex, thought something similar when I was with him.

"That's disgusting," Robbie states. "They should be with their own kind."

I don't know why this pushes me past the breaking point, but it does. I don't know if I'm just looking for an excuse to kiss Jayce again or if I feel I really need to make my argument, but I walk up behind Jayce, running my hands down his back and around his waist, pulling him around to face me. Rising up on my tippy toes, I bring my lips to meet his. It's a short kiss compared to our first, but it's still just as intense and sends tingles all over.

"I dunno," I say, pulling away slowly. "What do you think? Totally gross?"

"Mmm, disgusting," he says, nodding slowly with a grin.

I force myself to step away and am met with Robbie looking even more pissed off, and Ryan's looking pretty bashful. I can almost feel the burning glares from the girls back at the table.

"Let's go," Jayce says, grabbing my hand and heading for the exit. "I'm sorry about them," he says as soon as we get outside. "I guess you've found my thing?"

"Your thing?"

"My flaw. I have A-holes for friends," he says, unlocking his car.

We get in, and he starts the engine. "They aren't so bad," I lie.

"You handled that amazingly, by the way."

"I've had many conversations like that. Although, I usually shut them down a lot quicker."

"You didn't have to do that."

I shrug. "I probably shouldn't have kissed you. I'm sorry about that, but if I'm not going to stick up for my own kind, then I can't expect anyone else to."

"You never have to be sorry about kissing me," he says with a smile that I can't help but return. "Ever."

141

Aunt Kenna's right. I haven't spoken like this in a long time. I haven't even thought like this. Something's changed in me, and I'd like to think it's for the better.

"So, home? Or coffee?" he asks.

"You ask me that as if there's more than one possible answer. The answer is always coffee. *Always*."

He smiles and starts driving through the city towards the café.

"We could go somewhere else, not so close to the clinic?" he says as he pulls up outside our usual place.

"Nah. They won't know we're here unless one of them comes for coffee."

"So basically, they'll know within five minutes."

"We do drink a lot of coffee, don't we?" I say with a small laugh.

We find a table outside. The cool night air smells fresh—as fresh as it can get in the city anyway. Mix that with ground coffee beans, and I think I'm in heaven. Jayce goes inside to order.

"There's one thing I want to ask you," he says, sitting down with two coffees, handing one to me.

I take a sip and am surprised to find he knows my drink order without having to ask me. "Yeah?"

"You don't have to answer it if you don't want to. You've already answered so much for me and my stupid friends tonight," he says putting his hand on top of mine on the table.

I can't shift my gaze away from our hands. "But Ryan was right, wasn't he?"

Break the tension, make a joke. Stop looking at our hands. I force myself to make eye contact, a small smile on my lips. "That we're firecrackers in the sack? Well … from my experience, I'd say we're okay. A more educated conclusion could come from Ebbodine."

Jayce winces. "Eww, I am *not* asking my brother about his sex life." He sits back in his chair, letting go of my hand.

"I was one of them," I admit. "I was trained at the Institute to be a field agent."

"Field agent?"

"Well, we weren't an army like Ryan thought, but we were sent back into the real world to arrest others like us. I was in the field for three months."

"So that whole time that Mr. Brookfield was telling us 'Defectives need to be isolated,' he was sending you back out into society? He obviously couldn't have believed his own words if that were the case."

"Oh, Brookfield believed we were dangerous."

"Then why send you back out?" Jayce asks, confused.

"Because he knew we wouldn't jeopardise him or the Institute."

"Why not? Why didn't you all escape?"

We did. But I can't tell him about that. "Well … we wore

tracking bracelets, so they knew where we were the whole time. And secondly—and this is just in my case—Brookfield threatened the life of my brother if I was to do anything to go against him."

"So you knew Brookfield well?"

I nod slowly. "I knew Brookfield fairly well, unfortunately."

"And you have no idea where he is now?"

"None. If I did, the authorities would better hope they got to him before I did."

"So that's where you got your right hook from? From the training?"

"Sort of. Chad and I went through the training program together, but he trained me on the side to be more skilled, faster, better. He didn't want me to die in the field."

"Is that how he died?" Jayce asks quietly.

I shake my head. "There's still so much to tell you. I just don't know if I can go there yet."

"I understand," he says a little disappointedly. "I know it must be hard."

"You remind me of him, you know. Of Chad." I don't know why I thought it would be a good idea to say that. "The night you brought your neighbour into the clinic, I actually thought you were Chad. Only for a moment though. It's actually pretty clear now that the only thing that's similar about you two is your hair and the way you walk. You're almost the complete opposites of each other."

ACK

"You do know that's a normal reaction to have, right?"

"It is?"

"Psychologically speaking, your brain is projecting Chad onto other people as a way of comforting you, of surrounding you with familiarity."

"So I'm not crazy when I see him in some random stranger on the street? In his cousin Tate? Even in my brother?"

"Not crazy at all," he says reassuringly. "So how do Chad and I differ so much?"

I get the impression he may have been a bit disheartened by me saying that.

"You're completely laidback compared to Chad." I laugh a little and shake my head. "The fights Chad and I used to have … we practically hated each other in the beginning. He was arrogant, and I was naïve. I understood that his upbringing had a lot to do with why he was that way, but he was just so serious, *all the time*. If you asked anyone else, they would've said Chad never learnt to have fun. He really only showed his fun side with me and Tate. Robbie most likely would've ended up with a black eye if Chad had been there tonight."

"So he was violent?" Jayce asks.

"No, not like that. He was very protective of me. He hated when I put myself in danger. We fought a lot when I just wouldn't leave well enough alone. He was passionate about getting out of the Institute and equal rights for the Defective but not at the expense of my life. I wish he lived to see how we live now. It's not ideal, but I think he would've been happy."

"But you don't feel he would want you to be happy? Is that why you work at the clinic? Why you go to those political events with Paxton, even though you hate them? I'm still trying to figure out why you believe everything is your fault."

I squirm a little in my seat at his words. "I think we've talked about me enough tonight."

"I didn't mean to push. I—"

"It's not you. There's just a lot you still don't know, a lot to go through. I want to know something about you," I say, trying to change the subject.

"Well, where should I start? I grew up in the city, as you already know. My parents worked their asses off their whole lives so the three of us could go to top schools, do whatever we wanted. Jamie is a dentist, Jenna is … well, Jenna. Umm … I'm trying to think of something you don't already know." He leans forwards, resting his elbows on the table in front of him. "Here's something: I've never been in love."

"You've never been in love?" I repeat him.

He shrugs. "There have been girlfriends. None that really made me want to make an effort. Certainly none that I'd be willing to wait six months for before even being able to ask her out on a date."

"That Max girl seems pretty interested. I'm guessing the two of us aren't going to be besties any time soon."

"I went on one date with her a couple of months ago. She's not exactly getting the hint that there isn't going to be another one."

I try to hide a little relieved smile. "So that's it? That's your whole life in a bubble?"

"That's everything."

"You mean to tell me that you've never fallen for a secret agent spy who didn't hesitate in turning you over to the authorities?"

He chuckles. "Nope."

"No getting tortured for days on end?"

"Nope again."

"No falling in love with a fellow inmate, only to have them die the day you're truly liberated?"

Jayce looks at me, sharply. I realise I hadn't told him when Chad died. He slowly shakes his head.

"I wish I was as boring as you," I say, trying to move on from my last comment.

Jayce cracks a smile. "You will be. One day. Maybe even more boring."

"I don't think it's possible to be even more boring than *you*." We laugh, successfully lightening the mood. "I'm going to go get another coffee. You want anything?"

"Nah, I'm right with this one still," he says, holding up his cup that he's barely even touched.

Campbell's behind the counter when I walk inside. "Hey,

Allira!" she says excitedly. "I was wondering when you were going to come in tonight. I've got a package for you."

"A package?" My voice squeaks.

"Yeah. Some guy dropped it off today. He said he knew you'd be in tonight."

My heart beats in my ears. She hands me an identical orange envelope to the one I received at my home last week. My trembling hands take hold of it.

Opening it where I stand, I'm met with a familiar sight. Another photo and another note.

This photo is of Tate in his cell, the one that went viral, the one that Jayce's friends and I were talking about just a few hours ago. And a note:

He's lying to you.

CHAPTER TEN

Who's lying to me? Tate? It wouldn't be the first time.

Rubbing my temple with my left hand, I grip the photo with my right so hard my knuckles turn white.

"Are you okay?" Campbell asks.

"What did the guy look like? Has he been in here before?" I ask.

"Nah. He was an older guy. In his forties, I'd say. Bleached blond hair."

"Bleached?"

"It definitely wasn't natural."

"Like stylish bleached or 'I don't want anyone to recognise me bleached'?"

Campbell looks at me as if I'm crazy. "I don't know. I

assumed you knew him. He called you Lia."

"What?" My head snaps up.

"He said 'You know our Lia. She'll be in here for her regular Saturday night shift coffee.' I assumed he was family. I've heard your aunt call you that, so I figured you must be close to him."

I can't breathe. No man calls me Lia. Only Mum, Aunt Kenna, and Nuka call me Lia.

Jayce walks in. "Hey, what's taking so long to order a coffee?" he says lightly before seeing my face and my hands. "Another one?"

"It was dropped off *here,*" I manage to say.

"Allira," Jayce says, putting his hands on my shoulders. "This is getting serious. You have to go tell Paxton. Tell him everything."

I nod. "He's away again, just for tonight. They're coming back tomorrow morning."

"Do you have somewhere you can stay until he gets back? You shouldn't be in that apartment by yourself—this person knows where you live."

I shake my head. "I have nowhere else to go."

"Your parents?" he asks.

"I haven't spoken to my mum in months. I … I can't go there." Kenna is at work tonight and so is Ebb. I can't impose on Ebb's mum. There's nowhere else. "I'll be fine. I'll just make sure I lock the doors."

"You can stay with me," he says.

"No, it's fine. I don't want your sister finding out. I—"

"This is not negotiable," he says, cutting me off and surprising me with his forcefulness.

Jayce puts his arm around my shoulders and leads me back outside to his car. He opens the passenger door for me, and I get in without hesitation.

A million thoughts are running through my head right now. *Looks like Paxton isn't the only one with secrets. Jayce. Tate. He's lying to you. Jayce.* Why is it that these envelopes appear whenever I'm with Jayce? What does he have to do with all of this?

I'd be stupid to trust anyone at this point. It can't be a coincidence that I've been with Jayce each time I've gotten one of these. He says he's not hiding anything. He claims to be boring. *So did Drew when you first met him.*

"You know, I've been thinking," Jayce says. "It might be a good idea to tell Jenna about this."

"No. No journalists!"

"She's first and foremost my sister. I can guarantee she won't write a thing about it. I promise. She has access to resources to find this guy."

"I just don't feel comfortable with that. Not right now. I should talk to Paxton first. This still could be nothing. I'm overreacting," I say, trying to convince myself more than him.

"Just think about it?" he asks.

"Okay."

I keep running it over and over in my head until we pull up to a building in one of the nicer parts of the city. It's not exactly high class, but it's certainly more expensive than the part of the city where I live. Then again, anywhere is more expensive than our part of town. That doesn't stop my suspicions from going into overdrive.

"How can you afford to rent an apartment here?" I try to keep my tone as non-accusatory as possible.

"Don't get too excited. It's a ground-floor apartment, and Mum and Dad actually own it. It was their first apartment as a couple, so it's nearly paid off. Jenna and I just pay the leftover mortgage as rent."

"Oh."

I don't like where my mind is taking me. I want to trust Jayce. It'd be nice to know that there's *someone* who's never lied to me, who isn't hiding something from me. It sucks that I live in a world where the simplest of decencies has to be questioned.

We get out of the car which Jayce parks on the street. We enter the building and walk straight past the elevators, turn right down a corridor, and go to the end. Jayce gets out his keys and opens the door.

I hesitate for a brief moment. Am I a complete idiot for just having let Jayce lead me here? What if he's behind this? What if I've just walked straight into a trap?

Jayce cocks his head to the side, looking confused. "What are you thinking?"

"Oh, umm." *Act normal,* I tell myself. "Just that, it probably wasn't the best idea to come here."

"I have a couch," he says. "I'm not expecting anything to happen between us, if that's what you mean. You can have my bed all to yourself."

"That's okay. The couch is fine for me," I say, forcing myself to take a step forwards into the apartment. *You know krav maga. Jayce may be a giant, but you can take him. You took over an entire building before. You can take one person in a tiny apartment.*

"Jayce!" I hear a girl scream. *Make that two people in a tiny apartment.* "You should've told me you were bringing someone over," the girl screeches.

I see a flash of someone in a night camisole and tiny short shorts run from the living room into a bedroom on the right.

"Even if she wasn't here, I told you not to dress like that around the house. You're my sister—I don't want to see that," he yells after her.

They seem normal so far.

I tell myself to snap out of it. Nothing has changed. He's still Jayce. This isn't a big setup. He and his sister aren't about to tie me down and force me to spill all of my secrets … I hope.

"Hi, you must be Allira," Jenna says, coming back out of her bedroom fully clothed. I'm immediately envious of her long blonde wavy hair and her shining blue eyes that match Jayce's and Jamie's.

"Uh, yeah. Hi," I reply.

"I recognise you from the papers," she says. "So no Paxton James tonight?"

I find it funny when someone knows of Paxton but doesn't know him personally, so they use his full name in conversation—as if that's how we must address him, too, just because he's famous.

"Paxton's on the campaign trail. He's coming back tomorrow," I say.

"Ah, so while the cat's away, the mice will play?" She looks in between Jayce and me, a little suspicion in her expression.

"It's not like that," Jayce answers for me. "Something's happened, and Allira just doesn't want to be alone in her apartment tonight. I'm going to take the couch."

"No, I already told you—I can take the couch," I say.

"What's happened?" Jenna asks, concerned.

"Oh, just the usual harmless protestor. It happens being involved with Paxton, but it's still creepy nonetheless," I try to cover.

"I bet. Well, make yourself at home," Jenna says with a smile.

"Actually," Jayce says, "Do you have any clothes Allira could borrow? We didn't have time to drop by her place to pick anything up."

"Sure." She turns to walk away but hesitates. "Are you sure

it's just a protestor?"

I try to be as friendly and as diplomatic as possible when I say, "I appreciate your concern, but given the nature of your position, I wouldn't feel comfortable discussing this with you until I've at least spoken with Paxton. You understand that, right?"

"Oh! Of course, of course. I wasn't actually thinking of myself as a journalist when I asked, but I completely understand where you're coming from. Just know you can talk to me about anything—it will be strictly off the record, I promise," she says warmly, before disappearing into her room again.

"I told you," Jayce says with an arrogant smile. He walks over to the linen cupboard near the hallway that I assume leads down to his room and pulls out a pillow, a pillowcase, and a sheet.

"Yeah, yeah," I say, grabbing the pillow and pillowcase off him. "Your sister seems really nice, but you know I can't say anything until—"

"Until you've spoken to Paxton. I know."

Jenna comes back out and throws over a pair of three-quarter sweatpants and a T-shirt. She shows me where the bathroom is so I can get dressed, and when I return, both of them look at me funny.

"I know, right? The pants come down to my ankles. Is everyone in your family a giant?" I ask.

"Jamie's the runt, and he's still six feet," Jayce says.

I head for the couch, but Jayce quickly runs and beats me to it, sprawling out so I don't even have a place to sit.

"I told you, I'm taking the couch," he says.

I sigh. "Fine. Where's your bedroom?"

"Whoa, there's a sentence I never thought I'd hear you say. I like how it sounds, say it again."

I lightly push him back down as he gets up to lead me down the hallway.

"Just yell if you need anything," he says when we make it to his bedroom. He turns and walks back down the hall. Closing the door, I curse when I see there's no lock. I don't know if I'll get much sleep if I don't feel as if I'm in a secure room.

Climbing into his bed, I bring the sheet up around my shoulders. They smell like him, of fabric softener mixed with a faint scent of sweet aftershave and man sweat. I could live in these sheets.

Sleep doesn't want to come though, and by four a.m. when I look at Jayce's bedside clock, I'm about ready to give up. I contemplate snooping around his bedroom, but once I cross that line, there's no going back. If I find nothing, he'll never trust me again. If I find something … I don't want to find something.

Jayce's bedroom has a sliding door that leads out to a tiny courtyard. I guess that's one benefit of having a ground-floor apartment. I decide to get some fresh air, hoping that will make me sleepy.

I tiptoe out there—as if that's going to make me silent. My

eyes and head feel so heavy, but there's no way my brain is going to shut off long enough for some sleep. I may have fallen asleep here and there for maybe ten or so minutes at a time, but I could still feel myself alert in the present.

I'm not outside for long when I hear the adjoining sliding door from the living room open.

"Can't sleep?" Jayce asks. Even though I knew he was there, it still makes me jump when he talks. He jumps back, his hands going up in surrender. "Please don't hit me again."

"Did I wake you?" I ask.

"I heard the door. For a second, I thought someone had broken in."

"Oh. Sorry," I whisper.

We stand in silence.

"I wish I knew how to help you in this," he finally says, sitting down on the patio lounger and rubbing his hand over his face and hair, trying to wake up properly.

I shrug. "I've dealt with worse."

"I admire your strength."

I walk over and sit next to him. "I used to think I was strong. Now I look back and think I was just stupid. I never took anybody else into consideration, putting lives at risk all because I thought I was doing the right thing. And look where that's gotten me—a dead boyfriend, a job I barely tolerate, a mother who won't talk to me, a brother I never see because his husband and I can't be in a room without getting angry at each other, a phoney relationship with someone who's controlling nearly everything I do, and now this—threatening notes trying to tell me God knows what. How am I meant to figure it out? Why don't the bad people ever just send a note that says 'Oh, by the way, we're doing this because we don't like you, and our ultimate plan is to kill you. If you could be here on this date at this time, we'd appreciate it. Thank you for your cooperation in this matter.'? At least then I'd respect them." I notice Jayce trying to cover a smile at my rambling. "I know, I ramble a lot. Paxton tells me all the time."

"I wasn't smiling at that," he says. "Did you want to talk about any of it?"

I shake my head. "No. Yes. I don't know."

"Yup, those are all of the options."

"I've been thinking my mum was right. I'm a danger to myself and everyone around me."

Jayce's brow furrows.

"No one knows why my mother and I really had a falling out. They all think I'm the one shutting her out because of some petty reason like jealousy over my new baby brother. The truth is …" I can't quite find the words.

"The truth is …?"

I take in a deep breath and sigh it out, preparing myself to tell Jayce something I haven't told anyone. I know I probably shouldn't, but there's something about Jayce that makes me want to tell him everything. Maybe deep down I'm just trying to scare him off so he can leave. Make him hurt me before I get the chance to hurt him.

"For twelve months after Chad died, I was a wreck. I've really only just started getting back on my feet these last six … seven months."

"That's understandable," Jayce soothes.

"I actually have hardly any memory of those twelve months. There's this image in my mind of Shilah and Tate's wedding. I was standing at the altar next to Shilah, watching them exchange vows. I remember thinking 'I'll never have this.' Then I looked at the front row and saw my mum and dad with my eight-week-old brother. They looked so happy, so proud. I couldn't do it anymore. I wanted to forget. I asked my mother to erase my memory. She's Defective too—that's what she can do. I wanted her to erase Chad completely. She said she wouldn't do it, she didn't even know if she *could* do it. She was used to erasing conversations, or the last few hours, or days. She'd never erased people before. She refused."

"And so she stopped talking to you? That hardly seems fair."

I shake my head. "I'm not finished. You remember what I do, right?"

"Borrow abilities …" His mouth drops open in shock as realisation crosses his face. "You didn't, did you?"

A single tear finds its way down my cheek. "I did. I got angry and decided to help myself to her ability, totally screwing it up in the process. My memories of Chad were still intact, but I forgot an entire year had gone by. When I walked out into the living room the next day, my brother Liam was in his little bouncer thing. I was so confused. I thought we must've been babysitting someone's kid. I turned to my parents and asked whose baby it was."

"I'm assuming that didn't go down well?"

"They lost it. Mum yelled, I cried. I didn't completely understand what was going on because I didn't have any memory of what I'd done. We spent the next few days, just Mum and me, trying to get my memory back. She had never done that kind of thing either—she only knew how to erase memories, not put them back together. I ended up getting snippets here and there, but most of it was lost.

"I remember that moment at Shilah and Tate's wedding where I'd hit rock bottom. I remember the reason I wanted to forget in the first place. I thought that by forgetting Chad completely, I wouldn't be grieving anymore. Vague memories from that entire year come back to me occasionally, me lying on the couch for days on end watching crappy TV, being angry at anyone and everyone. They're only snippets and more like photos in my mind, but I remember how I was feeling at each of those moments.

"In the end, we gave up trying to get my memory back completely. Mum said I was a danger to myself and to Liam, and she didn't want me anywhere near him until I could get myself together. She's the one who suggested I move in with Paxton for a while. 'Just for a break' she said. It was only going to be for a little while. I wasn't meant to become Paxton's 'girlfriend.' I was just meant to attend a few banquets and functions. Here we are, six months later, and it's gotten a bit out of hand."

"You can't be blamed for your actions, Allira. You were

grieving. Loss makes people do crazy things. It doesn't excuse your behaviour, but she can't hold you to something you did when you were at your lowest. She should've accepted your apology and helped you move on in a different way."

"I never apologised," I mumble quietly. His disappointed look says it all. "I got angry. I blamed her for refusing to do it in the first place." I look down at my hands, and they're wet with tears from wiping my face. "I should've apologised. Now it's too late."

I don't tell Jayce about my true fears about what happened. The truth is, I'm missing a huge chunk of my life. That whole year is a blur, but there's one major thing that has me confused. I think something else happened that my family isn't telling me about, but my gut tells me it's true. I've been too afraid to ask about it because I don't know if I can handle what it would mean.

Jayce wraps his arm around me, and I lean into his shoulder as I sob.

"It's got to be hard carrying all of that around, plus what you're going through right now with these envelopes." He pulls his arm away from me, forcing me to look up at him. "I want to try something out on you. It's a theory I've been working on for one of my papers. So, you sit here and name your top three issues that you're dealing with *right now*, forgetting all the menial crap. By only focussing on those key three issues, you might find some insight on how to fix them."

I look at him sceptically.

"I'll go first. Number one is that I don't know how to help

you with this. I want to—more than anything, but I'm in way over my head. I don't know what to do. Two is my paper—the one I'm experimenting with right now—is due on Monday. Clearly, I'm a bit behind. And three, this is probably the biggest issue I'm having right now, and that is you look so damn good in those ridiculously long pants, your hair's dishevelled, your eyes tired. You look like someone I could wake up to … every morning."

My breath catches in my throat. I'm having a meltdown, and he thinks it's sexy? I just stare at him. I don't know what else to do.

"And now that I have clearly crossed a line, we're going to move on to you. Your top three. Go."

"Okay," I say slowly as a stalling tactic while I think about it for a moment. "One. I don't know who's sending me these photos, what they want, or why they're doing it. Two"—I take in a deep breath—"I don't want you to take offence to this. It has nothing to do with you, and everything to do with me, but I don't know if I can trust you. I want to, so much. But you have to understand that every single person in my life has lied to me. Every. Single. One. A part of me might always be waiting for the other shoe to drop."

He nods, but I can see the disappointment in his face.

"And three is"—I suck in an extra breath of air, hoping I can get the words out as fast as I can—"I know that when I give Paxton these notes, the photo of you and me together, he's going to force me to stop seeing you. And right now, that seems worse than anything these guys are threatening me with."

A smile finally finds his face, his arm wraps around me, and I get the distinct impression that we're about to cross that line again. He moves his head closer to mine and our lips meet. As much as it makes me feel better, I can't do it.

I force myself to pull away. "I'm sorry. It's just …"

"No need to apologise, Allira," he says warmly, unwrapping his arm from around me.

"I've been thinking. What if we don't tell Paxton today?"

"We have to tell someone," he says.

"I know. I have two people in mind. If we can find out what's going on without involving Paxton, I might learn the truth."

"You think Paxton won't tell you the truth? That he's hiding something from you?" he asks.

"It's what the first note said, didn't it? Paxton isn't the only one with secrets?"

"But they might not be secrets from you. They might mean from the world."

"What if it's both?" I say before even really thinking about what my words imply. What do I really think Paxton could be hiding from me?

"So, who did you want to tell instead?" Jayce asks.

"A friend I can trust. And someone you trust. Your sister."

"I'm in." I hear Jenna's voice from the door. We both flinch and turn to look at her, surprised she's even up at this hour. "I'm sorry. I didn't mean to eavesdrop. I don't know exactly what is going on, but I'm in. Whatever it is, I'm in. Anything for my little brother," she says, scruffing the top of Jayce's head. He swats her away with his hand.

"Everything will be completely off the record?" I ask.

"Of course," she says.

"Then let's go on a road trip."

"Where to?" Jayce asks.

"The Institute."

CHAPTER ELEVEN

"If we leave now, we'll get there just in time to wake him for breakfast," I say.

"Wake who?" Jenna asks.

"Going to pay the director a little visit."

"The director? You know Director Jacobs?" Jayce asks.

I have to laugh. "Director Jacobs is just Drew to me. Do you remember me asking you if you were only interested in me because you're actually an undercover cop sent to trick me into using my ability so you could arrest me?"

"Yeah?" he replies questioningly.

"That's how I met Drew. He was my boyfriend when he arrested me."

"Oh," he practically whispers. "Can you please tell me that

you have a not-so-intimidating ex hiding somewhere? Chad the Martyr, Drew the Director, and Paxton the Politician. Anyone else? An O.A.M. winner perhaps?"

"Nope. That's all of them," I say, smiling. "And Paxton isn't technically an ex, he technically isn't even a boyfriend," I say before pointedly looking at Jenna. She doesn't focus on what I just said though. She's still stuck on Drew arresting me.

"You mean it's true? There were Defectives working *for* the Institute?" she asks.

"There's so much you're about to find out," I say to Jenna. "And we have two and a half hours to get through it all."

* * *

Jenna insists on driving with me in the front passenger seat so I can get her up to speed on the situation.

I've borrowed more of her clothing to save me from going back to my apartment first. Her jeans are rolled up at the leg three times but they fit me. Knowing I'm heading to the Institute, I've also borrowed a short-sleeved T-shirt, not worrying about covering up my mark.

I spend the majority of the trip just catching her up on the truth about me, about Paxton's and my relationship, the notes, the photos, and what it all could mean.

"I agree with Jayce, as much as I hate to admit it when he's right," Jenna says with a smile. "It doesn't sound like a journalist or reporter to me—certainly none I know. They'd print a story, not mess with your head."

"Are we there yet?" Jayce complains from the backseat.

"Did you really just say that? What are you, five?" Jenna retorts.

We pull into the estate and Jenna finds a parking spot right out front. It's Sunday morning, no one will be here for their monthly check-up, so the parking lot is practically deserted.

We walk into the reception area, which is empty, and the lights are off.

"Where to from here?" Jayce asks.

"I doubt he'll be in his office at eight a.m. on a Sunday. I know where his apartment is," I say, leading the way through the back of the reception area to the elevators.

I still find it weird that Drew kept his old apartment from when we were agents, but he said it felt like the closest thing to a home he had. He'd already lived here for six years before I came to live here.

We make our way to room ninety-one, just two doors away from my old apartment. The same apartment I spent every day training in with Chad. He'd come over, let himself in without even knocking, and then help himself to my breakfast before walking me to our agent classes. Then we'd come back up on our lunch breaks for extra training. I let out a loud sigh at the memories as they threaten to take over me.

I knock on the door and we wait. A loud shuffling comes from inside. Drew opens the door, hair completely dishevelled, wearing only boxer shorts. He blushes beetroot red when he sees the three of us standing before him and quickly shuts the door halfway, standing his body behind it so only his head is showing.

"Please. I was your roommate for three months, you think I haven't seen it before?"

"What are you doing here?" he asks me groggily.

"We need to talk."

"Give me ten minutes to change," he says, yawning. "Meet me in my office." He closes the door gently, and we start to make our way back down to the reception area.

When I turn to Jenna, she seems a little flustered. Jayce doesn't seem to notice Jenna's weird behaviour though, so I assume I must be reading her through Drew's ability.

We arrive back at reception and head across to another hallway, down to where Drew's office is with its own little waiting room.

"How do you not get lost here?" Jenna asks as we take a seat and wait for Drew.

"Oh, it took me a good few months of living here to work it all out," I say. "I should probably warn you guys. Drew's ability is to read people. He's an Empath, so he basically knows how you're feeling." I look at Jenna when I talk. "You know, just in case you were having some … feelings that you don't want him to know about," I add, raising my eyebrow at her.

Jayce nods as if he understands, but I'm guessing he's totally confused. Jenna on the other hand is blushing but trying to hide it. I told her in the car on the way here that I borrow abilities, so I'm pretty sure she knows what I'm talking about.

"I'll try to control it, but damn! The new director is hot," she whispers.

I shrug as if I haven't noticed how good Drew's looking these days, even though I have. But he's always been good-looking.

Drew walks in not long after, wearing a suit and tie, dressed all professional-like. I resist the urge to bow sarcastically like I normally do. We all stand as he approaches.

"Now," he says, "what in the world has happened to make you grace me with your presence twice in the one month?" he asks with a smile while giving me a polite hug. "You're not back in the game of bringing Defectives here, are you?" he jokes, looking between Jayce and Jenna.

"Drew, this is Jayce and Jenna. Jenna is a reporter for the Daily News, and Jayce is ... I work with him at the clinic."

"Uh-huh," he says slowly and unconvinced. "So why are you here?" he asks, leading us into his office.

He sits in his big boss chair, and I put the envelope on the table in front of him. "There's another one, but I left it at home. This was left for me last night at the café near the clinic. Another one was dropped off last week via courier to my apartment."

"What is it?" he asks, pulling it towards him.

"Open it."

He pulls out the photo of Tate and the small note that reads "He's lying to you." He looks at it with a confused expression before looking up at me.

"What did the other one say?" he asks.

"The other one was a photo of Jayce and me walking along the street one night. The note said 'Looks like Paxton isn't the only one with secrets.' I don't know what it means."

"When did you say you got the first one?" he asks.

"Wednesday, so … eleven days ago. Why?"

He gets up from the desk and goes over to his filing cabinet. He pulls a drawer out and flicks through the files until he pulls out a nearly identical envelope. He hands it to me and my hand goes to my mouth in shock. It's addressed to me—here at the Institute. Even has room ninety-three written on it. I look at Drew for an explanation.

"That came for you on the Monday you were here. It arrived after you'd already gone home, though," he says. "I thought it was weird that you were getting mail here, so I figured it couldn't be too urgent and I'd just give it to you when I saw you again."

"Open it already!" Jenna yells, frustrated.

"Okay, okay," I say. I really don't want to, though. Tearing open the envelope, I immediately drop the photo when I see what it's of.

A photo of Chad. It's an older photo, maybe a year or two

before he passed away, and it looks as if it came from a school magazine or yearbook.

There's a note, too, of course. *'Miss him? Whose fault is that?'*

I stumble, finding the closest chair to sit down.

"Are you okay?" Jayce rushes to my side, bending down beside me.

"I'm fine," I say, shaking my head, as contradictory as it may be. "Who would do this?" I look at Drew.

He looks at the two parcels in front of him, studying them with hard eyes. "Well, there's the obvious," he says.

"Brookfield?" I ask. Drew nods. "Wouldn't he just kill me if he was back? Wouldn't he be after you and Paxton, too?"

Drew shrugs. "Maybe he sees you as an easier target. Paxton's surrounded by bodyguards, and I'm here twenty-four-seven. I doubt he'd come back here."

"Why would Mr. Brookfield want to kill her? Kill any of you?" Jenna asks.

"Ah, so Allira hasn't told you *everything* then," Drew says with a wry smile.

"It's getting to a point where I can't believe there could be more," Jayce says.

Drew gives a little laugh. "All part and parcel of being with this one," he points to me.

"Oh, we're not … it's not …" I struggle to say any more.

Drew sighs. "I was your roommate for three months, you really think I don't know when you're lying to me?" he says, throwing my words back at me. Jayce's mouth turns up into a smile. Drew looks at him. "Oh, and if you ever think of hurting her—"

Jayce scoffs, "Is this the overprotective 'If you hurt her, I'll kill you' speech?"

"I was actually going to say you better watch your back because she's damn feisty."

Jayce rubs his nose in memory.

"But I can see she may have already shown you that side of her." Drew laughs.

"You're the one she knocked out, aren't you?" Jayce assumes.

Drew's smile falters a bit, but he nods his head.

"I'm glad you find my violent streak entertaining," I say sarcastically.

"Wait up!" Jenna yells in excitement. "*She* hurt your face? You told everyone you walked into a door." She starts laughing uncontrollably.

Even I giggle at that. "In my defence, I thought he was attacking me, and I didn't know it was *him*."

"I so can't wait to tell Jamie," Jenna says between trying to breathe through her laughter.

Giving Jayce an apologetic look, I mouth "I'm sorry."

"It's not my fault she's trained like a damn ninja," he argues.

I look back at Drew, but he's ignoring our banter and is studying the envelopes again. "Okay, let's get all agent-like on this," he says, suddenly taking on a serious tone. "You said there was another one?"

"The note said 'Looks like Paxton isn't the only one with secrets.'"

"And the photo was of you and Jayce?" Drew asks. I nod in response.

Drew grabs a piece of paper from his desk, writes the words that were on the note, and draws a very inappropriate diagram of Jayce and me.

"I definitely wasn't doing *that* in the photo," I say, causing everyone to laugh.

Drew shrugs with a grin on his face. "It's just for reference. Okay, so, how do all of these come together?"

"Well, the first one is clearly indicating that Allira and Jayce are hiding their relationship from Paxton," Jenna suggests.

"But it says Paxton is keeping secrets, too," Jayce says.

"Couldn't that mean that he and Allira are hiding their true relationship from the media?" Jenna replies.

"Okay. We'll run with that theory for now," Drew says. "So the first one is about you and Paxton. The second one is about Tate?"

"So he's lying to me. It wouldn't be the first time. But I have no idea what it'd be about. Something about Shilah, maybe? But that doesn't make sense. Shilah would tell me if anything was going on with him."

"What if it has nothing to do with Tate, and everything to do with the photo?" Drew suggests. "We never found out where that photo came from. Paxton said it was on Brookfield's desk after the takeover."

"So Paxton's lying about the photo?" I ask. I'm so confused.

"We'll come back to this one," Drew says. "Okay, so the latest one. A photo of Chad. 'Miss him? Whose fault is that?' Clearly blaming you for Chad's death."

"How was Chad's death your fault?" Jayce asks me.

I hang my head. "If it wasn't for me, he wouldn't have been involved in the takeover."

"What takeover? The takeover of the Institute?" Jenna asks.

I turn to her. "This is still off the record, right?" Jenna just glares at me, clearly unimpressed that I've brought it up again. "Paxton didn't just walk up to Brookfield, threaten to turn him in, and take over his seat as easily as the media thinks. We had nearly the whole Institute on lockdown. We had Brookfield under control. We had a lot of people on our side. We just had to face the agents who were coming back from a mass arrest." My eyes start to fill. I haven't spoken about this since it happened. "The agents came back, and there was gunfire. Nine people were lost in total—four from the Institute's side. One of them was the person who shot and killed Chad. We didn't want it to come down to that. We —"

"Allira, it wasn't your fault," Drew says, gently.

I shake my head. "He wasn't meant to be there. He wasn't

going to come. What if I hadn't gone back to convince him to come with us? What if after the gunfire, someone actually thought to check Lynch for a gun? That should've been me. I should've checked everyone before trying to find him. He didn't even want to be there in the first place." I wipe tears from my eyes, trying to compose myself.

"How did all of that get covered up?" Jenna exclaims.

"Paxton's pretty resourceful," I blubber.

It's as if a light bulb goes off in my brain. Narrowing my eyes at the photos and notes laid out on the table, I sniff and wipe my nose as I stand up to get a closer look. "Hang on. You said you got this one on the Monday I came to visit you?" I ask Drew.

He nods. "It arrived in the mail, but it wasn't delivered until the arvo, and you were already gone."

"That would make the photo of Chad first." I rearrange them, reading the notes in order. "Miss him? Whose fault is that? Looks like Paxton isn't the only one with secrets. He's lying to you."

"What does it mean?" Jayce asks.

"Ignoring the corresponding photos, it's pretty clear whoever sent these blames *Paxton* for Chad's death. There's only one group of people I know who'd care about Chad's death," I say.

Drew looks up at me. "Belle. The Resistance."

CHAPTER TWELVE

"What's the Resistance?" Jayce asks.

"You know how you asked me why we didn't escape when we were agents?" I start.

"Yeah."

"Well, a few weeks before the takeover here, Paxton organised a way to get Shilah and me out. Chad had already managed to escape the Institute months beforehand and was assigned by the Resistance to watch over me while I was on assignment. Our escape didn't exactly go as planned." I look over at Drew with a smile.

"I kind of tagged along for the ride," Drew adds.

"When we did finally escape, we were taken to a compound out west where my mother had lived for eight years. We were free … well, it seemed like we were free."

"What made you come back and take over the Institute?" Jenna asks.

"There were a few reasons. Chad's cousin, Tate—who remained at the Institute—went missing. We found him like this"—I pick up the photo of Tate in his cell—"but he wasn't the only reason we came back. Life at the Resistance wasn't exactly …"

"Pleasant," Drew finishes for me.

"Right. Pleasant. We realised that being free came at a cost, and they were asking something of me that I wasn't willing to give. Not only that, Paxton had worked here at the Institute for years. He knew what went on, and he wanted to change it. He had a plan to take Brookfield out, and Drew and I put that plan in motion. We went to Brookfield, pretending to betray the Resistance, and organised a mass arrest of Resistance members. We smuggled in weapons and … well … we just told you how that ended. There were a lot of reasons for coming back."

"That's why you blame yourself for Chad's death?" Jayce asks. "That's why you blame yourself for everyone getting hurt on the streets?"

I nod and avert my eyes from his.

"That hardly seems like your fault. If you didn't do it, everyone would still be imprisoned here."

"They wouldn't be getting killed." My words are barely audible.

"No, but they'd still be enduring stuff like this." He points to the photo of Tate.

"What did the Resistance want you to do?" Jenna chimes in.

"Jenna!" Jayce glares at her.

"It's just a question. She doesn't have to answer it."

"I realise I say this to you a lot," I say, looking at Jayce. "But there's something else you don't know."

Jayce lets out a tiny laugh. "You'd think I wouldn't be surprised by that phrase anymore."

"I not only borrow abilities, but I can amplify other's abilities as well."

Jayce narrows his eyes. "You have two abilities? Is that even possible?"

"It is, but I've only ever met one other person like me. He was with the Resistance." I swallow, hard. "They wanted to try to make more of us with two abilities." I shudder at the memory of what they wanted me to do. The way they voted on it, ordering me to reproduce like a prized pedigree puppy.

"Are you saying he …"

"No. Cyrus didn't touch me. We didn't give him the chance to take it that far. We left almost immediately to come back here."

"So why would these people from the Resistance send you these?" Jenna asks, pointing to the envelopes.

"One of their leaders is Chad's mother. Chad was with them for over two years and was on track to become a leader himself."

"So we're just going to rock up at their compound and demand answers?" Jenna asks.

I look at Drew and we both smile at the same time. "Yup," we say in unison.

Drew stands and leads us out of his office. Getting his keys out of his pockets, he opens one of the doors in the waiting area to a supply of weapons and safety equipment.

"Are you two coming?" he asks Jayce and Jenna.

"You don't have to," I say. "It's a few more hours out to the compound, and by the time we get back, it'll be late. We'll probably have to stay the night. Jayce, you've got that assignment due tomorrow, and—"

"I'll get an extension. I'm coming," he says.

"Do you have work you need to be back for, Jenna?" I ask.

"I'll call them and tell them I have leads on an investigative report." She sees the look on Drew's and my faces. "Don't worry, I'll tell them it was a dead end after we get back. You guys really don't trust journalists, do you?"

"Nope," Drew says with a slight smile.

"Sorry," I tell her.

Drew places four bulletproof vests into an oversized bag, along with four locked gun cases.

"Is all of that really necessary?" Jayce asks.

"Purely cautionary. Okay, let's go," Drew says picking up the bag.

"I should probably call Paxton before we go. Tell him I won't be home," I say.

Drew nods and reaches over the receptionist's desk, picking up the phone and pressing a button to get an outside line. He hands me the phone, and I punch in the number to the apartment, hoping to get voicemail. I don't.

"Paxton James," he answers.

"Hey, it's me."

"Where are you?"

"I'm actually out visiting Drew at the moment. I was thinking of hanging out here and maybe staying the night." A long sigh comes through from the other end of the line. "I won't have many chances to come and see him once I'm out on the road with you."

I start feeling self-conscious having this conversation in front of Drew, Jenna, and Jayce. Turning my back on them, I pretend they aren't here.

"Is he the reason you wanted out of our deal?" Paxton says in a defeated tone.

I narrow my eyes even though I know he can't see me. "If he was?"

Paxton sighs with a tiny hint of a laugh. "It'd mean that Tate wins the pot."

"What?"

"He had eighteen months for you and Drew to get back together."

"Are you friggin' kidding me?" I yell. "You've been betting on me?"

"Calm down, Allira. It's not that big of a deal. He also thought you and I were going to end up together, remember? When can I expect you home?"

"When I'm home." I slam down the phone and tell myself to breathe. "Let's go," I say to the others and start heading for the door.

The phone starts ringing immediately. Drew looks at the caller ID and gives me a small nod. I shake my head. I'm not talking to Paxton again.

"Jacobs," Drew answers the phone. "Yeah, okay. I'll tell her," he says before hanging up. He looks up at me, hoping I won't shoot the messenger. "He said to remind you to be home for the benefit tomorrow night."

I roll my eyes. "Whatever."

Drew leads us down to the garage so we can take one of the Institute's cars. Jayce stops and grabs my hand to pull me towards him as Drew and Jenna walk over to the car, loading the bag into the boot.

"Are you okay?" he asks.

"I'm fine. It just looks like we have the same flaw. I have A-holes for friends, too."

"Yeah, I kinda heard Paxton through the phone. They were really making bets of when you would—"

"Seems that way." I shake my head. "Come on, let's go. I have bigger things to worry about right now." *Like seeing Chad's mother again. Ugh.*

By the time Jayce and I get over to the car, Drew's behind the wheel and Jenna's taken the front passenger seat, leaving Jayce and I to the back. We get in and begin the three-hour drive to the compound.

The longer I sit, the angrier I get at Paxton and Tate. I need to be rid of my mood before we get to the Resistance, that's for sure. Keeping a level head is imperative to deal with those people.

"So how do you two know each other?" Drew asks Jenna. I assume he's talking about her and Jayce, which I would've thought was obvious—they look like brother and sister.

"He's my *little* brother," she says, emphasising the word "little."

"Four minutes doesn't count," Jayce argues.

"Oh, sorry. I just assumed you were friends from the vibe …"

"Mr. Director, sir, you wouldn't happen to be using your ability, now would you?" I ask, in my mocking posh accent.

"Of course not," Drew says with slight sarcasm, actually making me smile.

"You could arrest yourself for that, you know," I say.

He smiles. "I'm sure I could work out some sort of deal with myself." I see him wink in the rear view mirror, and I can't stop the laughter from coming out.

"How do you and Allira know each other?" Jenna asks. "I know you arrested her, but how did you meet? At school?"

Drew looks back at me before answering. "She saved my life."

"Technically, we'd met before that, but he doesn't remember it. I fell over and he helped me up, then called me a bitch when I didn't say thank you." I turn to him. "And then I saved your life, and what did you do to repay me?"

"I arrested you." He laughs.

Jayce looks at me with pursed lips when he sees I'm smiling, too. "I think I'm missing the punchline," he says.

I shrug. "It happened a long time ago. We've been through so much since then, it almost seems funny to us now. Besides, he made up for it by saving my life in return, so I guess I can't hold it against him too much." I smile at Drew as we share a look of pure respect for each other.

Somewhere along the way, I tune out to the conversations around me and stare out the window, preparing myself to see everyone from the Resistance again.

Jayce reaches over, squeezing my hand. "Are you okay?" he asks softly.

I nod with a small smile. "I'll be fine."

He goes to remove his hand, but I hold onto it and grip it

tight. Meeting his eyes, I shake my head. No, I don't want him to let it go. He smiles and leaves his hand where it is as I stare out the window again.

We reach a small town on the outskirts of the radiation barrier that was set up decades ago. Last time I was in this area, this town was deserted and had been for a long time, but now it seems to be flourishing. Stores are open, cars are on the street, and people are everywhere.

"What's going on here?" I ask Drew.

"This is one of the things I've wanted to show you for a while now, but you keep running off every time I meet with you. It's one of the Institute's projects. We set it up a few months back. People aren't feeling safe in the city and the suburbs any more. There's too much violence, too many attacks, and not enough being done about it. They all started coming back to the Institute. We had the room to accommodate them but not their families as well. Not to mention it's such a depressing place to live, but I don't need to tell you that."

"So you set up and built a brand new town for them?" Jenna asks in awe.

"Pretty much," Drew says proudly. "The plan is to extend as far as we need to."

I'm speechless, and proud, and a little envious. Drew's actually making a difference in this world.

We drive for another hour before Drew pulls the car over to the side of the road. "Ready to walk?"

"We can't drive the whole way?" Jenna asks.

"Not if we want to go in undetected," Drew replies.

We all file out and gather around the boot of the car. Drew reaches into the car, grabs out two gun cases, and hands them, plus a leg and hip holster and a vest, out to me. I start gearing up as a wave of déjà vu hits me.

"Just like old times," I mumble to myself.

"You understand I won't be able to arm you guys, right?" He looks at Jenna and Jayce. Jenna nods, and Jayce actually looks relieved.

"That's fine. I've never actually fired a gun before," Jayce says.

Drew laughs while opening the cases to his two guns, and I do the same. "If you're going to be with Allira, I suggest you learn how. I'll take you shooting sometime if you want?"

Jayce raises his eyebrows. "Thanks," he says a little confused. I can't tell if he doesn't know if Drew was being serious about needing to learn or doesn't know if he was serious about teaching him.

"Are you really that much of a trouble magnet?" Jenna asks me as Drew throws her one of the vests to put on.

"You're currently dressing yourself in Kevlar. Does that not answer your own question?"

"I guess it does."

Drew hands me two cartridges, my hands trembling as I take one of the guns out of its case. I haven't held a gun since the takeover, but I find it strangely exhilarating to be doing it again, like I've missed it. I shake off my nerves and load the cartridges with ease, putting one gun on my hip and strapping the other to my leg. Pulling my hair off my face, I tie it together by knotting my hair into a ponytail. "Okay. I'm ready."

Jayce stands a few feet away, staring at me, his mouth slightly open. "Damn, that's hot," he mumbles.

"Jayce, I think you're drooling," Jenna teases.

"You're one to talk," Jayce retorts, nodding in Drew's direction.

Drew's stripped of his jacket, shirt, and pants, only wearing a white undershirt and boxer shorts. Drew seems oblivious to the perv-fest he's putting on for Jenna—either that or he doesn't care. He grabs a pair of jeans out of the boot and starts putting them on.

I can't help but laugh at Jenna, her eyes scanning over Drew's body. She sees me laughing and stands up straighter, shaking her head. "Sorry."

I shrug. "No need to be sorry. It's a bit hard not to stare," I whisper.

Jayce clears his throat, raising his eyebrows at me. "Oh really?"

"Eh. He's all right," I admit with a smile. Jayce just shakes his head, crossing his arms. "You want to get half undressed so I can perv on you, too?"

"Nah. I won't torture you like that." He smiles, nudging me with his elbow.

"We ready to go?" Drew asks, dressed and ready, seemingly oblivious to what the rest of us are talking about.

"I'm starting to think that maybe Jenna and Jayce should stay with the car," I suggest.

"Why?" Jenna asks.

"Like Drew said, he can't arm you guys. I don't expect us to need to use our guns, but … I think I'd feel more comfortable if we didn't have to watch your backs as well as our own."

"Then why did we even come with you at all?" Jenna asks.

"I'm not saying you need to stay here the whole time. We'll come back and get you once we've spoken to someone. I just don't know how they're going to handle our unexpected visit."

Jayce grabs hold of my hand, dragging me across the road and away from the other two.

"Are you sure this is safe?" he asks me.

"I'm like ninety percent sure nothing will happen, but … okay, I know this might seem emasculating, but the last time I dragged someone I cared about into something like this, he was killed. I don't want to be responsible for that again—even if there's only a really small chance of it happening."

Jayce half-smiles. "I'll stay with the car." He pulls me in for an unexpected hug and kisses me on top of my head.

"That was easy."

"You just admitted you care about me," he says, still holding on to me. I can hear the smile in his voice.

"You're not going to try to stop me from going?" I ask, pulling back surprised.

"If I thought for a minute you'd listen to me, I would. But I know you need to do this, and if you'd feel more confident with me staying behind, then I'll stay behind."

"Thank you," I whisper, leaning in to hug him again. When we pull back, our eyes meet for a brief moment before both Drew and Jenna start to wolf-whistle and holler.

Jayce rolls his eyes and leads me back over to them. "We're staying here," he says to Jenna.

"But—"

"We'll come get you as soon as we know it'll be safe," Drew cuts her off. He opens the front door and leans in, pulling something out from under the passenger seat. It's a clear plastic box. He opens it, pulling out a tangle of wires. "Here," he says, handing us all an earpiece that looks like a brown jellybean. I recognise it from when I was an agent with the Institute. "It's so we can keep in contact with each other. We'll take a microphone and receiver, and you guys will have one too, so you'll be able to hear everything while we're gone, and we'll be able to hear you." Jenna and Jayce nod, fitting their earpieces in.

"We'll be an hour, tops. We're about a twenty-minute walk outside the compound, and then we'll try to borrow a car to come back out to you guys. If they'll let us, anyway," I say.

Parting ways feels weird and unnatural. I feel wrong without

Jayce by my side but shake my head at that insane notion. I guess I can't say that it's only a crush; it has gone way beyond that. Ever since that kiss in the supply closet, I haven't been able to stop thinking about him. But I still don't even know him all that well, even though he clearly seems to know me.

We walk for a few minutes before Drew tests the earpieces.

"Just doing an equipment check, can you guys hear me?"

"Yup, we can hear you," Jenna says. "Are … almost … uh?" Static fills my ear.

"Can you repeat that?" I ask. Nothing. Dead silence. "Jenna?" Still nothing. "Do you think we should go back? Could something have happened to them?" I ask Drew.

"Nah, it'll be the piece of crap Institute equipment. We'll check again in a little while. We're probably just in a bad spot."

We make our way farther into the valley that leads to the back fields of the Resistance.

"Seeing as they can't hear us, did you know?" I ask.

"Know what?"

"About the bet?"

"The bet about how long it'll take for you and me to get back together?"

"Yup. That one," I confirm through gritted teeth.

"I knew. I still think I have a pretty good chance at winning, too."

My heart sinks. "You're in on it?"

"Technically. I told them they were insane and that we're never getting back together, and they took that as my bet."

"Really? You bet it would never happen?"

He raises his eyebrows at me. "What, you think it will?" he scoffs. "You know I haven't looked at you like that in a long time, right? Just like you haven't me. And don't lie, I know you haven't," he says, touching the side of his head.

"I know. I just … I don't know. I guess I always thought that when I'd be ready for another relationship, I'd start seeing you like I used to—like that would be my indicator that I was ready. But it just never happened."

"Because you know there's nothing there anymore. You can't blame everyone for thinking you'd come back to me once you got over Chad. Especially if you even assumed it yourself."

I sigh. "I guess that's true. Still pisses me off."

"They were only kidding around. I don't think money ever exchanged hands or anything."

"That doesn't make me feel much better."

"I've always known we'd never end up together. There've been times where I've wondered about the what-ifs. What if I'd told you who I was from the start? What if I managed to escape Brookfield and ran away with you when we were planning to leave with Shilah? Ultimately, it always comes down to me thinking we wouldn't have worked out anyway. You don't look at me like you look at him. You never have, even when we were dating … if you could even call it that."

"Looked," I correct him.

"What?"

"You said 'the way I *look* at him.' It should have been *looked.*"

Drew shakes his head. "I wasn't talking about Chad. I was talking about Jayce. Although, it is a similar look."

"I still don't know if I can trust him. I keep getting the feeling he's hiding something from me."

"I'm so sorry for that," he says quietly. "I think I damaged you."

"It's not just you, though. Everyone I've ever known has lied to me in some way or another. Some lies were just as bad as what you did to me."

"Sometimes it's necessary," he states. "For what it's worth, I can't sense anything but the best intentions towards you. Surely you felt it too?"

"Sometimes I don't even know if I can trust myself, even when I'm borrowing your ability. I keep thinking that I just sense what I want to sense and not the truth."

We continue to walk. I know we'll be reaching the compound soon. My ear starts to fill with static again—we're coming back into range. I open my mouth to check in, but Jayce's voice cuts me off.

"I hate that I have to keep this from her," he says. "You heard her, she's already had so many people betray her. I can't keep doing it, Jenna."

"Well, if you just stayed away from her like I told you to, you wouldn't have to lie to her. You want to keep her unharmed? Keep your mouth shut." Jenna's tone is cold and authoritative—not at all like the girl I've spent the last twelve hours with. Was her kindness all an act?

I look over at Drew, tears filling my eyes, but I refuse to let them spill over. *I was right.* The funny thing is, I'm not even surprised; the other shoe just dropped. Shaking my head, I let out a sigh in defeat.

"I'm sorry," Drew mouths, before trying to check in again.

"Jayce, Jenna? Can you hear me?" Drew asks. There's silence again but a different kind of silence—it's a startled silence. There's no doubt in my mind they just heard Drew. I wonder if they know that we heard them. "Jenna? Jayce?"

"We can hear you," Jayce answers.

"Finally," Drew says. "We've had nothing since we pretty much left you guys. How you holding up?"

"Uh … yeah, we're good. We're still at the car. No one's come by," Jayce says.

"Okay, we're approaching the back of the compound now. Hopefully we won't cut out again."

We don't get far before I hear the distinct sound of a gun being cocked behind us.

"Well, well, well, it seems Allira's up to her old tricks." Cyrus's voice is still as creepy as ever.

CHAPTER THIRTEEN

My hand reflexively goes for the gun on my hip as we turn to face Cyrus. He isn't alone; he's got a man on either side of him, and all three are armed.

"Nah-uh. Hands up," Cyrus instructs. We do as he says.

I hear Jayce's voice in my ear. "Allira? Who's that? What's happening?"

I ignore him.

"Why are you here?" Cyrus asks.

"I missed you, Cyrus," I say sarcastically. Drew nudges me with his elbow, making me sigh. "We need to talk," I say, more conciliatory.

Cyrus lowers his gun. "Okay." His two henchmen lower their guns, too.

"Okay?" I ask, surprised.

"Anything for the director. We'll go up to the town hall, and don't worry, someone's already picking up your friends."

Jenna's voice comes through the earpiece. "Yeah. There's a car approaching, what do we do?"

"Just go along with it," I try to say quietly.

"What was that?" Cyrus asks.

"I was just wondering how you knew we were here?" I say, trying to cover.

"New security system installed by one of the newbies. Thanks to you two, we don't need to recruit anymore. We have people coming to us."

My stomach churns. They're still growing in numbers, and power.

"You don't have to look so tense, Allira. You never did believe in what we're doing here. We're doing everything we can to stay out of the mess you guys have made, but we also need to be able to defend ourselves if we need to. All we want is to be completely independent from the rest of the country. We're striving on our own. And with more numbers, the more independent we become."

"You know, you need to advise the Institute of any sort of security systems," Drew says, cutting me off from yelling about how power-greedy and arrogant Cyrus is.

"Well, here you go, Mr. Director, sir, we have a new security system."

I'm beginning to wonder if anybody actually takes Drew seriously as the director of the Institute. I know I tease him a lot about it, but after hearing Cyrus do it, I'm starting to think maybe I shouldn't. He's doing an excellent job, better than Brookfield and Paxton combined, probably.

"Just make sure you fill in a form at your next monthly meeting. Unless you want your new security system confiscated."

"Speaking of confiscating—how about you give us those guns of yours. You have to understand we can't take the risk. The last time you two were armed among a group of people, we lost some of our best guys. Belle lost her son."

I wince.

"We're not going to just hand over our weapons," Drew states, again stopping me from yelling at Cyrus. "They're Institute property."

"Oh, calm down, Director Jacobs. You'll get them back before you leave."

Drew hands over his two guns and then glares at me, encouraging me to do the same.

"Fine," I mumble, handing them over.

As we walk past farmers in the fields where Drew used to work, I feel eyes burning into me. The feeling only gets worse the farther into the compound we get. We reach the door to the town hall, Cyrus stopping us before we enter. Jayce and Jenna arrive behind us, guarded by more Resistance members. We've been hearing them in our earpieces as we've walked along, but they haven't said much and haven't addressed us once.

I avert my eyes from Jayce, the fresh bitterness of betrayal hitting me. But what I see when I look across the narrow dirt road is worse. Brayden. I didn't know a thirteen-year-old could intimidate me so much. I've only met him once, but I've never been able to forget him. His older brother Hayden was part of our takeover plan. He was one of the ones who didn't make it out alive. It's my fault Brayden's brother is dead, and by the look in his wet, glassy eyes and the angered scowl on his face, he believes it's my fault too.

I'm relieved when we're dragged away from the street and led down to the front row of the town hall. We file in—first Jenna, then Jayce, me, and then Drew, and we sit patiently.

"Alert the others," Cyrus instructs his men.

"Is this normal?" Jayce whispers to me, making our earpieces ring a high-pitched noise and making all four of us jump. Drew reaches over me to turn off Jayce's receiver.

Pissed off doesn't even begin to describe how I'm feeling about Jayce right now. He's hiding something from me, and I've been nothing but upfront with him—well, mostly. I was right about him, and I'm so angry that I still allowed myself to fall for it, for him. I shake my head and look down at my hands as my knee bounces uncontrollably.

"Allira?" he asks, reaching for my hand.

I recoil at his touch. "Everything will be fine," I say curtly. "We're just going to ask them what they know and then leave."

He removes his hand, and a look of confusion mixed with worry crosses his face. *Good, let him squirm.*

Drew leans over, whispering in my ear, "Don't jump to conclusions. You don't know what it is yet."

I think I've already jumped to the worst conclusions. What Jenna said is repeating in my head—to keep me unharmed, Jayce has to keep their secret from me. It makes no sense. How does that keep me safe? I don't even know if that's what she meant by "unharmed." Maybe she meant it threateningly—he needs to keep his mouth shut or else? Is she even his sister? Is anything he told me the truth?

I'm brought out of my thoughts by voices coming through the doors. Drew and I stand up as we watch the council members walk down the aisle towards their table at the front of the room. Jenna and Jayce follow our lead by standing and wait until the council is assembled. Interestingly enough, there are still eight council members, only four of whom I'm familiar with: Cyrus; his second wife, Marlo; Connor, the old guy; and lastly, Chad's mum, Belle.

Belle seems to have aged ten years in the last eighteen months. I haven't seen her since Chad's memorial service they had out here, where she told me that his death was my fault and if she never saw me again, it would be too soon. I'm guessing it's still too soon.

"You can sit down," Cyrus says, and we obey. "So what is this visit all about?"

"Straight to the point, as usual," Drew says.

"We don't really have the time or patience for pleasantries

with you two. You understand, right?" Cyrus replies.

"We understand," I say. "We came here to ask you to get whoever it is you've got following me to stop."

Belle scoffs, "You think we care to send one of our men— who would be much more useful here—to the city just so we can keep an eye on you? Why would we want to do that?" Her tone is even icier than ever, if that's even possible.

"Why would you send me threatening notes? It's obvious you still blame me for his death." I can't even bring myself to say his name to her. "Are you doing this to torture me? You don't think I do that enough myself, without your help? You think that by threatening Paxton and me you'll get some sort of revenge for what we did?"

Belle sighs as if she's defeated. "I don't know what you're talking about." She looks up and down the line of council members, all of them shaking their heads and looking confused. "None of us know what you're talking about. I don't exactly know what you came looking for, but we can't give you the answers you want." Her words aren't laced with hatred like they normally are. I don't know what changed in the last thirty seconds.

Drew unfolds his arms, giving the council a short nod. They start to get up to leave.

"So that's it?" I ask Drew, whispering. "We're not going to question them any further? They just got here!"

"You know Belle. They're not going to tell us anything."

"Then why did we even bother coming?" I ask a little louder.

Quiet mumbling between the council members becomes louder as they get closer. They're complaining about how much of a waste of time this was and wondering what the hell is wrong with me. I hang my head as they walk by.

"I don't blame you for his death." Belle's voice comes quietly from in front of me. I lift my head to find her and Cyrus standing in front of us. "I did once, but I've since realised that you lost someone too, and you wouldn't have just let it happen. I know you tried to save him, I know you loved him." She's fighting tears. I've never seen her look weak before. Seeing it causes my eyes to water, but I refuse to cry here. "Do I still think you were reckless? Of course. But that doesn't mean it was your fault. You were eighteen years old and easily swayed under someone else's influence. We didn't help the matter by trying to force you to … well, let's just not talk about it anymore, okay?"

All I manage to do is nod, acknowledging what she's said. I think I'm in shock. Of all the things I was expecting today, Belle being nice to me wasn't one of them. She starts to walk off but turns back at the last second. "Give my love to your parents and that gorgeous little boy." She walks out, leaving me surprised.

I didn't even realise she and my mother were still in contact. It makes sense though. Mum worked alongside Belle for almost nine years. They were really good friends until I came along.

Cyrus is still standing in front of us. He's studying my face, and I can't help but shift in my seat uncomfortably.

"Maybe you should all stay for lunch. We'll talk," Cyrus says.

We don't confer with each other, just follow him to the cafeteria shed and sit where he tells us to. It's mid-afternoon, so it's practically deserted except for us and the rest of the council members at one of the other tables.

Cyrus goes to the kitchen and brings out trays of food for us. "So why did you think we were following you?" he asks, sitting down at our table and helping himself to some food.

I pick at some fruit on the platter and am reminded of how much I miss fresh farm food. It was an adjustment, but I finally grew used to the laboratory-grown food. I'd almost forgotten what this was like. I hear myself moan embarrassingly.

"Sorry, what?" I ask, a mouth full of mango. "Oh, right, the notes. They seemed to be blaming Paxton and me for Chad's death. We figured you guys would be the only ones who'd be concerned with that."

"There were notes?" he asks. "What did they say?"

Drew speaks up. "Are you actually interested in helping, or are you just asking for the sake of it?"

"I'll help if I can. Just start from the beginning."

We fill Cyrus in on everything—the notes, the photos, and the fact the bleached-blond-haired man called me Lia. He listens intently and doesn't comment until we're done.

"You said the photo of Chad was old?" he asks.

"Yeah. It looked like a yearbook photo or something. Probably from Eminent Falls High," I say.

"And you didn't think that if it was us, we would've sent a more recent photo?"

Drew and I look at each other, a little embarrassed that we hadn't thought of that.

Cyrus shakes his head with a smirk. "I thought you two were agents?"

"We may have overlooked that," Drew admits. "But we just want to get to the bottom of this. We have to follow any possible leads." '

"I know this might sound like it's coming out of left field, but have you given any thought to Paxton being behind this?" Cyrus says.

I narrow my eyes. "Why would he threaten himself?"

"I don't really see any threats being made from what you've told me. I see someone wanting to scare you. Perhaps Paxton was hoping you would turn to him if you were scared, instead of turning to Drew."

"But what would be the point? Why would he do it?"

"Because he wants to marry you," Drew says. "He could offer you ultimate protection."

"That's so wrong," Cyrus says. For a minute, I think he means because of the manipulation, but then he adds, "You with a normal person?" He shakes his head. "Such a waste."

Not this again. Jayce scowls, giving me the urge to reassure him that Cyrus's words aren't bothering me. But then I think better of it. I can't care about his feelings; I'll only get hurt.

"All I'm saying is, you wouldn't be the first one to be burned by Paxton's manipulative ways," Cyrus says.

"How did he burn you?" Jayce speaks up for the first time, slight anger in his tone.

Cyrus eyes Jayce and Jenna up and down. "What do you two have to do with all of this?"

"Nothing," Jayce says, shrugging. "We're concerned for Allira, that's all. I personally don't like Paxton *at all* or have any respect for him. I was just wondering why you felt the same."

That's news to me. I knew he wasn't exactly thrilled with Paxton's and my relationship, but to say he doesn't like him at all, that he doesn't respect him?

"I like him already," Cyrus says to me, nodding in Jayce's direction. "Allira here once accused me of being power-hungry," he explains to Jayce. "She didn't seem to notice that it was actually Paxton who was the greedy one. Still is by the look of it. Running for president? You wouldn't call that power-hungry, Allira?"

"He wants to make a difference in the world," I say, rather pathetically.

Cyrus lets out a tiny laugh. "And you thought *we* were trying to brainwash you."

"What do you mean?" I ask.

"Who do you think first alerted me to your double ability? I didn't know the nature of it, or what you could do, but Paxton had given me a heads-up about you the night I came to pick you guys up. When he contacted the compound for a lift, he specifically told them that I should come do it. Everyone thought it was weird as that wasn't my job, but it made sense as soon as I shook your hand. He wanted me to know about you."

"Why would he do that?" Drew asks, just as confused as I am.

"Probably the same reason he told me it would be interesting if we were able to recreate a double ability through genetics. All hypothetical, of course, all before I knew about you."

"No. I don't believe you. You're just trying to get me to turn against him. Paxton was so against the baby idea." *He's lying, he has to be.*

"I was surprised, too, when he voted against it in the meeting," Cyrus says. "I tried confronting him about it afterwards, but suddenly you were living at his place, planning the takeover. Everything happened so fast. You three forced us into a mission that only paid off because of pure luck. But at what cost? Paxton played us all, Allira."

"No. He was the only one helping us! He wanted to save Tate."

"Did he? Or did he just want control of the Institute? He'd been pitching the Institute idea to the council for years, pretty much ever since he joined the Resistance. He was elected to the council because of his innovative ideas, but once he became a leader, he became obsessive about putting them into action before we were ready. He took your escape from the Institute as an opening. No one at the Resistance would've followed him. He had to force us into it."

I try to take in what he's saying, but a big part of me doesn't want to believe him. I can't believe him. Paxton has been one of the only people who have been there for me.

I shake my head. "No."

Cyrus leans in closer to me, forcing me to meet his gaze. "I don't expect you to believe me after everything that's gone down between us, but I do hope you pay more attention to his actions from now on and see for yourself what he's truly like." He stands, preparing to walk out. "If you want a lift, I can take you back to your car."

We finish up with lunch and take up Cyrus on his offer. I sit up front with him so I don't have to be anywhere near Jayce. It also gives me a chance to think.

What Cyrus said can't be true, right? He's saying that Paxton's the one who put everything into motion, that he's the one who wanted me to feel unsafe with the Resistance. He planted ideas of double ability offspring in Cyrus's mind, knowing full well that Cyrus would jump at the chance to have another wife in his bed. All so we would agree to help take over the Institute? I don't buy it. The main reason we went back was for Tate.

We arrive at our car, and I start to get out when Cyrus grabs my arm. "Just watch his actions. You'll see. Paxton isn't the saint everyone seems to think he is." He lets go of my arm and I climb out of the car, not bothering to thank him or even acknowledge his words.

Drew, Jenna, and Jayce strip off their vests. Drew gets our guns back from Cyrus and puts them back in their cases, putting everything back in the boot. They all get into the car, but I find myself pacing back and forth in front of it. Drew reopens his door and comes to sit on the hood of the car, watching me pace.

"He's wrong," I say. "He has to be. He's wrong, he's wrong, he's wrong."

Drew sighs. "Are you trying to convince me or yourself?"

I stop in my tracks. "You believe him? You think Paxton tricked us into doing what we did? You think he's behind this?"

"Do *you* believe him?"

"No."

"Then why are you having such a hard time with what he said? There's a point where you have to ask yourself why you've resorted to listening to Cyrus. Of all people—Cyrus. It's Cyrus!"

"Exactly. He's wrong …" I hesitate.

"But?"

"But some of it makes sense," I say with a sigh. I don't want to admit it, but it does. Paxton's been so controlling lately. I think he was really counting on me to accept his proposal, to put this front on permanently, to secure his career even more. And if he was so desperate for an advantage in the polls that he was willing to marry me, what else would he be willing to do? What else has he done?

Drew gets off the hood of the car and takes me into a hug. The tears start falling as I bury my head in his shoulder.

"We'll work it out," he says soothingly.

I pull away to look at him, a small smile appearing through my tears. "Don't take this the wrong way, but what the hell happened to the world to make you the only person I can truly trust?" We both laugh as I wipe the tears from my face.

"We better watch out for other signs of the apocalypse," he says, pulling me towards the car. He undoes my vest, removing it for me, along with my waist and leg holsters. "We'll go back to the Institute and map it all out. We'll figure out what to do. It'll be okay," he says reassuringly, opening the car door for me.

I get in the car, sitting next to Jayce again but refusing to look at him this time. I don't know what to do about him yet, and I know I can't ignore him forever, but right now, I just don't want to deal with it.

We begin the long drive back. Looking at the time on the dashboard, I figure we won't reach the Institute until about dinnertime. I settle back in my seat and hope for a silent trip.

I don't get one.

"So what's the plan?" Jenna asks, back in her fake persona of nice girl.

"Allira and I are going to sort it," Drew says, losing the flirty edge to his voice that he had with Jenna a few hours ago.

"We can help," Jenna offers.

"How can you help?" I snap. I don't mean for it to come out angry, but it does.

Jenna shrugs. "Fresh minds that aren't close to the issue. We might offer some new kind of perspective."

"So tell us your theories then," Drew suggests. "Because Allira and I don't know who or what to believe anymore."

"Well, from what that Cyrus guy said, it seems Paxton has a lot to answer for."

"You have to understand that Allira and Cyrus have a history, though. He might be doing it to mess with her," Drew replies. "Allira and Paxton live together, they're a team. Cyrus might be trying to break them apart to spite them, or to even ruin Paxton's election chances."

Drew clearly doesn't trust Jenna and Jayce considering he's now defending Paxton instead of continuing with our theory that Cyrus might be right about him.

"But it's all fake," Jayce says. "Allira and Paxton aren't really together."

"Cyrus doesn't know that," Drew says.

"And it's not *all* fake," I interject. "Paxton and I might not be together, but we do have a relationship. It might be unconventional, and you might not like it," I say, forcing myself to make eye contact with Jayce, "but Drew's right, we're a team. Cyrus's accusations mean I have to question everything. Paxton is one of the only people I've ever trusted. Now that I have to question him, there's no way I can trust anyone. *Anyone.*"

"I know you feel you can't trust Jenna and me, and I know I can't do anything but keep reassuring you that you can, but you can trust us. I swear it on everything that I am."

I involuntarily let out a "pfft" noise. "No. I can't."

Thanks to Drew, I can feel just how much my words hurt Jayce, and I hate how much I care.

We get back to the Institute after a painfully long trip. I've spent approximately nine hours in a car today. I'm wrecked and ready to crash.

"I can organise some apartments for you guys for overnight. Lucky for you, Allira, your old apartment is vacant," Drew says. We make our way from the garage into the main building, all nodding in silent agreement. "Are you guys hungry or anything? I can have food delivered to the rooms if you want?"

"Yeah, thanks," Jenna says.

"I'll just go grab the keys from the office. Allira, do you want to take them up? There's enough rooms on our level for all of us."

"Okay."

I lead Jenna and Jayce up to level nine, only having to endure a few minutes of awkward silence until Drew comes up with the keys.

"Food will be delivered soon, guys. Jenna, you're in room ninety-two, and Jayce, you're in ninety-five."

They take their keys and head down the hallway. I go to room ninety-three, taking in a deep breath before I open the door. It's been a long time since I've been in here.

Drew's hand lands on my shoulder, strong but reassuring. "I'm sorry, I didn't think. I can get you a different room if you like?"

I shake my head. "Nah, I'm all good. I'm just … reminiscing." I open the door a little farther. Glancing around the room, I hesitate to step over the threshold.

"Seems like a lifetime ago, doesn't it?" he says.

"It really does."

"So do you want to get started on this tonight, or do you just want to go to bed?"

I raise one eyebrow at him.

"I meant go to bed in your room. I go to bed in my room, you in here," Drew stammers.

"Mr. Director, sir, are you blushing?" I can't help but laugh.

"Shut up," he whines.

"I knew what you meant, and yeah, I think I'm just going to go to bed."

"Okay. Sleep well. We'll sort this whole Paxton thing out tomorrow." He kisses me on the cheek before heading to his room.

I glance around the room one more time, preparing myself to enter. I take a tentative step forwards and then another. I turn to shut the door when Jayce appears out of nowhere. "Can we talk?" he asks.

"Okay. Talk."

"I don't know what exactly happened today, but I feel like I need to explain."

"Nothing happened today," I say, trying to shrug it off.

"Something happened with our communication earpieces. You couldn't hear us, but we could hear you. I heard everything. I know it's incredibly hard for you to trust people, and you have a completely good reason for that, but I need you to believe that I've never lied to you about who I am, and I never will."

Wow. Jayce is a better liar than I thought he'd be. "Okay," I respond.

"Okay? That's it?"

"I don't know what you want me to say to those obvious lies."

"I'm not lying."

"Okay."

"Will you stop saying 'okay' and just talk to me?" he pleads.

"I think I've done enough talking. I've shared things with you that I've never told anyone. I've shared more with you than I've shared with my best friend. Do you think Ebbodine knows why I really work at the clinic? Why I am the way I am? Why I'm not in contact with my mother? And you're standing there still claiming to be the same boring person you told me about? *Really?*"

"I *am* boring."

"I want to believe you," I whisper. "But I just can't." Averting my eyes, I look down at his feet. I'm sure if I hadn't heard the back end of his and Jenna's conversation, I would believe every word. I want to ask him what they meant. What are they keeping from us? But I'm scared he won't tell me. I've even more scared that he will. Maybe not knowing is better.

"I don't want you to walk away from what we have because of a misunderstanding."

I open my mouth to say something, but he stops me.

"I know we technically don't have anything, but I …" He takes in a deep breath. "I've never felt this way before. I've never wanted anyone as much as I want you." He steps forwards, his hands finding my hips. My whole body warms. "Please let me show you how much I need you to believe me."

My lip trembles from the memory of our first kiss—the intensity and heat behind it. My eyes find his, and my brain tells me to pull away. *This is all an act; he doesn't mean it. He's lying.* But when he brings his lips down to mine, all that logic goes out the window. I ignore the voice in my head that's yelling at me to stop and only pay attention to the voice telling me to never let him go.

My arms wrap around him as he pulls me closer. I feel as if I'm losing control. I've never felt anything like this. My skin is tingling and my heart hammering. I'm overcome by an agonizing need to be with him.

When I was with Chad, it was nice, but … *Oh God, don't think about him right now.*

It's surprising how quickly I'm able to push him from my

mind. That has never happened so easily before.

Jayce lifts me up, my legs wrapping around his waist confidently as he carries me into the room, closing the door effortlessly with his foot.

His mouth moves from mine, down to my neck as he lays me on the bed. Clothes are being pawed at, being thrown across the room. His hands roam all over me, driving me crazy, so much so that I know if I don't do something soon, I'm not going to be able to stop myself. And I need to stop this. I should stop this. I'm going to stop this …

I'm so not going to stop this.

CHAPTER FOURTEEN

Stupid, stupid, stupid. Waking in Jayce's arms, I shake my head at myself—not only for letting it get this far but for the effort now needed to get out of here without waking him. I went to sleep blissfully happy, not allowing myself to realise what I'd done was a colossal mistake. But now I know. Chewing off my own arm to get out of here is probably my best option.

It's still early, and the bedside clock says 5:22 a.m. I manage to get up and start getting dressed with Jayce only stirring a few times. Each time he moves, my heart stops. I silently tiptoe to the door, making my way outside of the apartment. I flinch when the door clicks shut loudly behind me. *Now where do I go?*

I step over the tray of food that must have been delivered while we were ... busy. What the hell was I thinking? I know for a fact he's lying to me, I know for a fact I can't trust him, and yet I do that? *What is wrong with me?*

Making my way down the hall to Drew's apartment, I hesitate before knocking. I don't want to wake him, but I have nowhere else to go.

It takes a while, but when the door finally opens, I'm shocked by the face staring back at me.

"Jenna?" I say, disbelievingly. Taking a step back, I look at my surroundings one more time, making sure I have the right apartment. "What are—" My eyes widen as I realise I wasn't the only complete idiot last night.

"Why are you up so early?" she asks.

"Oh, umm …" *Because I regret having sex with your brother and now I want to hide. Yeah, that'll go down well.* "Never mind. I'll just come back later," I stammer before heading for the elevator.

Stepping into the elevator in my daze of astonishment, I press the button for The Crypt without really thinking. Was it a force of habit from visiting Tate in his cell all those days after training? Or was it because I haven't been down there since Chad died?

Whatever the reason, I find myself walking towards it when the elevator opens. My feet are unsteady as they shuffle forwards, my gut pinching at the thought of reaching The Crypt floor.

When I reach the top of the stairs leading down to the main prison area, I don't know what I'm expecting to see. But whatever it is, I don't see it. Perhaps I expected pools of dried blood where nine people lost their lives or a blown light smashed from gunfire. Maybe some leftover shell casings or the doors to the now empty cells open from the finality of being liberated. I thought I'd see something that tells the history of this room. I didn't expect to see crisp clean floors, everything in order, nothing askew or out of place.

Before realising what I'm doing, I've descended the stairs and I'm standing on *the* spot. I'm taken back to when I was forced to say goodbye, when Chad's firm grasp became limp in mine, the moment I lost my will to fight.

The urge to lie down takes over me. The cold concrete floor stings my back, while tears fill my eyes until everything becomes a blur.

"I'm sorry," I whisper to Chad, trying to conjure him back into existence. I imagine his face, his body lying next to mine. I imagine his blond hair, his hazel eyes that bore into mine, and that smirk—his arrogant yet charming smile that made me both weak in the knees and annoyed because it usually meant he was mocking me.

Being brought back to the reality of the here and now, I have to wonder why in TV shows, dead loved ones always visit in a time of need, they give you signs, they let you know they're still there—but in real life, you find yourself lying on a cold, hard floor talking to yourself.

Footsteps approach and I don't even bother turning my head. Drew lies down beside me, right on top of my imaginary boyfriend.

"What did you do?" he asks quietly.

"I killed him," I whisper, choking on my words.

"You what?" Drew exclaims, sitting up.

"It's my fault Chad's dead."

Drew clutches his chest, his breathing becoming even again. "I was asking about Jayce. When you said you killed him, I was trying to figure out what to do with the body."

His distraction actually makes me giggle, but it's a sad laugh. "I didn't kill Jayce, but it's good to know if I ever do kill anyone, you'll have my back."

"Always."

"I slept with him," I whisper.

"Geez, woman! Do you have no self-control?" he asks, lying back down next to me. I know he means it in a joking manner, but it's a little too soon for that.

"Apparently not," I mumble. "Seems like I'm not the only one with self-control issues, though."

"Nothing happened between Jenna and me."

I wave my hand at him dismissively. "I don't care if it did. I just can't believe we were both so stupid."

"Speak for yourself."

When I don't laugh at his playful words, he realises how dark a mood I'm really in.

"Come on. Let's get up and get started on this Paxton thing. I'm already packed, so let's go back to the city."

"You're coming with me?"

"Of course. Now, get up," he says, standing and reaching his hand out for me.

* * *

"Are you sure you can be away for a few days from this place?" I ask when we make a stop at his office before going down to the car.

"I'm sure they'll manage without me. I've trained my assistant pretty well. You remember Licia, don't you?" he says, smirking.

"Licia?" I exclaim a little too loudly.

Of course, I remember Licia. She was my first and only assignment as an Institute agent. I saved her from being arrested. She was there when we took over the Institute, but I haven't seen her since. We lost touch ... well, I guess, I lost touch. I stopped talking to everyone after Chad died. She'd be eighteen now. Eighteen and already assistant director of the Institute. I'm not really all that surprised. She always was motivated and up for anything. She wasn't originally part of the plan to take over the Institute, but she insisted and practically forced herself into it.

"She's doing great. She'll make an excellent director one

day," Drew states.

"In many, many years to come, right?"

Drew shrugs. "Maybe sooner, who knows?"

"You don't like what you do? But you're so good at it."

Drew's eyebrows perk up in surprise. "Really?"

I tilt my head to the side and give an apologetic smile. "I know I rip on you about it all the time, but I only do it out of love. I thought you were doing a good job even before I saw the projects you've been working on yesterday. Now I'm seriously impressed. You're doing so well because you don't have a hidden agenda like Brookfield and Paxton. You actually care what happens to us, to our world."

"You don't think Paxton cares?"

"I used to. I used to think a lot of things about that man. Now I don't know what to believe."

"Then let's find out, shall we? I'm just going to leave Licia with a list of everything I'll need her to do while I'm gone, and we can head out."

I'm half-tempted to stay for a while, just so I can see Licia again. But I'm a coward and don't want to run into Jayce. I wince at memories of last night. *Stupid, stupid, stupid.*

"Stop beating yourself up about it," Drew states coolly.

"I haven't had to tune out my feelings from you in a long time, but I'll do it if you don't watch it," I grumble.

It doesn't take long for us to get out on the road. It takes even less time for the interrogation to start.

"Okay, spill," Drew commands.

"Spill what?" I play dumb.

"What happened with Jayce?"

"What happened with Jenna?"

"Nothing happened. We were talking."

I laugh. "Really? *Just* talking?"

"She didn't want to be alone. That's all." I don't miss the half-smile he's trying to suppress.

"You like her! Like, *like-like* her." I sensed they were attracted to each other, but I didn't think it would go beyond that.

Drew shrugs. "She's all right." He's clearly trying to act nonchalant. It's *so* not working.

"I wonder what it is about those damn Harrisons. Maybe they're Defective magnets."

Drew looks confused. "Why do you say that?"

"Oh, didn't I tell you? Ebb is going out with their older brother, Jamie. Love at first sight apparently. Although it's been almost a week, I'm not sure if they're still together."

"Well, nothing actually happened between Jenna and me."

"Then what did you talk about?"

"Stuff. The Institute, what I do, but mostly she just wanted to know about you and Paxton."

"What? Why?"

"She's worried you're going to hurt her brother." He raises an eyebrow at me.

Isn't that exactly what I've just done? I can't stop shaking my head at my actions. I know I've been sending Jayce mixed signals—telling him I can't trust him and then sleeping with him? *I'm such an idiot.*

"It may have been a mistake, but you can't be angry with yourself for following your heart for once," Drew says. I throw my head back on the headrest of the car seat, unsure of what to say to that. "I mean, look where following your head has gotten you in the past."

"The last time I followed my heart—which, by the way, is a totally lame way of saying 'did something stupid'—was when I fell for an Institute agent." I raise my eyebrows back at him.

"Yeah, that was pretty stupid of you," he says with a smile.

"I'm scared I'm doing it again," I admit.

"You don't really think he's some sort of undercover agent, do you? He doesn't exactly act like a cop."

"I don't know what it could be, but there's definitely something. Do you not care that Jenna is hiding something from you?"

"Jenna and I aren't together, so it's different."

I grunt in frustration. "Jayce and I aren't technically together either. Doesn't make it any less hurtful."

"You may not be together officially, but you've dated, you've been together, you've *slept together*, you clearly have strong feelings for him. It's different."

I sigh. "I'm done. I can't talk about this anymore. It's probably best if I just forget it ever happened to begin with. I'm leaving the clinic in a week. I won't have to see him after that. I just need to make it through this week."

Drew shakes his head. "Running away from him isn't going to help."

"Let's just do what we set out to do, okay? We need to work out why these photos are being sent to me."

"Fine, but this conversation isn't over," he says sternly. "So if Paxton was the one sending the notes to you, what would he hope to get out of it?"

"Well, the first note would be to make me feel guilty over Chad's death, which I already do."

"It may also motivate you to help try to fix the Defective community," he adds.

"The photo of me and Jayce? Maybe he was hinting that Jayce is hiding something, too? That I can't trust him? Which it turns out, I can't."

"It also made you paranoid about being followed, right?"

I nod. "The third one—Tate in his cell. What would that be about?"

"Turning you against your closest friend?" Drew suggests.

"But it's not like we've been close lately."

"You still feel you'd be able to turn to him in a crisis though, right?"

I shrug. "I dunno. Maybe. I guess Paxton wouldn't have assumed I'd come to you instead. I don't think anyone would've assumed that. Do you really think it's him?"

"It could be. How do we rule him out?"

"He's been out campaigning this whole time. He would've had to have someone follow me to take those photos and send the envelopes. If we can find out who he has on his payroll, maybe we can find the person he's paying off to do it. If he's doing it."

"So what do we do until then?"

We both think for a while. "Give him what he wants. If we do that and the notes stop—it will pretty much prove it, right?"

"Are you seriously okay with marrying him?"

"It won't get that far."

"You'd better hope not."

* * *

"I'm home!" I shout as we arrive back at the apartment.

Paxton appears from the hallway, taken aback when he sees Drew's with me.

"Jacobs," he says curtly.

"James," Drew replies in the same tone.

"What's going on?" Paxton asks me.

Drew is the one to answer. "Well, I thought I'd make an appearance at one of these benefit things. I get invited to them all the time, but I've never actually been. I thought I could tag along with you guys, if that's okay?" Drew puts his arm around me and watches for Paxton's reaction. Paxton gives him a scowl, and I think that's the answer Drew was expecting. He removes his hand and takes his bag over to the couch. "It's all right if I crash on your couch, right, Paxton?"

"Sure," Paxton says with a tone of confusion and relief. I guess he's relieved Drew didn't ask to stay in my room.

"So where's Nuka?" I ask.

"She's out with Linds for the day. I was hoping to talk to you about something."

"Sure."

Paxton looks over at Drew. "Could you give us a minute?"

"Anything you have to say can be said in front of Drew," I say as Paxton's eyebrows shoot up in surprise.

"Fine," he says, shrugging. "I just thought you wouldn't want your boyfriend knowing about the cop you've been spending your time with."

Cop? My heart sinks.

Paxton throws a file on the dining table. There's the photo of Jayce and me—the same one that was sent to me—and a police personnel file. According to this, Jayce *is* a cop. My brow furrows in confusion.

"How did you get this?" I ask.

"I asked a friend to look into him."

"How do you even know about him?"

"Why have you been spending time with a federal agent? It says right there, 'Special Response Unit,'" Paxton asks angrily, pointing at the file.

"You answer my question first. How did you even know I was spending time with him?"

"I don't have time for games, Allira. I did what I had to do. I need to know who you're with and what you've been doing. He's a federal agent, for crying out loud!"

"I didn't know he was a federal agent! And what do you care if he's an agent or not? He's the new volunteer at the clinic. I already told you about him."

"You didn't tell me you were dating him. Him *and* Drew, hey? I guess you're making up for lost time."

"Whoa, uncalled for, Paxton." Drew comes to my defence.

I shake my head at Paxton. "You're an asshole."

"No, I'm the only one looking out for you. You've been played again, Allira. Why do you think this cop has been sniffing around you? He's doing the exact same thing that Drew did to you."

I rub my head, sitting down at the table and looking at the personnel file. *Constable J. Harrison.* It has Jayce's address, birthdate, everything about him. Or someone exactly like …

"Are you okay?" Paxton asks.

"I'm fine. It's just a bit of a shock."

"I was expecting you to be livid! You're practically smiling."

"I guess I'm smiling because I always thought something was up with Jayce. Now I know what it is." *I know his secret.*

"You're not going to continue to see him, are you?"

I shake my head. "No. It's definitely over. I'm fully committed to you and your campaign," I lie.

"Oh, Allira, I'm so glad to hear you say that," he says, approaching me. He lifts me out of the chair and hugs me. I grit my teeth. "So no more slutting around, okay." It wasn't a question.

Don't punch him. Don't *punch him.*

"Also, you should go to the salon today. You're looking rather ragged."

"Uh, thanks?"

Paxton sighs as he pulls away. "Just go. You need your eyebrows and hair done. I'm paying, so treat yourself to a mani-pedi while you're at it."

I'd rather go to the dentist than get a pedicure. I think feet are gross. He should know that about me. He gives me his money card, and I'm sent on my way with a wave of his hand—like he's dismissing the help or shooing a stray cat.

"I just need to go get dressed into fresh clothes," I say, heading for my room.

I resist the urge to slam the door shut. I don't know how long I'm going to have to keep up this charade. It's already tiring. Now that it has been pointed out to me, I realise Paxton has never been supportive of me. He disguises his intentions with kindness, and he only has one goal—to become president any way he can.

I go to my bed where my copy of the photo of Jayce and me is under a pillow. At least, that's where it should be. It's gone. Paxton has it. He's been snooping in my room! I throw the pillow across the room in anger. How did it come to this?

Forcing myself to breathe in deep, I count to ten. I find clothes to change into, and I keep reminding myself that I need to play along. At least for now.

"You feel like being pampered today?" I ask Drew when I come back out.

"Sure, why not." He looks at Paxton. "That won't be classed as 'slutting' around, would it? I don't want to break any of your rules."

"Don't push it, Jacobs. Unless you want to spend the night in a hotel."

Drew and I go back towards the elevator to leave, when Paxton's voice stops us. "Make sure you look spectacular. It's going to be a big night for us."

I nod, sadly. "I figured as much."

Drew and I make our way back down to the lobby and out the front. There are a few salons within walking distance.

"You don't have to spend the day with me getting my hair done. It'll be boring." I actually only asked him along as an empty gesture, thinking he would say no.

"I just want to make sure you're okay. You don't seem too angry. I can't believe Jayce is a cop."

"Pretty funny, considering I had joked about it with him numerous times."

"You think it's funny? You're not going to turn all super-bitch like you did with me?" he asks, curious.

"I guess I just love him more than I loved you." I'm only joking, but the words fall out of my mouth so easily, I even surprise myself. I can't feel that way about someone I've only known a few weeks, right? Granted, it's been a few intense weeks, but still ... I shake my head. I think I'm insane.

"You do that a lot, you know," Drew says.

"Do what?"

"Shake your head while you're thinking. It looks like you have a nervous tic."

"Thanks."

"Oh, if only I could borrow Tate's ability. I think you'd entertain me for hours with what goes on in that head of yours."

"Are you going to be like this all day? I'm seriously surprised you and Ebb don't hang out more."

"Come on, let's get you beautiful. It's probably going to take *all* day."

I can't help but smile. He's trying to distract me from the mess that is my life, and I'm grateful for that. I'd be more grateful if he left me alone so I could go to Jayce's and talk this out.

I'm not so lucky. Drew spends the entire day by my side while I'm plucked, waxed, dyed, and practically tortured for hours. How women find this relaxing is beyond me. Drew even gets a pedicure with me, laughing every time I flinch when the girl touches my feet. *Gross.*

"Hey, why do you think Paxton was so against me going out with Jayce?" I ask Drew on our walk back to the apartment.

"I think he'd be against you going out with anyone. I don't think he's too pleased that I'm here."

"But he put a lot of emphasis on the fact that Jayce is a federal agent. You don't think he's … you know … breaking the law or anything, do you?"

Drew shrugs. "I don't know, but if what I've learnt about Paxton in the last twenty-four hours is anything to go by, anything could be possible."

"When he thought I was with you, he sounded disappointed

but not angry. I'm just starting to wonder what else he's hiding."

"Maybe he was angry *for* you. You did seem to take the news surprisingly well."

"I guess." We reach the apartment block, and I have to force myself to go in. "Let's do this."

* * *

Wearing yet another dress Paxton gifted to me this afternoon, I think I'm as glamourous as I'm ever going to get. My hair has been curled and left down, simple diamanté pins holding my fringe off my face. The ice-blue satin hugs me in all the right places; I just kind of wish the back wasn't so backless. I would've thought Paxton would want me more conservative and demur-looking for a political event, but he picked this dress, and I know if I go out in a different one, he'll just make me change like he did last time.

When we arrive at the intimate rooftop function, photographers are posted both outside and inside the venue as usual. I proceed to fulfil my duty of being Paxton's arm decoration.

After Paxton drags me around for a while, I finally have a moment to myself and find a tall cocktail table to lean against. I much prefer the sit-down formal events to these cocktail parties. At least at those, I can sit when my heels get too painful.

'Stop complaining about your feet.'

I smile and turn to see Tate standing behind me.

"No Shilah tonight?"

He shakes his head. "Nah, he's feeling a bit sick. I told him to stay home. You look gorgeous, by the way," he says, leaning in and kissing me on the cheek.

"Thanks."

I step back into a hard body. Arms wrap around me from behind, and lips find their way to my bare shoulder. I assume it's Paxton. "Hey, here you are," Drew whispers in my ear. Tate looks shocked which makes Drew and me laugh. "I thought that might get a reaction," Drew says, stepping away and reaching out to shake Tate's hand.

Tate raises an eyebrow, *'Drew? Really?'*

No. Not really. He's just enjoying pissing Paxton off.

'Why would he want to piss Paxton off?'

We have our reasons.

'We?'

Long story. A lot has happened in the last two weeks since you've been out campaigning.

'Like what?'

Oh, you know, the usual. I met someone, fell for him, received threatening notes in the mail. Went to see your aunt, Belle, and Cyrus at the Resistance, thinking they had something to do with it. Belle told me Chad's death wasn't my fault. Found out the guy I fell for was lying to me, slept with him anyway. Get home to realise I'm going to be stuck with Paxton for the rest of my life unless I can prove that he's behind the notes and that he has manipulated all of us for almost two years.

Tate sprays the champagne he was sipping everywhere, causing me to take a step back. "What?" he exclaims.

Drew looks between the two of us. "I really don't miss that about you two. Can't you talk out loud like normal people? Am I going to have to threaten you with being arrested? What are you getting all uptight and spazzy for?" he asks Tate.

"Allira's life is a mess," he says with a smile.

Drew smiles, and I hear him think, *'Damn straight.'*

"Why do I feel like both of you think I'm just being dramatic?"

"You can be as dramatic as you like. For a moment there, I thought I was hearing the old Allira come through," Tate answers, his eyes glistening in the dark.

Paxton's voice cuts through the crowd. He's up on the slightly raised platform, a temporary stage just for tonight. We all turn to him at the sound of his voice. "Can I have everyone's attention, please?" His voice is commanding but charming.

"What's going on?" Tate asks.

We're about to find out.

"You don't have to go through with this Paxton thing." Drew leans in to me.

"Yeah, I do," I say dejectedly as I start making my way up to the side of the stage by Paxton—where I should be.

"I want to thank you all for coming out tonight and supporting such a wonderful cause," Paxton continues. "Defective Genetics Laboratories is such an important asset for us to support. The research they are doing into genetic mutation is phenomenal. As all of you are aware, not only is my daughter Defective, but so is a very special person with whom I'm close. I'd like to ask her up on stage for a moment if I could."

Paxton holds out his hand, and as I look up at him, I force myself to smile. I force my feet to move, and I force myself to reach out for his hand. *He's not doing what I think he's doing, right?*

"Allira has been by my side ever since I became director of the Institute a little over eighteen months ago. She's stuck by me, she's encouraged me when I was second-guessing myself, and she's shown me what true love is."

I hear a collective "aww" from the audience.

Oh crap, he is going to do it. *Don't roll your eyes, don't roll your eyes.*

'I heard that,' Tate tells me telepathically.

I don't need you in my head right now. Bugger off.

'Don't do this' is his response.

You wanted me to do this a few weeks ago! You win.

'I wanted you to be happy. I didn't want this.'

I switch my brain off from him and block him out.

Paxton says more sweet things that are complete lies, and then he gets down on one knee. I find it hard to suck in a breath, and I'm choking on the surrounding air. This is it. I can't say no, not here, not now. He's forcing me into this, and he did it on purpose, knowing I don't have the heart to reject him in public.

"Allira Daniels, will you marry me?" he asks.

I want to scream *No!* But tears fill my eyes as I say, "Yes." Everyone will think they're tears of joy, but they aren't. They're tears of feeling manipulated and weak.

Applause within the crowd erupts. Flashes from photographers' cameras attempt to blind me. Paxton places the gigantic ring on my finger, stands, and wraps his arms around me. I feel his breath in my ear, and I involuntarily shiver.

"Are you okay?" he whispers.

"I'm fine. I just don't like everyone staring, you know that."

He pulls away, looks me in the eyes, and tucks a loose curl of hair behind me ear. Just like Chad used to do. I sigh as I think of how disappointed Chad would be with me right now.

"You're going to have to get used to people staring. Want to get out of here? We can play it off like we want some alone time."

I nod. "Just get me out of here."

CHAPTER FIFTEEN

I wake up with one goal—to get to Jayce's apartment. Drew ended up driving back to the Institute last night, against a lot of protesting from me. Licia had called and left a message on our voicemail while we were at the benefit saying she needed him back, there was some emergency, or a break-in, or something. I couldn't quite follow her rambling.

I'm dressed in my scrubs, ready to go to the clinic, but I'm not going into work today. The plan is to call in sick and then sneak away to Jayce's. I put the coffee machine on, waiting impatiently for it to warm up.

"Why are you wearing that?" Paxton asks, walking into the kitchen behind me.

"I have a shift at the clinic today."

"No, you don't, we have appearances and interviews we need to do."

"Paxton, it's one week. I only have a week left at the clinic, and then I'm all yours."

"I'm sorry to tell you this, but after last night, your number one obligation is to me."

I raise an eyebrow. "I don't even get to say goodbye to everyone at the clinic?"

"Who would you say goodbye to? You're not dying. You're still going to see Kenna and Ebb."

"Vic," I say.

"The other doctor guy? Really?" He sighs and looks at me sternly. "You want to say goodbye to your cop boyfriend, don't you?"

I shake my head. "He won't be there. His shift doesn't start until tonight."

"You can go tomorrow. We need to be in the public eye as much as possible right now."

"But—"

"No buts, Allira. Go get dressed, they'll be here within the hour. And no jeans!"

"They're coming here?"

"They want to put our own personal touch to the surroundings, and film it in the place we will share as husband and wife."

I grunt and storm off to my bedroom like a grounded teenager. I don't know what he's expecting me to wear, I practically only own jeans—nearly everything else I borrow from Ebb. Scrounging around in my closet, I find a tight red tunic dress near the back that I could wear with leggings and boots.

My hair still has some curls to it from last night, so I quickly pin it back so it's half-up, half-down, and respray it with extra strong hairspray. I apply my makeup and walk back out where I find Paxton talking with a woman, and other people fluttering about setting up lighting and cameras. It must have taken longer than I thought to get ready.

"Here she is," the woman says. She extends her hand for me to shake. "I'm Corrie. I'll be interviewing you two today."

Nerves suddenly kick in. I don't want to be interviewed. "Paxton, could I talk to you for a moment?" I ask in the nicest tone I can manage.

"Sure," he says, putting his arm around my waist. "We'll be right back."

He walks me to his room, I assume because it's meant to be "our" room.

"I can't do this, Paxton. Cameras, people, TV?" The panic threatens to take over me.

"You just have to sit there. I can answer the hard questions, but there shouldn't be any of those. It's going to be some fluff piece on how we fell in love."

"But we're *not* in love," I whisper, scared they could hear me.

"Allira, it's okay. You're just freaking out. You don't need to, okay? Everything will be fine." He hugs me to him, trying to calm me down, not realising that it's making me feel worse.

* * *

After filming for more than two hours, I find out through Paxton's answers that we're very overwhelmed by all the excitement of our engagement and are eager to get to the altar. Apparently, our wedding will take place before the election— if Paxton is elected he'll be too busy being president to work out wedding plans. I added some crap line about not being rushed, and if we had to wait years, I'd be okay with that— Paxton's commitment to the people comes before his commitment to me. "In our eyes, we're already committed," I said. I can't believe I managed to get that out with a straight face. Paxton seemed surprised by my words. I think he was pleased with my answer because it was good for his campaign, but I purely said it to buy *me* more time. There's no way I'm going to marry Paxton. I need time to formulate an escape plan.

Only now do I realise that I've been trying to escape something nearly my whole life. Shilah's ability, the Institute, the Resistance, and now Paxton. Will I ever feel truly free?

We're finally finished with the interview, and everyone is packing up. I go into the kitchen to get myself a glass of water.

"You did great." Paxton stands in the entryway to the kitchen.

"Thanks. I'm going to go to the clinic now."

"No, we have a photo shoot and a magazine interview next. I told you we will be doing interviews all day."

"No. You said interview. *An* interview, one."

"I'm pretty sure I said interviews, plural. And then we're having dinner tonight in town as a publicity op. It will be our celebratory engagement dinner. Just you and me."

"Great. Can't wait." I can't hide the sarcasm in my tone.

"You can see your boyfriend tomorrow. Today you're mine," he growls and walks out.

I drink the water and try to swallow my anger with it.

* * *

After what feels like an eternity of answering the same questions, pretending to gush over my engagement ring, posing for photos, and looking lovingly into Paxton's eyes over dinner, we arrive back home, and I'm absolutely ready for bed.

But when the elevator doors open to our apartment, we find Tate sitting on our couch. He stands as we enter.

"What are you doing here?" Paxton asks, not even trying to

pretend to be polite.

"I came to see if anything has changed with the campaign now you two are 'hooked up.'" I smile at his air quotes. "I didn't see you guys after your engagement announcement last night—I couldn't even get close."

"Sorry about that. I didn't think it would get that crazy with the photographers and all that. We left pretty much straightaway."

Bullshit. He loved every minute of it and was expecting it to get crazy because our car was already ready when we made our way out of the building.

'I actually came tonight to see if you're okay. Shilah's worried about you.'

Then why didn't he come?

'Because he can't talk to you in private like this.'

"So is there anything I should know? Schedule change, different campaigning tactics, anything?" Tate asks Paxton.

"Not that I can think of right now, other than Allira will be coming with us from now on and will probably be taking your spot by my side at speeches and photo ops."

"Oh, okay."

I need your help.

'Anything.'

"Would you like to stay for coffee, Tate? Maybe you and Paxton can work out the finer details," I offer. *I need your car.*

"That won't be necessary, Allira. We'll sort it on the road. I'm going to head to bed. I suggest you do the same. We have a big day tomorrow," Paxton says.

"You said I can go to the clinic tomorrow."

"Yeah, to say goodbye. I'm sure that won't take long—we can squeeze five minutes in somewhere."

Okay, now I really need your car.

"I might stay for a coffee, if that's okay? I wouldn't mind catching up with Allira. You know, seeing as we barely get to talk anymore. We'll try not to be too loud, Paxton, if you're still wanting to go to bed."

"Why don't we go down to the café?" I suggest, my voice and words sounding uptight and fake. "We can get that nice coffee, not the crappy stuff Paxton buys." I look at Paxton. "No offence."

"Don't be out too late. Like I said—big day tomorrow."

I'm surprised he's actually letting me go, but I don't question it and head for the elevator.

"So where are we really going?" Tate asks when the elevator doors close.

"Jayce's." Tate raises his eyebrows at me. "I'll explain on the way."

We make our way down to his car, and I begin to explain everything. It seems that all I'm doing these days is explaining myself. *I want a normal life.*

"Who are you kidding? You love this kind of drama," Tate says, invading my thoughts once more.

I try not to smile. *Maybe I do thrive on this kind of thing.*

"You really do. I've seen more light in you in the last twenty-four hours than I have all year. Sneaking around, performing espionage on your roommate … sorry, fiancé, it's like you're you again."

"Let's just go, already," I say, getting in his car.

"Where to?"

"Midtown."

He drives and I continue to explain. I mainly focus on the notes and the theory that Paxton's behind them. I ask Tate about the photo of him, and why it says that he's lying to me. He swears he knows nothing about it, and while I believe him, he seems to be working really hard at keeping me blocked from his mind. I'm sure I'm reading into it, but I counter by keeping him out of my thoughts and my suspicions about him. He asks me questions about Jayce and how we met. I think he's more interested in that side of things than the meaning behind the notes.

"You do realise if it's Paxton, it means he's somehow keeping me from hearing it in his head? He's never been good at that sort of thing before," Tate says.

"I know you don't want it to be him. I don't want it to be either. But … what if … I mean, what if he just wanted to make us *think* he's not good at blocking us out?"

"Do you think he's really that manipulative?"

"If you asked me a month ago, I would've said no. Now? I just don't know what to believe anymore."

"Should we be worried that the same car has been following us since we left your apartment?" Tate suddenly asks.

"Really?"

He nods, looking in the rear view mirror. "Pretty sure."

"How do you know?"

"You do remember I was in the recruiting game for the Resistance a lot longer than you were an agent for the Institute, right?"

"So what are we going to do?" I ask, looking in the side mirror at the silver SUV that's following us.

"I'll take a few random turns, see if he really is following."

Keeping an eye on the car behind us as we start making turns, my heart skips a beat every time it turns with us.

"Okay, we need to lose him." Tate puts his foot down, heading in the direction of the closest motorway.

"Who do you think it is?" I ask.

"If I had to guess, I'd say it's one of Paxton's guys."

"Paxton has guys?"

"We need them out on the road but usually not while we're home."

I think back to all of those times I felt as if I was being watched. Has Paxton had someone following me this whole time?

"Maybe we should stop and ask him some questions. Maybe he's the guy Paxton hired to send me those photos," I suggest, half-jokingly.

Tate glances at me and back at the road before he quickly pulls on the handbrake and spins the car so we're facing the opposite direction on the wrong side of the road. I narrowly avoid hitting my head on the window as we turn.

"A heads-up would've been nice," I mutter.

The silver SUV honks. A hand sticks out the driver's window, giving us the finger before the car speeds off into the distance.

"Do you think he knew his cover was blown?"

Tate shrugs. "Or we're just being paranoid. What did you want to do? Keep going towards Jayce's?"

I let out a defeated sigh. "We better not. No one can know I went there, and if someone's following us ..."

"So back to the apartment?"

"I guess so."

"You okay?" Tate asks me by the time we're nearly home.

"Just exhausted. I want this to be over with already." I stare out the window, tears finding my eyes. "But I won't have anywhere to go when it's done." My voice trembles in a whisper.

"That's not true. You have Shilah and me, Ebb and her mum, your aunt, Kenna, even your parents. I'm sure they'd take you back."

No, they wouldn't.

"Yes, they would. If you just explained—"

"Please don't. You don't know the full story."

'Yes, I do.'

"You do? How?"

"It doesn't matter how I know, I just know. Okay?"

"They're still angry with me, just like you are."

"I was never angry at you, Allira. I just couldn't watch you suffer like that. I understand you were grieving, you still are, but it was as if you didn't want to help yourself. You didn't even try to move on. I know I haven't been the best friend I should've been, but do you know how hard it was to sit back and watch that? Not to mention how hostile you were to everyone. We all understood you were upset and irrational over losing Chad, but that didn't give you the right to treat people like shit without so much as an apology for it later."

"I know I lashed out at a few people, but I don't think I was that bad, was I?"

"You don't remember how bad you were," he states calmly.

He really *does* know what happened between me and my parents.

"Let's just say there were quite a few times that you blamed me for everything that went wrong in your life, even though I never asked you to come rescue me. When I would argue that Chad was right, that you shouldn't have risked everything to save me, you'd call me many names that I don't care to repeat right now in front of a lady." He raises his eyebrows at me.

"I'm sorry. I didn't know."

"I was getting frustrated because I know Chad would've hated seeing you like that. I think you knew it, too, but you just couldn't see what you'd become. You needed that push, but even when you started to do things—attending benefits with Paxton, working at the clinic—you never really smiled. Not a real, genuine smile. It was as if you were going through the motions of doing what a normal adult does, without actually investing yourself in it. I could see your pain, and so I kept trying to get you out of your comfort zone. I'm sorry things have been so bad between us, but I thought I needed to be cruel to be kind. I didn't know how else to help you."

He's right. I wasn't helping myself.

"Clearly you just needed to get laid. That seemed to fix you right up."

"I know you did not just say that!"

"I was never angry with you," he repeats himself, turning serious. "I'm just glad to have you back. I've missed you."

I try to inconspicuously wipe a stupid tear that has escaped.

'I saw that.'

Tate drops me back off at the apartment with the promise of helping me find out the truth. If Paxton truly is guilty of what

Cyrus says, it changes everything.

When the elevator opens and I step into the apartment, I'm met by Paxton, looking weary and annoyed, and a man I've never met. He's mid-twenties, tall and broad. His long dark hair is tied in a ponytail at the nape of his neck.

"Allira, this is Thom. Thom, Allira," Paxton introduces us. I step forwards to shake his hand. "He's the man you almost killed tonight."

I raise my eyebrows in surprise. "Oh. Sorry about that." *Although, technically, it was Tate who almost killed him,* I want to say. "Why were you following us?" I ask, taking back my hand.

"He's your bodyguard," Paxton explains.

"Well if we'd known that, I'm sure Tate wouldn't have done what he did."

"Who did you think was following you?" Paxton asks.

"Uh … I don't … we weren't sure." *Come on, Allira, lie!* "A journalist, maybe." *Lie better!*

"And you thought the best way to deal with a journalist would be to run him off the road?" He turns to my new bodyguard. "Thanks for tonight, Thom. I'm sure Allira will be more cooperative tomorrow." *Why did that sound like a threat?*

"Sorry again," I say bashfully.

Thom just gives me a curt nod and proceeds to leave. I realise he hadn't spoken a single word while he was here.

Paxton looks less than pleased. "Okay, you need to tell me what's going on. You said you were going for coffee, why were you heading into the city?"

"We just went for a drive. We were talking. You know how it's been with Tate lately, I thought we should keep going while we were on a roll. Then we noticed we were being followed."

He tilts his head. "What's really going on?"

"Nothing's going on. I'm going to go to bed. We have a big day tomorrow."

"Allira," he says in his fatherly voice he uses when Nuka's in trouble.

"It's nothing, really, but I just can't shake the feeling that someone's following me. Turns out, I was right. Are you sure today was Thom's first day?" I raise my eyebrow at him, wanting to see his reaction.

"This again? I'm sure it's nothing." He doesn't give anything away with his tone or body language. *Nothing.*

"I know, I'm just being paranoid. I'm going to go to bed."

"Goodnight. I'm just down the hall if you get scared."

I put on my winning fake smile to save me shuddering with contempt. "Goodnight."

* * *

Looking at the giant diamond on my finger and the way the kitchen light shines off it, I raise my glass to take a drink, wondering if the diamond is even real. It'd have to be at least sixty years old if it was. It would have to be one of those lab-diamonds, not that they're much cheaper.

Placing my glass back on the sink, my stomach churns at the idea of yet another evening campaigning, another formal political event to attend. Apparently, this one is rather important. Then again, Paxton seems to think all of these silly parties are important. This one is actually *for* Paxton, though. Some campaigning party or rally … or something. I should really pay more attention when he tells me things, but I'm struggling to concentrate on his words while trying to figure out what he's hiding from me.

Funnily enough, in the past week since we got engaged, I haven't had a single note or photo sent to me. So my mystery person has just vanished? Does this mean Cyrus was right?

I haven't been able to get away from Paxton, or the goon squad he has following me around all day and night. I haven't seen anyone from the clinic, I haven't seen Jayce or Drew. My life has basically been filled with Paxton, Shilah, Tate, and my new constant shadow, Thom. I'm starting to think he wasn't hired to protect me but to keep tabs on me and report back to Paxton. I haven't been let out of his sight.

Ebb did call once and left a screaming message for me to call her back. I'm assuming she's upset with me because the last time she saw me I was off on a date with Jayce, and then two nights later, I was suddenly engaged to Paxton. I'm too chicken to call her back—I don't want to be yelled at, and I don't want to explain why I'm doing this.

"You look beautiful," Paxton says, startling me out of my daze. "Are you ready to go?"

"Uh, yeah. I'm just …" *What was I doing? Oh right, drink.* "I'm just getting a glass of water."

Paxton has been remarkably affectionate and kind this week. He's back to his normal self. Or is it his fake self? I can't be sure.

"Are you okay?" he asks.

"Yeah. I guess I didn't realise standing still and looking pretty would be more exhausting than working at the clinic."

He laughs. "It can get pretty tiresome."

I shyly nod and try to move around him to exit the kitchen when he gently grabs hold of my arms. He brings me in for an unexpected hug that feels stiff and awkward, not at all how Paxton and I used to be.

"I realise I haven't thanked you for doing this for me," he says in my ear.

I pull away, glad that Paxton isn't Defective with an ability like Tate's or Drew's. If he was, he would know that there's no chance in hell that I'm doing this *for him.*

I manage a half-smile before walking off to grab my gold clutch that matches my dress, and then head for the elevator.

Getting into our limousine, I feel as if I'm forgetting something or missing something. It isn't until I climb in and slide across the seat that I find what I thought was lost, sitting in the seat opposite me.

"Thom." I nod in his direction.

"Miss Daniels," he replies cordially.

I open my mouth in mock horror. "It speaks." It's a rare occasion that he does open his mouth, but when he does, it's usually only a few words. "I know you're smiling on the inside," I remark at his stone-like expression that he always seems to have.

"Stop teasing the man," Paxton says lightly, settling in next to me. "He's just doing his job."

"Where's *your* bodyguard?" I ask Paxton. "Why is it that only mine seems to be always two feet away?" I talk as if Thom isn't even here, but he doesn't seem to care. Is that part of his job? To pretend he can't hear private discussions?

"He's up front, as usual. I would've thought you'd appreciate Thom being so close seeing as you're being 'followed'," he says condescendingly and using air quotes.

I refrain from showing my anger but find myself shifting in my seat uncomfortably. Is Thom the real reason the notes have stopped?

We ride in silence to the convention centre where tonight's event is being held. Once we make our way through the throng of media outside and the dedicated voters and supporters inside, we find our table, which is right in the middle of the room. I'm assuming this is so Paxton can be on display all night. I'm bodyguard-lite now that I'm inside, but I can still see Thom lurking along the wall on the other side of the banquet room.

The night seems to drag. This is evident by the fact that when I look at Paxton's watch I realise we've only been here for twenty minutes. I sit, staring at the floral centrepieces, telling my mind not to wander. But it does. It wanders over Jayce's soft lips, strong arms, and firm touch. I think of the night we spent together and about the fact that he hasn't even tried to call or get in contact with me since. Not that I *could* talk to him if he did, but it would be reassuring to know he still wanted to. Is he really that angry at me for leaving him? I sigh at myself—that was a pretty shitty thing to do. I guess getting engaged didn't help much either. Actually, come to think of it, I'd be amazed if Jayce ever spoke to me again.

I'm brought out of my … I guess I could only call it wallowing, by someone whispering in my ear. "Cheer up. It will all be over soon."

I stand and throw my arms around Drew, relaxing a little at his presence. Then I see whom he has with him.

"Licia!" I exclaim, moving away from Drew to wrap her in a hug. She looks the same, just as energetic and peppy as she always was.

Paxton stands to shake Drew's hand while swiftly grabbing me around my waist with his left hand, pulling me away from Licia and back into his side.

"I'm surprised you could make it," Paxton says with a smile, but I can hear the grimace behind his voice.

"Wouldn't have missed it," Drew replies with an obviously fake smile.

"Licia?" We're interrupted by Shilah screeching.

He approaches with Tate, and Shilah wraps Licia in a hug while Tate comes to me.

When Shilah finally pulls himself away from Licia and turns to me, I scowl at him. "Should I be offended that you went to Licia before your own sister?"

"I haven't seen her for months. I see you all the time these days," he says, leaning in and kissing my cheek.

"So what made you tag along?" I turn back to ask Licia, taking a few steps closer to her as the others break out into their own conversations. Paxton moves with me as though his hand is now fused to my hip.

"I've been trying to get Drew to bring me to one of these things for ages. When I found out he attended one last week, I got all pissy at him for not bringing me. He doesn't like it when I get mad." She smiles proudly. "He promised he'd take me to the next one."

"So, you're enjoying working with him then? You seem pretty close," I ask, one eyebrow raised. I'm surprised Drew could be affected by Licia pouting at him.

"We are. He's such a great teacher, and he has high hopes for me." She looks at me and realises what I was implying. "Oh, yuck. Nothing like that. He's like a brother to me. Besides, he won't stop talking about some girl he's met. I'm yet to meet her, but apparently she's captivated him—his words, not mine."

"Oh really?" I grin. "She wouldn't happen to be tall, blonde, and gorgeous, would she?"

Drew's voice comes from behind Licia. "Nope. She's short, brunette, and a pain in the ass. Stop talking about me."

"Word at work is he's had a late-night visitor a few nights this week," Licia says scandalously, ignoring Drew's request.

"Really? Jenna would drive all that way just to see you?"

Licia's jaw drops in excitement. "Allira knows her?"

He groans, making us both laugh. "And I always begged my parents for a sister," he says, shaking his head and making his way over to the bar.

"I just have to go check on a few things. You'll be fine here, right?" Paxton asks me.

I nod. "Of course." I'm actually relieved he's leaving; I don't feel pressured to be the person he expects me to be.

"I'll make my speech in about half an hour. You need to be up on stage with me when I do," he orders. He kisses my cheek and then walks away in a hurry.

Drew comes back with a beer and takes a seat at the table.

Sitting with the four of them, I realise I haven't felt this good in a long time. The conversation starts flowing easily, and I find myself smiling, joking, and truly enjoying myself. I think it's a first for a political event.

"If someone had told us while we were with the Resistance that this was going to be our life, would you have believed it?" I randomly blurt out mid-conversation.

"Pretty insane, huh?" Drew says.

"Uh … Allira? Do you know that guy over there?" Shilah butts in.

"What guy?" I raise my head and see him. Jayce is standing near the entrance, glancing over the crowd, looking for someone. Looking for me. My breath hitches, and my heart starts pounding.

"Yeah, that guy. Because he obviously knows you, and it's going to turn ugly if you don't get him out of here before Paxton gets back," Shilah warns.

"I'll be right back," I say, practically leaping out of my chair.

I get a glimpse through Shilah's ability that Jayce isn't going to leave until he talks to me. Managing to catch Jayce's eye, I start walking away from the stage, getting him to follow me to the hallway where the bathrooms are and away from the prying eyes of the media and Paxton.

I lead him to the end of the hall, past the bathrooms, and around the corner to a small alcove with an emergency exit at the end. It says it's alarmed, so I don't open the door. He catches up quickly.

"Jayce," I start, with more whine in my voice than I expected. He looks good in his suit, which I have to assume he wore so he would blend in. "You can't be here, how did you get in, anyway?"

"My sister's press pass."

I raise my eyebrow at his answer.

"I had to come. I need to hear it from you," he says cryptically.

"Hear what?"

"That we're over. You won't return my calls, you haven't even shown up for your shifts at the clinic. Your aunt can't even get a hold of you."

"What calls? You haven't called me. Neither has Aunt Kenna."

He looks at me, suspicion and disappointment on his face. "Allira, we've all been trying to contact you. Especially Ebb."

"Ebb? I got one of her messages but was too scared to call her back. She sounded really pissed off."

"Allira, even your parents have tried to get a hold of you. They have been for a while now. Are you telling me Paxton hasn't told you any of this?"

My brow furrows. "You're mistaken. Mum and Dad wouldn't want to get in touch with me. Unless ..." Maybe they think I'm grounded enough now that I'm engaged, that I'm stable enough.

Jayce lets out a sigh. "I got in contact with them."

"You what?" I exclaim.

"After what you told me about them, I wanted to let them know how you've changed. You've grown, you're strong again. They can't keep punishing you for something you did while you were grieving."

"Why did you do that?"

"I was hoping they could talk sense into you, seeing no one

else can. Why are you engaged?"

I sigh as he reaches for my hand, his thumb running over my giant diamond. It takes all of my strength not to kiss him right here in the hallway.

"I need to work some stuff out. Until I do, I have to pretend to be happy where I am. With Paxton. It's killing me to be away from you, but I have to do it. I was wrong to leave you without an explanation, but I was confused, and angry, and I didn't know what else to do." I pause to take a breath. "You shouldn't have come, Jayce. I need you to leave."

"I'm not leaving until you tell me what's going on," he says sternly. I'm surprised by his rigid tone. "I know I said I would never pressure you, but I feel as if I've lost you. I can't … I don't … Please let me be here for you," he says, his voice softening.

I take a step closer to him. "You're not losing me. I just can't let you get involved in this. It's too dangerous, and I can't lose you, too. I can't lose you like I lost …" I take in a deep breath. "I'm hoping it'll be over soon."

"You're in too deep, Allira. You need to pull out of whatever it is. You can't let him take your life away from you, your choices."

I smile as my eyes begin to water. "I'm not going to let it get that far. I know what I'm doing."

I take another step forwards so we are pressed up against each other. His hands find my back as mine finds his shoulder and makes its way to his chest. He presses his forehead to mine, our lips centimetres away from each other. I breathe him in as his warmth fills me.

Don't let him kiss you, I tell myself. If I allow that, I run the risk of running out of here right now on Jayce's arm and never looking back.

Paxton's voice startles me out of my Jayce trance. But it's not coming from behind us; it's coming from a speaker, from the main room. He's started his speech.

"Shit. I'm meant to be up there with him. I have to go," I say reluctantly.

I pull away and go to walk back into the room when I'm met with a familiar face blocking my path. He's wearing a security uniform, with a baseball cap, but I can see the bleached blond hair under it. I've come face to face with my stalker, and it's not Paxton. It's not Brookfield. I would recognise that monobrow anywhere.

CHAPTER SIXTEEN

"Nice to see you again, Miss Daniels. How about we take a ride?" he says, gesturing to the emergency exit, an evil smile on his face.

"No thanks, Zac, I really need to be getting back," I say casually, taking another step forwards, trying to walk around him. I know it's no use but I thought I'd at least try.

"You don't want to be out there. Trust me," he says with a chuckle.

I narrow my eyes. "What did you do?"

"What you should've done by now," he says, his tone downright scary.

A gunshot explodes from the main room, and I fall to the ground on instinct. From my new vantage point, I see my "shadow" farther up the hall, near the entrance to the bathrooms. He's on the ground too, but the pool of blood around him lets me know he won't be getting back up. *Shit.* Thom is dead.

Jayce is on the ground next to me. Worried doesn't begin to describe his expression.

That's when my brain clicks. "Shilah! Tate!" I whisper in a panic.

"That's our cue," Zac says as another shot goes off, accompanied by the screams and sounds of panic from those back in the banquet room. "Now move. You too, lover boy," he says, giving me a gentle kick to get me to stand up.

"I'm not going anywhere with you," I say, pulling myself off the ground. If I can stall him long enough, surely people will start heading this way to get out and will see us. He'll be powerless to do anything then.

I prepare myself for a fight. Even though I'm in a tight dress and heels, I'm sure I could still kick Zac's ass. Jayce stands beside me. I turn to face him and grab hold of his hand reassuringly, but it starts trembling. It isn't until I look back at Zac that I realise why. Zac has a gun and is pointing it at Jayce's head.

"Move. Now," Zac says, cocking his head to the side.

"Do as he says," I instruct Jayce calmly.

We leave through the emergency exit. The alarm sounds, but amongst the mad panic, it wouldn't be drawing any extra attention. We're led into a dark alley and away from the crowd pouring out onto the street around the corner. I can't see anyone, but I can still hear screaming. Less than a minute, that's how long it took Zac to get us outside. It felt so much longer, but according to Jayce's watch that I was stealing glances at, it was less than a minute.

Tate! Tate! I cry out in my mind, hoping he can hear me. I don't get a response. *If you can hear me, it's Zac. I don't know who's shooting, but Zac's got Jayce and me. I don't know where he's taking us. Tate!* Still nothing.

"Crap," I mutter. I take a different approach. I concentrate on Shilah's ability as we walk. Maybe I'm just out of range. I can't hear anyone's thoughts, but I do get a vision.

Zac is taking us to an old warehouse. I can't see exactly where, but there's a few of them close together. I guess it must be near the business district of the city. Tate—if you can hear me, it's a trap. He wants Drew. Tell Drew not to come. Please hear me. Please. I'm begging. I fear it's no use, that Tate is out of range, or worse, dead.

I tell myself to revert to the last time Zac had me captured, torturing me for days. I need to be strong like I was back then. Now is not a time to break down and cry. For all I know, everyone inside the hall is fine. I can't worry about them right now. I need to focus on myself and Jayce. I need to keep Jayce safe.

I stand taller, walk more confidently, and ward off the tears that threaten to come. I'll find a way out of this.

"So what's this all about?" I ask gently.

"Oh, Miss Daniels, don't try to play nice now," Zac sneers.

"Are you at least going to tell me where we're going?"

"All in due time, Miss Daniels. Right now though, we're going to get in this car."

Basic survival knowledge kicks in, telling me to not get in the car. Rule number one is to never allow your kidnapper to take you to a second location. Maybe I can knock him out while he's driving. There's two of us and one of him. We could distract him, crash the car ... there has to be something.

"Here you go," Zac says, holding up car keys. "You didn't think I was going to drive and turn my back on you, did you? You drive, Miss Daniels. And don't even think about leading us astray. One wrong turn will result in a bullet in lover boy's head."

Damn it. Taking the keys from him, I climb into the driver's seat. Zac ushers Jayce into the back. I drive, making sure I pay close attention to Zac's directions and where we're going so I don't take a wrong turn, and also so I can relay the information later if I get the chance.

"Are you going to tell me what the plan is yet?" I ask, glancing at Zac in my rear view mirror.

"The plan? The plan is for you to shut your mouth before I shut it for you."

I shrug. "I only ask because if you wanted to just kill us, we'd be dead now. You could kill us, right here, right now. But we're useful to you somehow."

"Only your arm is, sweetie. And if you don't shut up, I'll take it with me and dump the rest of you in the gutter, got it?"

I nod and return my eyes to the road. When I look back again,

Jayce is white. He may even throw up. There's nothing I can do to reassure him.

Zac instructs me to drive into the business district, past the commercial offices and buildings, and through to the far end where there's a row of warehouses. I can only hope that Tate's okay, that he heard me earlier and will send help.

"Give me the keys," Zac orders. I turn the ignition off and hand him the keys. He gets out of the car, but before he shuts the door, he waves the gun in my direction. "Don't even think about trying to outrun me. Wait here." He starts moving towards the warehouse door to open it.

I turn to Jayce immediately, not knowing how much time we have. "Everything will be okay. I know you're scared, but I can handle this."

"I'm only scared for you, Allira. I don't want anything to—"

"It's okay. I've dealt with Zac before—I endured days of what he can dish out. I'll be okay. No matter what happens in there, don't worry about me. Don't do anything stupid and heroic. I can handle it. Okay?"

Jayce nods before his eyes go wide. Zac's back, opening my door and pulling me out of the car by my hair. I let out a scream but try to stifle it for Jayce's sake. I don't want him to do something stupid like try to stand up to the guy with the gun.

Zac turns to Jayce. "Think about taking off and she's dead."

Zac drags me into the warehouse, binds my hands behind me with duct tape, and then sits me down on a wooden chair, taping my ankles together. He walks back out and brings Jayce in, doing the same to him.

"Now what?" I ask as he finishes restraining Jayce.

"Now, we wait," Zac responds, walking over and taking a chair for himself.

He turns a lamp on next to him, lighting up half of the room. A shadowy figure of a couch and a TV are set up on the dark side of the room, and a fridge sits over in the other corner. It's only then do I realise that we're in Zac's home. He's been living here.

Scanning the room with my eyes, I search for anything I could possibly use as a weapon or a knife to get me out of my restraints, but in the dim light of just a small lamp, I can hardly see anything—just shadows.

We sit in silence for what feels like hours, Zac staring at me, me staring at Zac, both of us determined to gain the upper hand. He smirks whenever I break his gaze to look over at Jayce to make sure he's okay.

Most of the time Jayce just looks confused as to why we're at a standstill. "Why are you doing this?" he finally breaks the silence.

"Oh, so he does speak, does he? I was beginning to think you were dating a mute."

"We're not dating, it's not like that," Jayce says.

"I'd say what I walked in on tonight would state otherwise. You're seriously telling me nothing is going on?"

"Yup," Jayce answers confidently, but even I notice the spike in his heart rate as he says it.

Zac breaks out into a smile, looking at me. "You haven't told him about me? I'm offended."

"You can't lie to Zac," I say. "He's a walking lie detector."

"Oh," Jayce says.

"What does your *fiancé* think of your boyfriend?" Zac asks.

"Well, he wasn't all that pleased," I answer.

Zac laughs. "You know, my little presents were meant to make you see the truth about Paxton, not make you want to marry him."

"What truth? How was I supposed to work out your nonsensical notes? The photos didn't make sense either. It's as if you didn't want us to know the truth. If you did, why couldn't you just write 'Oh hey, Paxton is a horrible human being for these reasons,' and then list why you're after him."

"I thought you were a graduate of the Institute's agent program! Or were you too busy sucking face with that other one during classes? You know, the Williams kid."

I wince and look away.

"Ahh, touchy subject that one." Zac smiles. He's enjoying this. He must miss his old job and is making up for lost time. He pulls his chair closer to me. "What was so difficult to understand?"

"I got that you wanted me to feel guilty for Chad's death

because of what we did at the Institute—"

"Wrong," he interrupts me. "I wanted you to look for who was truly responsible. With a little investigating I thought you would've figured it out, and if not, the note about Paxton certainly would've tipped you over the edge."

"I'm just as responsible as Paxton when it comes to what happened that day."

Zac shakes his head. "You're so blinded by him. What kind of spell has he put you under to not see him clearly?"

"I don't understand. Drew, Paxton, and I know we made a mistake. You don't think we're torturing ourselves more than you ever could? Why are you coming after us?"

"I need to list *why* you all deserve this? How about this: ten months. Ten months of jail time for a crime I didn't commit. You thought the Institute was bad? Try being Defective in prison. You don't think Paxton deserves to be punished for causing that?"

"You tried to kill me! I think ten months was more than fair."

"Allegedly, Allira. You can't prove it was me who attacked you in the hospital. And that was more Brookfield's doing anyway. He knew the minute you and Drew showed up that something was off, but the mass arrest at the compound was too good an opportunity to pass up; he had to do it. He pulled me aside and gave me one mission—that if anything was to happen to him, I was to find you and kill you. I was just following orders."

"Nothing happened to Brookfield! He escaped because of

you!" I yell.

"Wrong again," he says, shaking his head. "I had no idea where you put him. I did my part, then got the hell out of there. I was going to kill Paxton and Drew, too, but I couldn't get to them. You were too easy. A few days later I was found and arrested on aiding and abetting a fugitive."

"If you didn't let him out, then who did?" My eyes widen with realisation. "Paxton," I whisper. "But why?" I ask myself more than anyone else.

Zac touches his nose and smiles. "He's a piece of work, that fiancé of yours."

I shudder. "Can you please stop calling him that?"

"I thought you would've taken action by now. I thought you would've worked it all out. Didn't you learn anything during your agent training? It was a pretty simple formula. Get you thinking about your dead boyfriend and whose fault it really was. Point out that you and Paxton clearly have issues in your relationship, the main one being he's a lying, manipulative son-of-a-bitch. Then, make you realise who was truly responsible for the near death of your best friend, the entire takeover of the Institute, and for the loss of all those people. Paxton did it all."

I shake my head. "No. I know he can be controlling and manipulative, but he wouldn't … he couldn't have done the things you're saying."

"Oh, but he did. He came to me one day, told me that one of the prisoners in The Crypt was a confirmed Defective but still wouldn't reveal his ability. He told me to take him to where they kept the double ability Defectives, to starve him for a few days and rough him up. Where do you suppose Paxton got that now infamous photo?"

"No," I whimper. "Paxton wouldn't do that to Tate. You're lying."

"Am I?" he raises an eyebrow.

"Why would Paxton set Brookfield free? You're just trying to confuse me. It doesn't make sense."

"Oh, but it does. Convicting Brookfield on such little evidence of his crimes would be difficult, wouldn't it? It would almost be just Paxton's word against his. You don't really think they'd take all the Defectives' accounts of what happened in that place as fact, do you? Paxton let Brookfield go so there would be no one to dispute his claims."

"What stopped Brookfield from coming forward since then? Where has he been all this time?"

"He still would've faced criminal charges. Paxton made him an offer that was a little too hard to refuse. He was hiding out in this warehouse when I found him."

"What?" My voice shakes. I begin to look around the room, waiting for Brookfield to jump out at any moment. I hate that that man still has an effect on me.

"Oh, calm down. He's moved on. Freaked out when I found him after I got out of prison. This building is actually Institute-owned property. Brookfield and Lynch used to do 'after hours' kind of work here to hide it from Brookfield's wife. I knew of this place but didn't know where it was.

During one of my obligated monthly meetings to the Institute, I snuck into the records room and found the address."

"Where's Brookfield now?" I ask.

Zac shrugs. "I took over this place when he refused to help me. I thought we were friends. I don't know where he's gone now or how he's living. I can't even get a job, I don't know how a fugitive with such a high profile like him would be getting by."

"Why did you come back? Why now?"

"Do you know how hard it is out there to be a convict and Defective? I've resorted to squatting in this hellhole, because of *you*. How anyone expects us to live on the Defective pension is ridiculous. I'm lucky if I have enough to buy food each week." He's getting angry, and I can't say that I blame him. "No one will hire me, how am I meant to make money?" He pauses, cocking his head to the side, listening to something I can't hear. "Ahh, and here's the other person responsible. Come in, Jacobs, we're about to get to the exciting part."

Damn it, Drew!

The door opens, and Drew comes in, gun poised.

Zac just sighs and rolls his eyes. "Really? I mean, I didn't expect you to come *unarmed*, but did you really think I wouldn't have planned for this?"

When I turn back to look at Zac, his gun is now raised to my head.

"You're going to kill me anyway, so just get it over with," I suggest.

"Allira," Jayce scolds.

"What? I'm being realistic here." I can feel myself giving up.

"Where's the girl who was so willing to fight me all those many moons ago? You endured four hours of electrotherapy. *Four* hours before you passed out. That was impressive." Zac shakes his head. "Bring her back. She was feisty, and I liked it."

I shake my head at how sadistic Zac is. "Paxton killed her." It's certainly not far from the truth from what I've learnt about him this last week.

Paxton orchestrated everything: my escape from my life as an agent, my uncomfortable feelings with the Resistance, and the thing that pushed me to be involved in the takedown—saving Tate's life from a prison *he* put him in. That was his insurance to get us to agree to the takeover.

"Drew, do come and join us, please," Zac says politely. "Here, you can even take my seat." Zac stands, his gun still pointing at me.

"No thanks, I'd rather stand," Drew replies. I can hear him stepping forwards slowly.

"I wasn't offering," Zac says more firmly. "Sit."

This is what I saw in my vision. I don't know what is going to happen from here. The last thing I saw was Drew being taped to the chair, just like he is now. He surrenders his gun, and I close my eyes. It's over.

"I'm assuming you didn't come alone. Where are the others?" Zac asks.

"There's no one else," Drew says. "The Institute doesn't have agents anymore, remember?"

"So you won't mind if I go and check the perimeter?" Zac asks. He raises an eyebrow, and I wonder if he's trying to get a reading on Drew. I can't tell if he's lying or not. Surely, he didn't come by himself?

Drew shrugs. "This is your barbecue, do what you want. Are you seriously going to leave the three of us in here though, *by ourselves*?"

"It's not like you're going anywhere," Zac says, going out the warehouse door to check outside.

"I told you not to come," I mutter.

Drew looks at me, his face marred with confusion. "No, you didn't."

"What happened to Tate?" I ask. Drew's face pales, and I close my eyes tight. This can't be good.

"I hope you've got backup on the way," Drew says to Jayce.

I laugh but not because it's funny. "You've got the wrong Constable J. Harrison, Drew," I say, shaking my head.

"You *know*?" Jayce asks me.

I nod.

"Wrong Harrison?" Drew asks, and then he realises what I'm saying. "Jenna," he whispers.

"You thought I was a cop?" Jayce asks.

"Paxton found her personnel file. It had J. Harrison on it, as well as your address and birthdate. It was missing gender though. Paxton and Drew assumed it was you," I say.

"How did *you* know it wasn't me?" Jayce asks with a proud smile on his face.

"You told me that you never lied to me about who *you* were." I smile back at him, glad that my hunch about him was correct. I turn to Drew. "I'm sorry I didn't tell you. I didn't realise you were still seeing her until earlier tonight."

He laughs, but it's a sad kind of laugh. "Like you aren't revelling in the irony of it all—me, falling for an undercover cop?"

"I know. I'm sorry. And it's only a little funny," I say, trying to hide my smile.

Drew looks at the door. "He's taking a while. I hope he hasn't found her."

"Who?"

"Licia," he whispers.

"That's who you brought to help?"

"You know her—she was begging for me to bring her."

Zac comes back in then, and Drew and I let out a collective sigh of relief when we see he doesn't have her. He seems pretty satisfied that no one was out there.

"You'll know when to make your move," Drew whispers to

me. I subtly nod.

"Let's check in on the others and see how they're going, shall we?" Zac says, walking over to the TV and turning it on. He swivels the screen so it's facing us.

And there on the news, right in front of me, Paxton and Tate get shot.

CHAPTER SEVENTEEN

My vision blurs. I try to blink the tears away, but they're coming too fast, too freely. I'm vaguely aware of someone screaming … I think it's me.

I manage to stifle my screams enough to hear that both Tate and Paxton are in critical condition at the city hospital.

After everything I've learnt about Paxton, I know I shouldn't care. I should hope he dies, but right now, I find myself hoping that they're both okay.

Then a thought occurs to me. "It should've been me," I say, but it comes out wispy and breathless. "I was supposed to be standing by Paxton during his speech."

"Don't worry," Zac smiles, "You'll be joining them soon enough." He turns the TV off and walks back over to us.

"Who was working with you? Who shot them?" I ask.

"Remote trigger," he says, taking a small device out of his pocket. "You screwed everything up by disappearing with your boyfriend. You're right—you should've been up there with Paxton. Not that it matters now. Plan B is working out just fine. I even got Jacobs here," he says, patting Drew on his shoulder. "I thought I was going to have to get him another time. Your funeral was an option."

"You're the one who broke into the weapons unit at the Institute," Drew says.

"What?" I ask.

"That's why I had to go back after your engagement. I thought I must've left the cabinet unlocked from when we went out west, but my assistant swore we were missing weapons and a remote trigger."

Zac can't contain his smile. "You know, if you paid more attention to me when I came to visit you, this may not have happened. You were always too busy to see me at my monthly meetings."

"I didn't want to hear anything you had to say," Drew grinds out.

"Well, it would've at least been smart to change the codes and locks when you took over."

"Noted. Thanks for the advice," Drew says sarcastically. "I'll be sure to implement that when I get back."

Zac lets out a laugh. "You won't be going back. Now, where should we begin?" he asks, putting his gun in the waistband of his pants and taking off his jacket and hat.

Drew catches my attention. He leads my eyesight down to his feet. He's standing on something, his foot slowly rocking back and forth on top of it. I can't see what it is, but I think he has a plan. I need to distract Zac.

"Start with me. My *fiancé* is the one who ruined your life." I try not to shudder as I say that word.

"Allira," Jayce says authoritatively. "Just because you *can* endure his treatment, doesn't mean you should."

"I'll be fine. I'm sure Zac hits like a little bitch anyway. Isn't that why you got Eugene to do all of your dirty work at the Institute?" I spare a quick glance at Drew and realise he was hiding a knife under his foot. He's bent over to his side, cutting off the tape, and preparing to jump Zac at the first chance. I smile at Zac, trying to pass it off as smugness from my comment.

"I wouldn't mind seeing the look on the guys' faces while I beat the crap out of you." Zac smirks.

I swear I almost hear a growl come out of Jayce before I feel a slap across my face. I let out a laugh before I'm smacked again. This time his hand is so forceful that my head jolts back from the momentum.

"What's funny?" Zac asks.

"I was right, you do hit like a bitch," I say, even though the whole left side of my face is burning.

I start laughing, somewhat hysterically. I don't know if the blows to the face have made me drunk with pain or if I've finally realised how screwed up this situation is.

"What is so funny, Miss Daniels?" Zac spits out.

"Oh, just that you not only kidnapped the next potential first lady but also the director of the Institute *and* a police officer's brother." I hit a whole new level of uncontrollable laughter. It earns me another hit to the face, which sobers me. It's really beginning to hurt.

Zac starts pacing the room as the reality of what he has done crashes down on him. I look at Drew and see that his legs are now loose. He's begun working on his wrists behind his back. At least it's more subtle now though—he doesn't have to bend to stretch his arms to his ankles.

"Your sister's really a cop?" Zac asks Jayce.

"Yep. Oh, and I should probably mention that I'm wearing a wire." Our heads snap in his direction. He shrugs. "She wanted to get dirt on Paxton at the party, which thanks to you"—he looks at Zac—"she has. If you want to make a deal with her, I'm sure the police department can work something out."

"Wait. You're wearing a wire? Your sister's investigating Paxton? Why?" I ask.

Jayce shrugs again. "I don't know. I try not to get involved in her work."

"Until me," I say, rather pissed off. "Were you helping investigate him? Were you using me to—"

"I didn't, I swear I didn't. I wouldn't tell her anything."

"And why should I trust you? You've been lying to me for a month. Were you ever interested in me? Or were you just after Paxton?" I yell. I don't actually feel this way—maybe a tiny part of me does, but I'm just trying to cause more of a distraction until Drew can get free.

"I'm not going to discuss this while you're being irrational, Allira," he replies.

"Me, irrational?" I yell louder.

"Oh, here we go with the drama again." Jayce rolls his eyes. "I'm beginning to think you aren't a drama magnet at all. You willingly go out looking for it! It doesn't come to you, you seek it out!" he yells back.

I've never seen Jayce lose his cool, but clearly I've pushed him over the edge. There's something in the tone of his voice though, something isn't right. It's almost as if … I smile but try to suppress it. He's noticed what I have. Drew's almost free, but Zac is watching Jayce and I fight as if we're on a teenage soap opera.

"Well, that's better than being *boring*," I say.

"You only think I'm boring because your life is one insane crazy person after the other wanting something from you."

"That actually seems pretty true right now," I admit.

"Enough!" Zac yells.

"Can I just ask what were you expecting to happen today?" Jayce asks Zac. "The fact that I have a sister on the police force shouldn't make a difference to your plan. You don't actually think you'll get away with killing us, do you?"

"That was the original plan, yes. But that also involved killing

Paxton and Allira at the convention centre, then getting the hell out of there."

"So now what are your options?" Jayce asks, calmly. He's using his counselling voice, one that I have succumbed to a lot since meeting him.

"I don't have any," Zac says.

I don't think that was the answer Jayce was hoping for, because in this moment, all four of us realise the plan is for none of us to get out of here alive. Zac has nothing to lose.

"You do have options," I say, trying to stall further. *What the hell is taking Drew so long?* "I'm sure that with all of the dirt you have on Paxton, you have more than enough to do some sort of plea bargain for leniency in the shooting. Paxton and Tate might even pull through yet—it won't be murder charges you're facing. Right now, you haven't done anything to the three of us. We're just talking. You haven't crossed that line yet."

"Your face begs to differ," he retorts.

"Meh, it's just a black eye. It doesn't even hurt."

"And that bodyguard of yours?"

"It was nothing he didn't deserve. He was super annoying." *Okay, now I'm just rambling.* "You're right about me, though. I did ruin your life. You and Brookfield offered me the world by letting me back into society, and I blew it by running away. I shouldn't have done that."

He paces, thinking for a moment.

"If you cooperate with them, they may even get you to help in the search for Brookfield. You found him here when no one else was able to locate him. That's got to count for something. You were smarter than anybody else when it came to finding him. They could use your skills. They need someone like you."

He shakes his head. "No. This needs to end now. I'm not going back to that hell hole of a prison."

He reaches for the gun in the waistband of his pants, but before he can aim it at me, Drew jumps on him from behind. The knife in Drew's hand goes flying in Jayce's direction. Jayce, still bound by duct tape, is quick to dive for it. He wriggles over to the knife while Drew and Zac struggle with each other. This is my chance.

I close my eyes and focus on Licia somewhere outside. I breathe in and imagine myself in duplicate, standing next to myself. The woozy out of body sensation I experienced the first time I ever borrowed Licia's projection ability is strong, and when I open my eyes, I see me, unconscious, still sitting in the chair.

Jayce stops struggling for the knife. He's too busy freaking out about seeing me use my ability for the first time. It only lasts a second before he's back to reaching for the knife to cut himself free. Drew and Zac are still wrestling each other; the gun must have been knocked to the floor in the scuffle. I have to find Zac's gun or Drew's gun. Where did Zac put that?

Zac suddenly drops Drew to the ground on his back and starts beating the crap out of his face. I run, still in my heels—*Why didn't I take them off already?*—tackling Zac off Drew. I straddle him, like he was doing to Drew, and start punching him, over and over again.

Adrenaline is coursing through me, and I just keep punching him. I can't stop myself, even long after Zac stops struggling.

"Allira, that's enough," I hear Drew say, but it's not enough.

"Allira." I feel a comforting hand on my shoulder and know that it's Jayce without having to look up. I stop my assault and turn into Jayce's arms as he picks me up off Zac, my body shaking uncontrollably.

"It's okay, it's over," Jayce soothes. I stay in his arms, just waiting to calm down, but it doesn't seem to be happening.

"Is he … ?"

"I don't know," he answers me. We stand there a few moments more. I don't want to turn my head and look at Zac, at what I did to him. "Uh … this is kind of weird. Could you maybe … uh, become one person again?" Jayce asks.

Forgetting that I'm in a projected state, I pull away. "Sorry!" I close my eyes, breathe in deep, and go back into my body. I realise I'm still restrained when I try to stand. "A little help? Please?"

Jayce comes over and cuts me free. He helps me over to Drew who's sitting on the ground, his head in his hands and his elbows resting on his knees. I lift his chin. He's pretty badly beaten. I hug him, and he hugs me back.

"Thanks," he sputters, turning his head to spit out some blood.

"Anytime," I smile. "So, tally-wise, I think we're about even now."

"I think you'll always be one up on me. You've saved me in more ways than I can count."

"Don't get all mushy on me now," I say, assessing his face. I think his nose might be broken.

Zac groans from the ground. Part of me is thankful that I didn't kill him; the other part of me wants to find a gun and finish what I started.

My eyes dart around the room, searching for the two guns I know are here somewhere. One's across the room, and I run to it, picking it up off the ground and pointing it at Zac. Jayce finds the one that was Drew's on the counter where Zac must have put it earlier. He doesn't point it at Zac though, he just holds it—I assume so Zac can't get to it.

"Do it," Zac says huskily. "I'm ready to die. I want this."

I stare at him with furrowed brows. Could I really kill a person? I know I just came close, but to do it like this? While he's lying on the floor, begging me for it? Would this be doing him a favour?

"Allira, you don't need to do it," Jayce says. "We're safe. He's contained."

"He tried to kill me. *Twice.* You don't think he'll come back and try again?" I'm trying to rationalise what I really want to do.

My hand begins to tremble. It's as if I have my own devil versus angel thing going on in my head, only my anger is the devil, and Jayce is the angel. I know that killing Zac like this would be wrong. It's not self-defence. If I do this, I'd be just like him. But what happens if he gets out of prison and comes to find me again?

"Allira," Jayce says soothingly. "It's okay."

Before I have the chance to make a decision, the door to the warehouse flies open. Men and women in black head-to-toe protective gear rush in, guns aimed at us.

"Drop your weapons!" a deep commanding voice yells. "Put your weapons down on the ground." Jayce and I do as we're told. "Hands up and walk slowly over to the far wall."

Over at the wall, the intruders start to cuff the three of us.

Jayce is next to me, and I recognise the blonde hair under the protective helmet of the officer arresting him. My suspicions are confirmed when I hear Jenna's voice.

"Hey, little brother. I told you to stay away from her, didn't I?" she says in a playful tone. "Mum's going to be so pissed when she hears about this!"

"What can I say—I just couldn't stay away," he says, smiling at me. "Is this really necessary anyway? We're not the bad guys here. Allira and Drew just saved my life, in case you were wondering."

"You still wearing the wire I gave you?" she asks in a hushed tone, as if she doesn't want her co-workers to hear he has it.

"Yeah. Still wearing it."

"This should be easy to sort out, then. We'll need you all to come down to the station, answer a few questions, give statements." She looks over to me. "Is that okay?"

I nod. "Drew might need to go to the hospital though. He's been beaten pretty badly."

"I'm fine," Drew disagrees on the other side of me.

"Can you tell me if Tate and Paxton are okay?" I ask, my voice breaking.

"There's no news yet," Jenna responds quietly. "Nothing they have told us anyway. We'll get your statements down quick and get you to the hospital as soon as we can, okay?"

"Okay," I reply barely above a whisper.

I don't know what I'm going to do if Tate isn't okay. I don't want Shilah to go through what I went through. I don't want Nuka to lose her father either, even if I could kill Paxton myself right now.

The officer fastening my cuffs turns me around to face Jenna when he's done.

"You don't seem surprised to see me here," she states, confusion written all over her face.

"Allira worked it out," Jayce answers for me.

"Oh," Jenna mutters.

"I tried to come and see you, numerous times. But since Paxton and I got engaged, he's kind of had me on a short leash, and I couldn't get away."

"Why did you want to come see me?" she asks.

"I wanted to help with your investigation. Not to mention I wanted answers."

She narrows her eyes. "And who do you think it is that we were investigating?" she asks, glancing at Drew.

"I assumed it was Paxton. I've learnt a lot about him this last week—more than I ever thought he was capable of."

She nods. "We'll talk at the station."

As we're escorted outside, the tension between Jenna and Drew becomes palpable. Before we're put in a police van, Licia comes running over to us from her hiding spot. Other officers are quick to come after her, but she's fast.

"You're okay?" she says, reaching Drew and throwing her arms around him.

"You did good, kiddo," he says proudly.

"I didn't do anything."

"Yeah, you did," I say, winking at her.

"And you got the cops here," Drew adds. "And you listened when I said I didn't want you in harm's way." He kisses her on the cheek in an overprotective, brotherly way.

I can't help giggling at the pang of jealousy coming out of Jenna. Drew feels it too and has a giant smirk on his face.

We're loaded into the van, Licia included, and taken to the police station. We're each led to a different interrogation room, mine eerily similar to the one I had when I was first arrested and sent to the Institute. This one is cleaner at least.

My arresting officer un-cuffs me and tells me to sit. He leaves the room and I'm left to ponder what they're going to do to me.

I watch two hours go by, according to the clock on the wall. It's six a.m. now. That means Zac only had us captive for a few hours. It felt so much longer than that. Finally, Jenna comes in, no longer in tactical protective gear but a business suit, her long wavy blonde hair resting below her shoulders.

"We listened to the tape ... well, enough of it anyway," she says.

"So we can go then?" I ask.

"We just need to go over a few things first."

"Okay ..."

"What did Jayce mean when he asked if you could become one person again?"

I look down, guiltily. "I may have been borrowing a Defective ability," I admit. There's no point in hiding it.

"We're not going to press charges, if that's what you're worried about—you used it in self-defence, and anyone would clearly be able to hear that if they heard that tape. I was just kind of curious. You said you wanted to help our investigation?" she asks, changing the subject.

I nod. "I will if I can, but to be honest, I don't know all that much. Paxton has been manipulating me for almost two years—ever since I met him. I don't even know what's real about him and what isn't."

"He isn't our target," she states. "Brookfield is."

My heart beats loudly in my ears. "B-Brookfield?" I stutter, suddenly feeling faint.

"Are you okay? Do you want a glass of water or something?" she asks, and I nod. She doesn't even move, but an officer comes in with a glass of water. Clearly, this interview is being watched. "Brookfield's been our target from the beginning, but you're right about Paxton, too. It's odd that Brookfield was able to just disappear like that. No money, no means of living. How do you suppose he's managed to stay hidden for so long?"

"His wife?" I suggest, not liking where this is going.

Jenna shakes her head. "We've been on her for the last eighteen months. She wants nothing to do with him."

"Are you saying that Paxton's behind it?"

"Paxton makes a deposit to a side bank account every month. It's not a lot of money, but it's enough to live comfortably. Do you know who he would be sending money to?"

My eyes widen when I realise what she means. "No. He wouldn't. He wouldn't be funding Brookfield's life. Why? Why would he do it? Why wouldn't he just turn him over? Brookfield tried to kill me. Paxton wouldn't be giving him money. The money is probably for his ex-wife or something." I know I'm borderline ranting, but I can't help it.

"It could be. We haven't been able to locate her. Have you ever met her?"

"No, but she abandoned Nuka when she was a year old. I

don't expect she would come back for her. Could it just be a savings account for Nuka?"

She shakes her head. "The money is always withdrawn within a couple of days, always at a different ATM, always in a different part of the city."

"Don't those things have cameras?"

She sighs. "You don't think we've checked that out? All we know is it's a man, and he always has his face hidden. Big sunglasses, baseball cap, hooded jackets, sometimes facial hair, sometimes not. That's why we don't think it's his ex-wife—unless she's getting her boyfriend or someone to get the money for her. But why hide his identity if that were the case?"

"You're sure it's Brookfield?"

"Fairly certain," she replies, reaching her hand out, placing it on top of mine.

"But why?" I whisper, more to myself than her. Why would Paxton do this?

"The AFP weren't aware of the hostile takeover until you told me about it last week. That was a major cover up on Paxton's behalf. The only theory we can come up with as to why Paxton is abetting Brookfield is that he doesn't want Brookfield's side of the story to come out. Before that, we had no idea what his motivation would've been."

"Paxton should want Brookfield captured just as much as me. He tried to kill me!"

"So did Zac, evidently. He's going away for a very long time.

So will Brookfield when we get him. Okay?"

I nod. With Cyrus telling me Paxton orchestrated the whole takeover, Zac telling me Paxton organised the torturing of Tate and the escape of Brookfield, and now Jenna telling me Paxton has been funding Brookfield's freedom, all I can wonder is how I was dumb enough not to see it earlier: Paxton is a sociopath and a pathological liar. For him to hide this, especially around Tate and me … he must even believe his lies himself, or we would've heard his deceit in his thoughts.

My revelation floors me.

"I just need to get your written statement of the events of what happened last night and this morning, and then we can get you to the hospital to be checked out, and you can visit your family," she says, placing a pen and paper in front of me.

"Are … Is …"

"They're not telling us anything at this point. All we've been told is they're both still in critical condition."

She gets up and goes to walk out, but I can't stop myself from asking. "Did you … was Jayce …" I don't want to ask the question.

"Was Jayce helping us?" she asks. I shyly nod. "No. In fact, he's been driving me crazy. He wouldn't even tell me if you'd mentioned *anything* that could help my case. Not until you were willing to tell it all yourself."

"When we went to the Institute?"

She nods.

I can't help smiling. I understand now why he wanted me to go to Jenna with all of this. He knew she could help, but he wasn't going to betray me or his sister by outing either of us.

"Tina was a confidential informant of mine from another case. The AFP put her up in our building in a safe-house type situation. Jayce didn't know that—he just thought she was a new neighbour. It was my job to make sure nothing happened to her. I was out one night, and he found her beaten. When he got home from taking her to the clinic, he told me about the hot reception girl. We'd been surveying you for a while, and I was really hoping he meant that Ebbodine girl and not you because of how involved you were with Paxton. I told him to stay away." She shakes her head, "He didn't listen, of course, and next thing I knew, he was volunteering and spending every day with you. He didn't even want to cover for me with the fake journalist crap, but he knew if he didn't, and he was to expose me, I could've lost my job, and he could've been charged. He never wanted to lie to you. He didn't even want to wear the wire last night. I told him I wouldn't give him the press pass if he didn't wear it."

I try to hide my ever-increasing smile but fail miserably. "How did you fake the news article? And the press pass?" I ask, remembering the article by Jenna Harrison—the one about the clinic.

She looks at me condescendingly. "We're special ops. We have the ability to use public media to our advantage. I have a connection to the editor of the *Daily News*. We needed to put focus on the clinic and your aunt to draw Brookfield out. We figured he wouldn't be happy to know that the Institute was funding such a cause. It was a long shot, but we're getting desperate to find him." She comes close to me and whispers,

"I also figured that even if it didn't help our case, it would've helped your clinic. Jayce was right—people need to know what you're trying to accomplish there."

"Thank you."

"Oh!" she says, her smile unwavering. "I heard your negotiation with Zac on the wire. You could make a career as a negotiator. Unlike my stupid brother who backed himself into a corner by making the target realise he had no other options, you played to his ego and managed to distract him for eight more minutes. Do you know how critical those eight extra minutes are in tactical situations? Jayce is going to make a great psychologist one day, but I think he's more suited to sorting out the messed-up problems of soccer mums than actual psychotics like Zac and Brookfield."

"Thanks," I say, managing a smile. She goes to leave, but my stupid mouth keeps talking. "Have you spoken to Drew? Was he part of your investigation, too?"

She sighs and turns back around to face me. "He was in the beginning, but from what I've found out about him—apart from him being a total workaholic—he has nothing to do with the shady money deals that Paxton was involved in while he was the director of the Institute." *Shady money deals, too?* She breathes in again and holds it. "I haven't seen him. I don't think he'll want to talk to me."

"I don't know about that. Even if he is pissed off at you, just remember that's how Drew and I met, and I've forgiven him. It took a while, but we've never been closer."

"I'm not exactly hoping to *only* be his friend, Allira." She walks out before I can stop her again.

I fill out my statement, providing as much detail as possible, and then sit and wait to be released. I put my head down on the desk in front of me for what feels like a minute, but when I hear the door click open, and I jump up startled, I'm wiping drool from my mouth. Maybe I fell asleep.

Jayce enters the room, and I'm out of my seat and in his arms before he can even say anything.

I feel his breath on my neck, his strong arms around me, and I can't be any more thankful that he's okay.

"I didn't think you'd ever talk to me again when you found out about Jenna. Especially after that night we … you know," he says, relief filling his voice.

"I have a confession to make," I say, pulling away but remaining close to him. "I knew you were lying to me before we slept together."

"What?" he asks stunned, taking a step back.

"You know how we couldn't hear you, but you heard everything we were saying through the earpieces that day?"

He nods.

"We overheard you and Jenna right before we came back into contact. You said you couldn't lie to me anymore, and she told you to keep your mouth shut."

"That explains why you were so pissed off after we left. Why didn't you just talk to me about it?"

"I didn't want to know the truth. I was worried about what it could be, and I figured ignorance is better than finding out what it was."

"But you still slept with me," he says, his brows wrinkling in confusion.

"I know." I smile at the memory. "My brain was telling me to stop it, but my body wouldn't listen."

"That's why you left in the middle of the night?"

"I thought it was a huge mistake because I knew you were lying to me, but I did it anyway."

He smiles back at me. "Maybe your body has known all along."

"Known what?"

"That we are meant for each other."

I don't mean to scoff, but I do. "I don't know if I'd go that far."

"Oh?"

"Don't get me wrong, I want to be with you, but I don't really believe in 'meant for each other.' I've learnt relationships are hard and take work. If fate, and soulmates, and 'meant for each other' was real, then why is it so difficult?"

"Because the obstacles make it worth it."

I stare at him blankly.

"Then do you care to explain the inexplicable need I have for you?"

"Hormones?"

It's his turn to stare blankly.

"I'm just that awesome?"

He laughs at that.

"All I'm saying is, if fate brought us together, then fate is a bitch." He raises his eyebrows at my words, intrigued. "Imagine how much fate would've been responsible for, just to bring us together. The release of all the Defectives from the Institute, the death of Chad, the fact your sister chose to become a cop *and* was assigned to Tina who got beaten up while she was off duty … there's just too many variables to say that that was all done so you and I could be together."

He's still smiling. "You're cute when you're trying to make a point. You can believe what you want. I know differently," he says cockily.

Smiling, I just stare into his eyes, take in the look of adoration on his face, and savour this moment.

"So you're *not* a cop," I eventually say.

He shakes his head. "Nope."

"And you never lied. I mean, not technically. Thinking back, I realise you never once told me Jenna was a journalist. *I* said it, and you didn't dispute it."

"You're really not angry about the whole Jenna thing?"

"It's not like you had a choice. And you never lied about yourself."

"Actually …" he says, taking a step back from me. "I did, once."

I swallow, hard. "Oh?" My voice is groggy. My heart starts pounding. What else did he lie about?

"I told you that I've never been in love. I may not have known it at the time, but that was a big, fat lie. I've been in love with you since the moment I saw you."

I smile before hitting his chest, pushing him farther away from me. "You jerk!"

He laughs, stumbling backwards. "I tell you I love you and you're hitting me?"

"I thought … when you said you'd lied, I thought it was about something serious," I say, telling my heart to slow back down.

"I couldn't be any more serious," he says, closing the distance between us again.

He brings his lips to mine, and I let him kiss me as hard and as intense as he wants to. I don't push him away, I don't think I could even if I wanted to. I've never felt this wanted, this *needed*, this loved. I have an inexplicable need for him, too.

I know Chad and I had something special, but I feel as if it was situational love—the kind of love between two people who had been through similar experiences, endured the same hardships. We were thrown together, forced to find comfort in each other, and we fell in love. I loved Chad, so much. I still do. A part of me always will. But I yearn for Jayce.

"I love you too," I murmur against his lips, surprised by how easy the words come. When I pull away, my eyes find his chest, watching my fingers as they play with the top button of his shirt. "When Chad died, I thought that was it for me. I didn't think I was going to find anyone who could be there for me the way he was. I was pretending to live without actually living. I wasn't expecting to find you, and even when I did, I didn't think it was possible to feel this way about you—to fall so hard, so fast. You made me want to live again."

"I don't think that was me," he whispers. "You could probably thank Zac for that as well."

"Huh?" I screw up my face.

"While you were trying to work out who could possibly be threatening you, you practically started glowing, like you had a purpose, like you were doing what you were born to do. I may have helped you want to live again, but actually doing it? It was all you. You're stronger than you give yourself credit for."

He smiles before taking my mouth with his again. I don't know how long we stay like that, lips locked in a state of euphoria, but we only stop when we're interrupted by Jenna.

"We can take you to the hospital now," she says, a smile gracing her lips. "I've got some clothes for you to change into, too. I'm sure you don't want to be wearing that bloodstained gown anymore," she adds before walking off.

"So what happens now?" he asks, his arms still wrapped around me.

I almost state the obvious—that I go to the hospital to make sure Tate's okay. Then I realise what he's actually asking. Technically, I still have a fiancé. One who was shot last night.

One who doesn't deserve to be my friend, let alone fiancé. I can't let Paxton manipulate me anymore, but with the campaign, and the publicity aspect of what happened last night, I'm not so sure it will be easy to get away from him.

Ugh. Now I'm even thinking like him. Who cares what the media thinks? *You do, Allira.* I sigh at my thoughts. The truth is, I do care what the media thinks, because Paxton getting shot—and by a Defective, no less—is only going to isolate the Defective community even more.

"I don't know."

"Want me to come with you to the hospital?" Jayce asks.

I nod. "I want you to come everywhere with me." I wince. "Eww. That came out way cornier than I was expecting."

"I like corny."

"You would. You believe in fate."

CHAPTER EIGHTEEN

"Where's Drew?" I ask Jenna as she opens the door to a squad car, motioning for us to get in.

"He was released earlier and sent to the hospital for treatment," she replies in an obviously forced casual tone. I'm guessing she's trying to hide the fact she's worried about him.

"He'll be fine," I reassure her. "He may end up with a crooked nose, but it should've been illegal for him to be that good-looking in the first place. This will just be karmic justice."

She cracks a smile, but I can tell she's just being polite. She really is worried about him. Either that, or she truly thinks he won't speak to her again now that her secret is out.

I pause to look at her before getting in the car. "Jenna, I of all people know what it's like to be betrayed like that, but I think it's completely different. Yes, you were investigating him and started seeing him under false pretences, but you never arrested him—in fact you cleared him of any wrongdoing. You didn't destroy his family. You didn't sit by and watch him get tortured for days. If I found it in my heart to forgive *him*, he should be able to forgive you. And I plan on yelling at him if he doesn't." I smile at her, and she returns it—a real smile this time.

"You've been hanging around Jayce for too long. Stop reading me," she says lightly before practically pushing me into the car.

Jenna and Jayce are silent all the way to the hospital. I'm not talking either, but it's not for lack of trying. I need a distraction, but they're not giving me one. I keep telling myself that until I know anything for sure, Tate will be fine, Paxton will be fine.

It annoys me that I still want Paxton to be okay. I may not want anything to do with him anymore, but I don't wish him dead. I have no idea why—I should want him to suffer, just like he made Tate suffer, just like he made Chad suffer. I guess a big part of me does, but there's a stronger part of me hoping he pulls through for Nuka's sake.

"Nuka," I whisper when I think about what this all means for her.

"She's with her nanny," Jenna says, thinking I was asking about her. "They're at the hospital."

I narrow my eyes, realising she may know more than she's letting on. "You know something, don't you?"

"We're almost there. I think it's best you hear it from the

doctors yourself."

My hand starts trembling, Jayce grabs hold of it to try to calm me, and it helps a little, but I can't stop my mind from thinking the worst. They're both gone.

My legs feel weak climbing out of the car when we arrive at the hospital. Jayce takes my hand again, and I use him to steady myself. The simplicity of the three-story building makes me wonder how it can be so intimidating. And that's when I notice the media waiting outside.

My hand releases Jayce's, flying to my side in an instant. But it's too late.

"Miss Daniels!" one of the reporters shouts. Within seconds, a swarm of news crews converge on me.

Questions are thrown at me. "Where were you when Candidate James was shot?" "Why haven't you been here?" "Is it true you were having an affair?" "Is that your boyfriend?"

I furrow my brow, screwing up my face at that one. *How did they know?*

"Just keep moving, Allira," Jenna's voice is in my ear. Both Jayce and she wrap their arms around me, protecting me from the encroaching crowd.

The doors to the entrance slide open as we near them, and suddenly I want to run the other way. I don't want to go in there, but I can't go back through the throng of media either. The only way is forwards.

Jayce must feel it when my whole body stiffens with anxiety.

"It's okay. I'm here for you," he whispers in my ear.

They usher me inside, and Jenna stalks off to talk to the receptionist. I wait patiently, still in Jayce's arms. When Jenna's done, she starts leading us down a hallway.

As we get closer to the intensive care unit, I don't think I've ever felt more elated than when the thoughts of everyone around flood my head.

"Tate's alive," I gasp with relief, my legs wanting to collapse underneath me.

"How do you know?" Jayce asks. "Oh, right. Telepath thing."

Where are you?

'Ward B, Room twelve, bed two,' he replies.

Are you okay?

'I'll live. You should visit Paxton first.'

No. He doesn't deserve it.

'Allira. Don't hold a grudge against him for whatever he's done. Now's a time for forgiveness.'

Why should I forgive him?

'Because if you don't do it now, you won't get another chance. You need to let your issues with him go.'

What's going on?

'Just go to him first, okay?'

Okay.

DEFECTIVE

Jenna turns to me as we near the end of the hallway, coming to a T section. "Tate's room is down that way," she says, pointing to the left. "Paxton's is this way," she says, pointing to the right. "Where to?"

"Right," I say, surprising both Jenna and Jayce. "Tate told me to go to Paxton first." I tap the side of my head.

We turn right, and Jenna pushes a button to open the glass ICU doors.

Jenna leads me to Paxton's room, but I freeze just outside the door. "You can go in, I'll go find a doctor for you to talk to," she says, walking off.

"Did you want me to come in with you?" Jayce asks.

I try to talk, but only air comes out. I nod instead. What am I going to see when I walk in there?

My feet take reluctant steps into the room. My nose is assaulted with that strong hospital smell, making my eyes sting and my stomach feel queasy. The sound of machines beeping and a ventilator huffing oxygen fills my ears. All I can do as I reach the foot of his bed is stare at him. He's unconscious with tubes coming out of everywhere.

A plethora of emotions fills me. Hate, anger, compassion, and grief consume me.

There's a knock at the door, and a doctor in a lab coat walks in with Jenna behind him. He's in his fifties and has a thick greying beard and glasses.

"Hello, Miss Daniels," he says, reaching to shake my hand. "I know this is a difficult time for you, but there are some things to discuss and decisions to be made."

"Decisions?"

Jayce comes up behind me, placing his hands on my shoulders in a comforting manner.

The doctor seems distracted by the move before he continues. "As Paxton's only family, you have power of attorney over his medical decisions."

"But we're not … we're not even married yet," I say, confused, taking a step away from Jayce in a move of political correctness. The doctor is still staring us both up and down.

"The only blood relative Paxton has is his six-year-old daughter. You don't expect her to make this decision, do you?"

"What decision?" I ask again.

"Your fiancé is currently in a coma. The machines are breathing for him. His brain scans show little activity …" The doctor continues to talk about things I don't understand. I don't know what half the words mean. All I'm getting from it is Paxton doesn't have much hope. "I can give you a moment to think it all over," he says as he finishes his spiel that sounds as if he's said it many times before.

"So you're saying I have to make a decision on whether to leave him in a coma and hope that he wakes up, even though the chances of that happening are small, or to switch off the machines and let him go," I clarify his words.

He nods. "Keep in mind that with little brain activity, if he does pull through, he won't be the same person. We can't be sure of the amount of damage sustained to his brain just yet, but chances are he'll most likely need help doing the simplest of tasks—and that's best-case scenario. You have to think about what Paxton would want."

"He's a fighter. I know he'd want to fight for his life, for Nuka." *That's understating it.*

"You don't have to make a decision right now," the doctor says. "I'll give you a while to think about it, and I'll come back and see you during afternoon rounds."

He leaves, and I'm left stunned and overwhelmed. I can't make this kind of decision. But if I don't, who will?

"Could I have a moment alone with him—to think this over?" I ask Jayce and Jenna.

Jayce kisses me on the cheek. "We'll be right outside," he says, leading Jenna out of the room.

Taking a seat in the chair next to his bed, I just stare at him for a long time. He doesn't even look like the man I know … the man I *knew*. He looks almost villainous, even in the vulnerable state he's in.

It's only now that I realise this is the man he's always been, I've just been too blind to see it—too wrapped up in my own crap to really notice who I was living with. I trusted him completely, I thought I was doing right by everyone.

I'm interrupted by a nurse coming in to 'check on him. She gives me a sympathetic look, putting her hand on my shoulder. "You know, they say that even in a coma he may still be able to hear you. It helps if you talk to him."

I smile politely, waiting for her to do her thing and leave before I start ripping into him. I don't care if he can hear me or not, I need to get this out.

"Why did you do it? Why did you set us all up? Why are you giving Brookfield money to live when he tried to take my life away? Why did you …" I stop to slump forwards on his bed, grabbing hold of his hand that lies next to my head. "I don't know what to do. Tell me what to do," I plead, tears starting to form in my eyes but refusing to spill onto my face.

'He would've come after us. I'm not sorry.'

"You can hear me?" I ask, sitting up straighter.

'Yes.' His body doesn't even flinch or register anything.

"So you *are* still in there?"

'I'm weak. I can't take much more of this. I keep telling myself to wake up, but I can't. This is the end. I can feel it. Let me go.' He's silent again for a moment before I hear *'I was going to make a difference in the world.'*

I try to contain my anger towards a dying man, but I can't. "Make a difference no matter whom you hurt in the process? You almost killed Tate, Chad died because of you—"

'Everything I did was for Nuka.'

The anger inside of me is urging me to stand up and pull the plug. If he didn't just say Nuka's name, I'm sure I'd do it. I want to scream; I want to yell. Paxton deserves it … actually he deserves so much more than that. He may have done so much good in this world, but he achieved it by doing evil things. He supposedly loved us like family, but he was willing to throw any one of us—me, Tate, the entire Resistance—under the bus if it got him what he wanted.

Can I really allow him to pull through this? If he does survive this, and he does need constant care, who will that fall on? I'm not going to spend my life caring for the man who was responsible for Chad's death. I know I played a big part in that, too—I didn't need to agree to Paxton's crazy plan, but he manipulated every situation I've encountered since leaving the Institute. I feel like a used puppet.

'Let me go' I hear him think again. *'I don't want to live like this. Let me go, let me go, let me go,'* he begs. I don't know if he realises I'm still here or not. It almost sounds like he's begging to a higher power or deity.

"I'll let you go," I tell him reassuringly.

'Look after Nuka for me.'

My mouth goes dry as the weight of his request hits me. I wait for a few moments to try to compose myself before stumbling out of the room and into the hallway. Jayce and Jenna are sitting at the end in a tiny waiting room. Jayce sees me and rushes to my side, holding me up as I begin to feel faint and almost fall over.

"Are you okay?" he asks. "Sorry, stupid question. Clearly you're not okay."

"He wants to die," I whisper. Tears threaten to come, but they don't, even though I'm not stopping them. Does that mean I'm not sad over him? Should I be sad? I don't know what to feel anymore. I wrap my arms around Jayce and bury my head in his chest.

'*He's awake?*' Jayce thinks, probably more to himself than me, but I answer him anyway.

"Not awake," I say.

"Oh. So he can still think and hear?" he asks, pulling back to look at my face. I nod solemnly. "So you're letting him go?"

"It's what he wants. He asked me to take care of Nuka," I say. Not wanting to look at Jayce's reaction, I bury my head in his chest again.

Jayce doesn't say anything, and I don't want to hear his thoughts, so I try not to focus on him, but they come through anyway. '*Surely there's somebody else who could take her.*'

I pull back and glare at him as realisation crosses his face. "Sorry. I didn't mean it like that. I understand why he'd want you to take her, but you're so young. You're only twenty, and he's asking you to be responsible for a six-year-old?"

"I know it'll be tough, but she doesn't have anyone else. I have to do it."

"Then we'll make it work," he says, wrapping me tightly in his arms once again. '*I don't know how, but we'll make it work.*'

Arms are suddenly pulling me away from Jayce and into another hug. Shilah's grip is deathly, and he's squeezing so hard I think my ribs are being crushed.

"I'm so glad you're okay," he says, pulling back and examining my face which I've only just remembered wouldn't look too good from the beating Zac gave me. It's not too painful, but I'm sure I look hideous.

"How's Tate?" I ask. "Can I go see him?"

"He was just given more pain meds. He'll be out of it for a while, but he's okay. You two will have matching battle scars," he says with a smile. "I saw what was about to happen but didn't get to them in time. Tate heard me shout his name at the last second and moved, but the bullet nicked his left shoulder."

I reflexively reach up to touch my right shoulder, running my finger over my scar where I was shot when Chad was killed.

"That's what that mark is?" Jayce asks, lightly brushing over it with his hand and down my arm. It sends tingles down my spine so fierce I actually shudder.

Shilah looks at him and then back at me.

"Oh. Jayce this is my brother, Shilah. Shilah, Jayce."

Shilah nods. "Tate's told me about you. I wish I could say my sister had, but she's kept pretty tight-lipped about you." He gives me a less than pleased look, smirking at me.

"Well. it's not like I could tell you about my boyfriend in front of my fiancé. Wow, does that sentence make me sound like the worst person ever."

Shilah and Jayce laugh. "It's not like he was really your fiancé though," Shilah reassures me.

"I know that should make me feel better, but it kind of doesn't."

"Lia!" I hear Nuka yell from down the hall as she comes barrelling towards me.

"Shh, Nuka, this is a hospital," I say, winking at her to let her know I'm only saying it to make people think I'm scolding her. She smiles as she runs towards me. As I kneel down, she runs into my arms, and I give her a big hug, but it doesn't seem like enough in our current situation.

"Linds told me you got away from the bad man and was hiding. I'm happy you don't have to hide anymore. Now you can be here with me and Daddy."

I mouth "thank you" to Linds for not telling her where I really was, but then I look back down at Nuka and realise I'm going to have to be the one to tell her that her daddy is never going to wake up.

"Do you know what happened to your daddy?" I ask.

She nods before looking down at her feet. "He was shot, but it's okay, because you were shot and you're fine now."

I lead Nuka over to some chairs, away from the others who are talking amongst themselves on the other side of the waiting room. We sit as I hold her hands in mine. I take in a deep breath as I begin to contemplate how to break this kind of news to a child.

"Do you remember when I got shot?" I ask.

"I remember visiting you in the hospital."

"Well, I was shot in my shoulder, so that's why I'm okay. Your daddy wasn't shot in the shoulder."

"Where was he shot?"

"He was shot somewhere that couldn't be fixed."

"But he's going to be okay?"

My nose starts running, my eyes begin to overflow, but I tell myself to be strong for her. "Do you remember my friend Chad?"

"Daddy said he died, and that's why you're always upset."

"I'm upset because I can't see Chad anymore."

"Why not?" she asks with the kind of innocence only a child could possess.

"When someone dies … it means they're no longer with us. We can't see them or talk to them anymore because they're gone."

"Did Daddy die?"

"You know the machines in his room, the ones that are beeping and making lots of noise?" She nods as I continue to talk. "They're living for him. They're breathing for him. So when the machines are turned off, he won't be able to live anymore."

"Why are they being turned off?"

"The machines?" I stall. *How in the world do I answer this?*

She nods again, staring up at me with glassy eyes.

"They need to be turned off because he's not going to wake up."

She's silent in thought. I don't know if she really understands what's happening, or if she's just trying to process it all. Leaning in, I hug her and don't let her go until she tells me to.

It takes a long time, but she eventually wriggles out of my arms.

"Do you want to go and say goodbye?" I ask, my voice cracking slightly.

She nods.

Taking her hand in mine, I nod to the others to let them know where we're going and lead her to Paxton's room. I don't let go of her hand, and she never once tries to let go of mine.

"You can talk to him. He can hear you," I say, even though I'm pretty sure he can't anymore. His mind is blank. She just shakes her head. "You want me to do it for you?"

She nods.

"Nuka wants you to know that you are the best daddy in the whole world. She doesn't want you to leave, and she loves you very much." I don't take my eyes off her as I talk.

"I don't want you to go, Daddy," she says as tears overflow onto her cheeks. "But Lia says that you have to. I'll miss you every day."

She's doing a remarkably good job at holding it together. I, on the other hand, am about to lose it. Nuka doesn't deserve this, even if Paxton does.

There's no response in Paxton's brain, no thoughts, nothing.

The alarm on the machine starts beeping madly at us. Doctors and nurses rush in, pushing us aside and telling us to step out while they work on Paxton. I want to tell them there's no use. I know he's gone.

* * *

Linds offers to take Nuka for a while, so I can get home and have a much-needed shower and sleep. Jenna drives Jayce and me to my apartment, all three of us silent for the whole trip.

I overheard Jenna talking to her boss on the hospital phone, saying that their investigation on Paxton is essentially dead now that he's gone. I cringed at her choice of words, but to be fair, she didn't know I was eavesdropping.

"Thanks for the lift," I say as we pull up. Jayce goes to get out of the front passenger side when I put my hand on his arm. "You don't need to come up, I'll be fine."

"I'm not leaving your side ever again," he replies, getting out of the car and shutting the door.

"I didn't realise he could be so bossy," I say to Jenna.

She laughs. "I think it's a new trait he's developed since meeting you."

"Hmm, that's not exactly a good thing."

"Yes, it is. Jayce has always been kind of ... wishy-washy, a flake. He hasn't cared about anything enough to commit to it. Until you."

Jayce taps on my window. "Coming?"

I say goodbye to Jenna and open the door, taking Jayce up to Paxton's and my apartment. *What's going to happen to the apartment now?*

We barely even talk. We don't need to. I shower first, changing into pyjamas and jumping into bed while Jayce showers after me.

I'm vaguely aware of the bed sinking a little under the weight of Jayce's body. His hand rests on my hip, his body spooning mine, but I'm far too tired to acknowledge him.

I'm awoken by voices coming from the living room. *Who's here?* I squint and look at the time. It's early evening and we slept the entire afternoon. Jayce's side of the bed is cold, and he isn't beside me anymore. I strain my ears and hear him talking to someone … is that … Mum's voice?

Jumping out of bed a little too quickly, I find myself having to hold onto the bed to stop from falling as the dizziness hits me. Quickly throwing on some black jeans and a white singlet, I rush into the living room, coming to a sight I couldn't have imagined. Mum and Dad are sitting on the couch, facing away from me. Drew, Ebb, Jamie, and Jayce are standing near the entrance elevator talking. Shilah and Liam are on the opposite couch to Mum and Dad. Shilah's eyes meet mine when I enter, but Liam's too busy playing with his toy to notice me.

Mum and Dad follow Shilah's gaze and stand when they see me. Dad rushes over to me, hugging me tightly.

"I've missed you so much," he says in my ear.

Mum approaches me cautiously, glancing at her feet and then meeting my eyes. "How are you doing?" she asks quietly, glancing away again.

I know I shouldn't be angry. They're here, making an effort. I screwed up, I know that. Now is my chance to apologise, but this insane rage I have building up inside of me won't let me let it go. "Really? You don't talk to me for five"—I start counting—"six, seven months, and that's the best you can come up with? *How am I doing?*" I have the attention of the whole room now. "Well, let's see. The person you shipped me off to live with was a narcissistic, manipulative jerk who controlled me to get what he wanted. You didn't check on me once to see how I was doing. The only time you did call was after Jayce spoke to you about me, but I didn't get that message because apparently Paxton had been intercepting all of my calls. Then … what else … oh, I just spent the last twenty-four hours being kidnapped, tormented, and then arrested, only to be released to go to the hospital and find out Paxton didn't make it. So now I'm suddenly going to be the parent of a six-year-old girl. I think that pretty much sums everything up. How are you doing, Mother?"

I'm breathing heavy after my rant. My mother stares me up and down, and I stare right back at her, unflinching.

"Maybe this was a mistake," she says to Dad. "I don't think she's ready." She goes to walk off but doesn't get far.

"Ready for what?" I ask through gritted teeth.

Shilah stands up from the couch, picking Liam up with him. "It doesn't matter if she's ready anymore, Mum. She needs to know before she"—he looks over to Jayce and then back at me—"gets in too deep."

"What are you talking about?" I ask Shilah while glancing at

Jayce.

Drew, Ebb, and Jamie are staring, wide-eyed and quiet.

Dad grabs my hand, leading me over to the couch. "It has to do with your memory."

I close my eyes and hang my head as my stomach sinks. *This is it.* They're going to tell me what deep down I already know. I've just been too scared to acknowledge the possibility.

I have to force myself to look over at the child in Shilah's arms. My breath hitches in my throat, and my chest heaves as I start hyperventilating. There's no mistaking who he is. The blond hair, his hazel eyes—he looks nothing like Shilah or me. When I look at him, all I see is a ghost.

"Allira—" my mother starts, but I cut her off.

"I know Liam is mine."

CHAPTER NINETEEN

Liam *is* mine. "William," I say. "Named after his father." I'm still looking at William, snuggled happily into his uncle's chest. *Uncle. Not brother.* "What kind of mother wants to forget her own child? Why did I do this?" I whisper frantically.

"Mother?" Jayce blurts out before shrinking back into the couch, embarrassed by his outburst.

"You okay, Jayce? You're looking a little pale," Drew says, a small smirk on his lips.

"Lia," Mum says slowly. "What exactly do you remember?"

"I don't remember anything. I … it's hard to explain. I just know. Apart from William looking like the spitting image of Chad, I've always wondered about that morning I walked out of my room and asked whose kid we were babysitting. The look on your face and Dad's, your reaction, it was … weird.

The more I thought about it, the more I realised why you reacted the way you did. But I didn't want to acknowledge it. I couldn't. I've had this tremendous amount of guilt over Chad as it is, I couldn't add the guilt of what I did to William on top of that. I told myself that he was yours so many times, I almost believed it. *Almost.*"

"When Liam was born—"

"William," I correct my mother reflexively.

She lets out a little laugh. "You never did like us calling him Liam."

I gape at her. I don't remember that. I don't remember anything to do with him. Again I ask, "Why? Why did I do it?"

"You were doing fine … well, relatively fine, up until he was born. We don't know if it was post-partum depression, or delayed PTSD from the shooting, but you kept looking at him and muttering that he looked too much like Chad. That it was too painful, that you couldn't do it."

"So you just *let* me cover it up? Sent me away to … to what?"

"We sent you away to give you space," Dad answers for her. "You needed to heal without the constant reminder of losing Chad. That's what William was for you—just another reminder of what was lost."

"We knew having you around William wasn't good for you, or for him. Not in the state you were in," Mum says. "You left a note before you erased your memory, saying that he'd be better off without you as a mother. You said you were doing it for him, but I think we all knew that you needed it for yourself, too."

I shake my head at what I'm hearing. "You told me I was trying to erase memories of Chad. I thought I'd screwed it up somehow."

"Your note said you were going to erase all memories of Chad, knowing that it'd mean you'd forget who Liam was," Mum says. "Sorry, William," she corrects when I glare at her. "That's going to be hard to get used to. Anyway, something did go wrong, and you only managed to wipe out your memory of William instead. In the end, we thought it best to just give you time."

I feel sick to my stomach, guilt coursing through me like adrenaline.

"You don't need to feel guilty, Allira," Drew says. "You're not a bad parent. If anything, you did the right thing by William. You knew you weren't fit to be a mother, so you left him with the two people you knew to be great parents."

"Who else knows? Oh my God, Belle! That's why she was suddenly nice to me. I'm the mother of her grandson. Has she seen him? Has Chad's dad seen him?"

"They've visited him, yes, but they don't know what you did. We were worried she'd try to take William to the Resistance with her and claim that you were an unfit mother. Whenever she came to visit us, we told her you weren't up to seeing her after what happened with Chad."

"When we went to the Resistance last week, and she mentioned Liam, I thought you were going to realise what she meant," Drew says. "But you had bigger issues to worry about and didn't think much of it."

"And you all vowed to never tell me?" I ask.

"We always planned to tell you," Mum says. "When you were ready to hear it."

"Why now?"

"Shilah told us about Nuka. You really have to think about your own responsibility before taking on someone else's. I know you think we haven't been checking up on you, but we have more pairs of eyes watching over you than you'd expect. I call Aunt Kenna every other day asking how you're going. Shilah's been keeping us updated, Ebb, Drew, we even got an earful from Jayce about how well you've been doing." She smiles over at him.

When I look over at Jayce, he's green. It's been a long twenty-four hours for both of us.

"So what happens now?" I ask Mum and Dad.

"We'll be here for you, whatever you decide. If you want us to keep looking after William, we will. We just thought that before you take on Nuka, you may want to think this whole thing through," Mum says.

I rub my hand over my face. "Nuka has no one else," I state quietly.

"William should have his mother, though," Ebbodine finally speaks.

"Two kids," I mutter. "*Two*."

"We'll be there to help any way we can," Mum says, putting a reassuring hand on my shoulder. "We could even discuss the possibility of taking Nuka for a while, or ... I don't know ... whatever you need, we'll be here. It was so hard to watch you go through what you went through. We didn't know what to do, and you wouldn't let us help you. Please let us help you now."

A rush of warmth fills me as I take in my mother's words. We haven't had much of a relationship over the years, and just when I thought things would get better, they got worse because of my stupid actions. Yet here she is, by my side, like I never thought she would be. She's always looked out for me, even though I never saw it that way.

William's fallen asleep against Shilah's chest. Tears fall again as I realise how much I've missed of his life, how much I don't remember. "Is he ... ?" I swallow hard.

"He hasn't shown any symptoms. But he's only nine months old," Mum answers.

Inexplicable relief washes over me. I know it doesn't matter either way if William is Defective or not—not to me, but I guess there's a big part of me that doesn't want him to have to face the same struggles that the rest of us do.

"How is he even possible?"

"Uh, Allira, if you don't know that, I think we have bigger problems," Drew says.

Mum sighs at him before answering me properly. "It's actually a miracle William survived at all. All that we could figure was you had conceived a day or two before Chad died.

You were shot, your body was in shock, you'd lost a lot of blood, and yet the embryo still attached anyway. Your bloodwork after the shooting didn't indicate pregnancy; it was too early to detect. It wasn't until a few weeks later that you realised you hadn't had a period, and it was a few more weeks after that before you told anyone. Aunt Kenna almost couldn't believe it when you had a sonogram showing a healthy eleven-week-old foetus."

"You were almost happy when you found out," Dad adds. "You said it was Chad's way of making sure he didn't leave you completely. But then William was born, and it was just too hard for you."

"How can I ever forgive myself for what I've done?" I ask no one in particular. "How will he ever forgive me?"

"Stop beating yourself up," Jayce says. My eyes dart over to him in surprise, and angst. *What about us? What will happen to Jayce and me?* He breaks eye contact with me and flicks between looking at me and the floor as he continues to talk. "I told you once before that people do some really crazy stuff while they're grieving. This isn't your fault. You did what was best for you and for William. I have no doubt about that. You needed this time apart to heal. But now you need to make a choice. What are you going to do now you know the truth?" His leg bounces with nerves, not to mention the uneasy feeling I can sense through Drew's ability.

I'm speechless. I don't know what I'm going to do. All I can focus on right now is the guilt.

"Stop it," Drew says. I scowl at him.

"I think I need some air," I say, standing and rushing out of the room.

Making my way outside, up the external stairs on the balcony, I go to my spot on the roof I found a few months back and stare out at the darkening city before me. I haven't been up here in a while. When I first moved in here, I'd come up here a lot. It was therapeutic. I'd look into the belly of the city and make up stories of people I'd see walking the streets below or the people who left their curtains open giving me a view right into their lives.

I don't understand how people think that just because they're twenty or so floors up, they don't need to close their blinds. Uh, *hello*, there are other buildings just as tall and close enough for easy viewing access.

Making up stories about other people's lives made me feel better about myself. Sometimes I'd give them all happy stories—usually when I needed to have some sort of faith that everything could be right with the world. Other times I'd wonder how many people they'd lost in their lives, how many mistakes they'd made.

The sun has just set, the city lights beginning to brighten the sky. Today I look for families on the street and wonder how they came to be a family. Did they all freak out when they found out they were going to be a parent? That they *are* a parent?

I guess that's the difference between me and them. I don't have months to come around to the idea of being a parent. I already am one. *Bam,* life changed forever.

I still can't stop wondering what kind of mother abandons her two-month-old child. *What kind of mother abandons her nine-*

and-eight-year-old child? My inner voice has a point. But I know when Mum disappeared for eight years, she was doing it for us. Can I really say the same?

I give in to my emotions and let myself cry. The tears continue to come long after I thought possible. I'm sitting in a ball on the ground when Jayce finds me. He wraps my black jacket around me. I didn't realise how cold I was until I feel its warmth.

"Really stupid question here, but, are you okay?"

"Sorta?" I choke out.

"Was that a question?" he asks, sitting on the ground next to me.

"I don't know."

"Pretty crazy, huh?" he says after a lengthy bit of silence.

"There's the understatement of the century." We both manage a smile. "I'm sorry I didn't tell you, but I didn't know for sure. I think a big part of me always knew, but I didn't want to deal with it. I couldn't."

"Want to play the Top Three game again? Your biggest three problems—go."

I breathe in and hold it, only letting it out when I begin talking. "One: I just found out I'm the mother of a nine-month-old boy. That in itself is enough to elicit a panic attack. Two: My dead fake fiancé left me with his very real six-year-old daughter. Three: And this is the biggest issue I'm having right now, I'm scared that this is all too much for you, and that I'm going to lose you because I can't turn my back on either of *them*. I just can't. When you told me you loved me this morning, I'm sure 'instant family' isn't exactly what you had in mind. It certainly wasn't for me. But if you're willing … we can make this work," I say warily.

He doesn't respond, no nervous twitch, no narrowing of the eyes. He's almost like a statue.

I realise the kind of pressure I'm putting on him and begin to backpedal. "Look, we still don't really know each other all that well. We still have so much to learn. So in light of that, I'm giving you a 'no hard feelings' easy out. If you want it. It's okay. I understand."

He stands, making his way over to the cement railing that faces the city. There's a brief moment of hesitation before I stand to follow him.

"I'm not going to lie to you," he says without turning to look at me next to him. "When I found out about Nuka, I freaked out a little. I know you know that, you could hear it in my thoughts. And then to find out about William as well … I just … it's a lot to take in."

"I know. It's a lot for me to take in, too, but coming up here and clearing my head, I've realised that I can't run from this anymore. I've been ignoring it for too long, and I can't deny what I now know to be true. It's one thing to suspect and ignore it, but to know the truth? I can't do it. It's scary, and daunting, but I owe it to William, I owe it to Chad, and I owe it to me."

"So maybe we need to take a step back," he suggests quietly. My heart sinks, but I understand. "You need time to get to know your son, and Nuka needs time to get over her dad.

We'll take it slow between us. But Allira"—he turns to look at me now—"believe me when I say that you're not going to lose me just because you're a mother. Those kids are lucky to have someone as strong and as caring as you to be their parent. It'll be an adjustment, but in the end, I know you're going to be a great mum. I just don't know if I could live up to Paxton or Chad in the father department—if and when the time came. I realise that's an unfair statement considering they're both dead—"

I put my arm around him. "We don't have to worry about that right now. We'll cross that bridge when we come to it, okay?"

"Okay," he agrees, wrapping his arm around me and kissing me on the side of my head.

We stand there in each other's arms, just watching the city. "So are you thinking fate had a hand in this, too? What do you think of that bitch now?"

"You're right. She is a bitch. But that doesn't mean this wasn't meant to be."

"I wish I had that kind of faith."

"You don't need to. You just have to trust me."

"I do."

CHAPTER TWENTY

It turns out Paxton's will confirmed he wanted me to take Nuka, and I'm officially her guardian now. Mum and Dad have agreed to have William for at least a few more weeks, if not a few months, until both Nuka and I are more settled and I'm ready to take him. They're bringing him by every day so I can slowly get used to being around him, get to know him, and start bonding with him as a mother should.

I don't know if I will ever get over my guilt of leaving him, but I've promised him, and myself, that I'm going to spend the rest of my life making it up to him. Mum constantly reminds me that I was just doing what I thought was best— just like she did when she left us. I was desperate and made a desperate choice. It doesn't excuse my actions, but it doesn't make me the bad person I feel I am.

The interesting part about Paxton's will was it was drafted just after he became director of the Institute. Had he always planned for me to move in with him and become his political beard? Or was I merely named for the fact he had no one else he was remotely close to?

Paxton set up a trust fund for Nuka which she'll receive when she's twenty-one, but apart from that, there was no money left for her upbringing. The apartment was left to me to raise Nuka in, under the proviso I'll take over the mortgage payments. I had to shake my head at that—surely Paxton would've known I couldn't afford the repayments, even with the apartment being fifty percent paid off. I'll stick it out for as long as we can. I don't want to put Nuka through too many changes too suddenly, but I do have the right to sell it, which I'll probably have to do sooner rather than later. I've already had to let Linds go. It will take a few months before the will is settled completely, though, and the bank has put a hold on the mortgage until then, so we at least have that time to work out what to do.

I'm making my way back to the hospital right now to talk to Tate. I asked Mum and Dad to take Nuka for the day, too, seeing as I have to address the media about Paxton's death right after I speak to Tate. I don't really want her there for that, and I've already put it off for a day. It can't really wait any longer.

I sneak into Tate's room and sit by his bed, waiting for him to wake up.

"I'm awake," he says, his voice husky.

"Hey, how are you feeling?" I ask, leaning forward to hold his hand on his good arm.

"Better. I'm so ready to get out of here. They tell me I need a few more days though."

"You should be revelling in all the glorious hospital food and the sexy gown you get to wear." I smile, but he doesn't seem as entertained as I am. "There's going to be a press conference," I say, suddenly serious.

"There is?"

"The promising presidential candidate is dead. The AFP have asked me to address the media. I have no idea what to say, or if I'm to introduce a new candidate, or if that's even my job." I look to him for the answer.

"The world is definitely not ready for a Defective president yet. There'd be no point in me running."

"Are you sure?"

"Maybe in a few years. After what Zac did, there's no way a Defective will come close this election."

"About that. The AFP were persuaded to cover up the fact that Zac's Defective. It's already bad enough out there with the hate crimes."

Tate kind of laughs. "Politics, hey? Anything is possible to cover up." His face loses the smile. "It still isn't a good idea for me to take Paxton's spot. I'm just being realistic."

"Okay, I'll let everyone know." There's a silent pause before I ask him about Paxton. "Did you know what he did?"

"Paxton?"

"He was the one who put you in that cell," I say, keeping my voice low.

Tate sighs. "I had my suspicions, but I told myself I was being crazy. I always wondered about that photo. And after the stuff you found out about him … I had to stop thinking about it. I didn't want to deal with it."

"That's not all." I haven't told anyone about what else I've learnt about Paxton. Drew knows the stuff Cyrus told us. Jayce knows what Zac said. No one knows what Jenna told me. "Paxton was giving Brookfield money."

"What? Why?"

"So his side of the story wouldn't get out."

Tate's thoughts suddenly hit me like a tidal wave. Expletive after expletive, and anger so intense I find myself flinching in surprise. His face still seems indifferent.

"You can hear that?" he asks, surprised himself.

I nod sheepishly.

"Sorry."

"You know you're allowed to be angry, right?" He's clearly hurt if he can't even block me from his thoughts.

"I know. I just don't want to put that on you."

I gesture for him to move over and lie down on the hospital bed next to him. I'm reminded of when I was shot, and he climbed in my bed to comfort me.

"We both have the right to be angry at him. Paxton claims he did everything for Nuka and would do the same again, given the chance," I say. "Part of me hates that he died, that I didn't get a proper chance to confront him, yell at him, tell him I'd no longer let him manipulate me. It's not fair."

"That's all good in theory, Allira, but you and I both know that if he was still alive, he'd just find another way to manipulate the situation to get what he wants." He shakes his head. "You know, I thought you living with him was helping you. I couldn't see that you were losing more and more of yourself each day, until it was too late."

"Do you think that's why he picked me? Because I'm easy to manipulate?"

"You're far from that. He originally picked you because of who you are—Persephone's daughter and my best friend. I don't think he planned for Chad to die in the takeover, but your grief gave him the opportunity to use you further."

"I hate that I have to go on pretending like we were in love. I want to scream, and yell, and tell everyone about what he did."

"But you can't," Tate says dejectedly. "Just like I can't let my anger get the better of me."

"I know. It'll set back all the progress we've made where Defectives are concerned. Not to mention it would crush Nuka. I can't do that to her."

"We really only have one other option."

I nod. "We have to let it go and forget."

He sighs. "Man, this sucks."

That's an understatement. "You know what else sucks? With Paxton gone …" I trail off.

"Brookfield's going to come back," Tate says for me.

"Yup. I'm working with the AFP to try and entice him out of hiding."

"Is that the reason for the press conference?"

"The press conference was going to happen either way, but he's the reason I'm doing the talking."

"How does Jayce feel about that? You'll be on TV practically daring Brookfield to come after you."

I half-smile. "His sister is special ops in the police force. He doesn't like that I'm putting myself in danger, but he's learnt from Jenna that it's all part of the job. There's no point in trying to convince me not to do it."

Tate's taken aback. "Talk about the opposite of Ch—" He cuts himself off, staring at me through the corner of his eye before glancing away.

"I know," I agree quietly. Chad was always big on keeping me out of danger—hence why he didn't want me to be involved in the Institute takeover.

"How's he taking the whole mother of two thing?" he asks. "Liam was another reason why I was pushing you so hard to get better and find your way back to us."

"I'm grateful for that," I whisper, shame filling my quiet voice.

"I thought for sure we'd all be in trouble for lying to you again."

"It sucks, yeah, but even I can understand why you did it this time. I must've been a wreck to do what I did. Sometimes lies are necessary," I admit.

"She finally gets it!" he exclaims, throwing his good arm up in the air, before wrapping it around me as I snuggle into his side.

"I'm so glad we're back to normal."

"Me too," he says, kissing the side of my head.

I love you.

'I love you, too … butthead.'

* * *

Lights blind me. Murmurs whisper around me. I stand next to a podium, unable to see the faces of the shadowy figures sitting in front of me, waiting for me to be introduced. The press room is lined with police officers. I don't even know if this will work—standing in front of every news channel in the country, lying to everyone, telling them that Paxton was a loved man, that he was a good person, that he was doing the right thing by being a Defective advocate—all of this in the hopes of flushing out Brookfield? I think it's a long shot, but with Paxton dead, and his funding source gone, it might be easier to get his attention now, unlike the small newspaper article Jenna organised.

The police commissioner completes his briefing about Paxton's death and introduces me. I step up to the podium and open my mouth to talk, but barely a squeak comes out. I look down at my note cards, and tell my hands to stop trembling. Clearing my throat, I try again.

"Two days ago, the Defective community lost its best ally, the world lost a great man, and I lost the man I was going to spend the rest of my life with." I tell myself not to shudder as I say these words. "Paxton James lost his life standing up for those who have been discriminated against, those who have been ridiculed for their shortcomings, and those who are targeted for the mere fact they were born different.

"Like many battles of the past that have been dissolved with time and new generations, this too will be resolved. But even as new generations are formed and revolutionary ideas are adapted, there will always be hate. Discrimination is not genetic, discrimination is taught. We can only hope that with the right attitude and correct information, it will scale down over time, eventually to a point where it won't exist among the majority. Only then will the Defective population truly be safe.

"I urge each and every Defective person out there to continue our fight. Many have resorted to going back to the Institute, which is now what it should have been all along—a sanctuary, a refuge, a home. And while the Institute will always be there for us, it's imperative that we don't let the biases of others drive us back to the place that once caged us. For Paxton's legacy to continue, we need to ensure we fight for what this country needs most—equality for everyone.

"I'd like to take this opportunity to thank you all for coming out today and for respecting my family's need for privacy during this difficult time."

I let out a deep breath of relief, but as I go to walk off stage, the yelling begins. So many voices cut through the crowd, all trying to get me to answer their questions. Some are really personal like "How is Paxton's daughter coping with the loss?" There are political questions like "Who's going to run in Paxton's place for president?" And then there are the ridiculous questions like "Did you have anything to do with Paxton's death?"

I pass the question portion of the press conference over to Paxton's campaign advisor, a man I've only met a few times before. He's here to let everyone know that no one will be running in Paxton's place, but there are high hopes for Tate's campaigning ventures in the future.

I've done my job. I'm going to go to my parents' place, spend some time with William, take Nuka home, and put Paxton behind me. My new life starts today.

* * *

Parenting is friggin' hard … and I've only been doing it for a short time—part time as well, since William is still living with my parents.

He's with me today though, and I'm trying to get the apartment ready for a get-together for Tate. He's coming home from the hospital, so I thought it'd be nice to throw him a barbecue. Shilah insisted he needs rest, not a party, and now I'm wishing I'd listened to him because I didn't realise how little time I'd have to get everything ready. I'm too busy chasing William all over the apartment to prepare. Who knew how dangerous an un-baby-proofed apartment could be to a nine-month-old? He's only crawling, but damn, he's fast. Not to mention I'm also trying to be there for Nuka, who's wandering around the apartment as if she's lost without her daddy here.

I'm not a complete idiot, I knew it'd be hard, but how am I meant to cook food, run after William who's getting into everything, and console a distraught almost seven-year-old?

Is it too immature of me to want my mummy and daddy? Because right now I just want them to hold me while I apologise for ever having been a child and putting them through this.

Giving in to William, I lie down on the floor and let him climb all over me—at least he's no longer exploring drawers and cupboards, pulling himself up on couches, or putting anything in his mouth. Nuka's gone back to her room, not wanting to join in our game.

The buzzing noise from the security intercom startles me. *Crap! Is everyone arriving already?* But when I go over to let them in, security informs me it's Jenna downstairs, and she wants to see me. She was at the press conference a few days ago, but we didn't get a real chance to talk. I tell security to let her up while wondering why she's come. I can only hope it's to tell me Brookfield's been found.

The elevator dings open, and she strolls in, dressed casually, holding a manila folder. I pick William up and pop him on my hip.

"Wow, nice apartment," she says in awe, looking around the expansive living room.

"It better be, for how much it costs," I mutter.

I still haven't come up with a money solution, and I have no job. Kenna offered me my old job back, but the hours aren't exactly suited to a single mother. Plus Ebb's informed me of how good the new volunteers are, so I'd feel guilty going back when it's only a job to me—not my passion. Kenna even offered one of them my old paid position when I said I couldn't return. Jayce is out of a volunteering job, too, because the others are actual nursing students and can help with treating patients, as opposed to only administrative stuff that Jayce was doing.

"So … have they found Brookfield?" I ask Jenna. "Did the press conference work?"

She looks apologetic. "No. Sorry. I probably should've opened with that. At this stage, it looks as if the press conference was a bust. There's been no movement on that front. We're starting to wonder if we'll ever see Brookfield again. He hasn't even checked his bank account. I guess when Paxton died he just knew the payments would stop. We're keeping an eye on it though. I actually came by to drop this off for you," she says, handing me the folder.

I take it with my spare hand but can't open it while holding onto William. "What is it?"

"The officer who was guarding you before the press conference said you mentioned something about being interested in joining the force. That's all the paperwork you need to apply."

My mouth opens a little in shock. "Uh, yeah, I may have mentioned something to him, but it was kind of just for conversational purposes. I couldn't actually join the police force." *Could I?*

"I think you'd be great."

"Not exactly the right kind of hours when I have two kids at home now," I say, looking for an excuse not to follow through on a spur of the moment idea that randomly popped into my head while making conversation with a complete stranger. "I'm guessing Jayce has filled you in on my … situation?"

She nods. "He did, but you know what the good thing about being a public servant is? Really cheap childcare. The government would even subsidise getting Nuka's old nanny back."

"How do you know about her nanny?"

Jenna shrugs. "Paxton's case. General background check. I also looked into how much her wage is and how much the government would fund her job for you. It's all in the folder."

"Why?"

She rolls her eyes. "You mean apart from the fact you're my twin brother's girlfriend and it would make you happy, in turn making him happy?" She pauses for a response I don't give her, so she continues. "How about that I want you on my team? That your investigative abilities, self-defence, and problem-solving skills rival that of some of my co-workers. Not to mention everything we heard on the tape of your kidnapping. The way you kept calm, kept Zac talking, took a beating so Drew could get free. We need someone like you with us."

My eyes focus on William; I'm unable to look Jenna in the eye as I ask what's going through my head. "When you say 'someone like me,' do you mean Defective?"

"No. I don't. What I mean is, we need someone with your kind of drive and determination."

"You barely know me."

"I know enough. You can't stand there and tell me this doesn't interest you. I can see the glimmer in your eyes as you're contemplating it."

"Are there any other Defective officers out there?"

She purses her lips. "No. You'd be the first."

I'm hesitant but excited at the same time. I could be on the right side this time, not trying to arrest innocent people like when I was an agent for the Institute.

No. This is crazy. "I—"

"Weren't you the one who was on television just a few days ago, asking everyone to not back down? To make a difference? Teach the world to rid itself of discrimination? Every person in this country has seen your speech, don't you think being the first-ever Defective police officer would drive your point home?" she cuts me off.

I smirk. "Did you practice that speech? It sounded rehearsed."

"Maybe." She looks at her feet sheepishly. "Doesn't mean it's not true."

"I'll think about it. Thank you."

"That's all I can ask you to do. There's a recruitment test scheduled for next month, and then there's a six-week training camp you'd have to leave for, so I guess there is a bit to consider with the kids, et cetera, but I can assure you it'd be worth it. I know why you were working at the clinic. You want to make a difference in the world, and while this job isn't curing the world of its stupidity, or ending the war you face on a daily basis, it's a step in the right direction. You don't belong in a treatment room, patching up someone who's been wronged, you belong where you have the chance to prevent such an act to begin with." She stares at me for dramatic effect. I'm guessing that part of her spiel was rehearsed as well. When I don't respond, she starts back towards the elevator.

"Did you want to stay? I'm throwing a barbecue for Tate coming home from the hospital. Jayce will be coming later. Jamie too, he's coming with Ebb."

"Thanks, but I should probably get going."

"Drew will be here," I add. This makes her freeze. "Still haven't talked to him?"

She shakes her head, turning to face me. "To be honest, I haven't tried."

I sigh. "Stay. Talk things out with him."

She nods slowly. "I won't know what to say to him."

"Just tell him the truth," I say, taking a step closer to her. She nods again. "So you'll stay?"

"I'll stay. Anything I can do to help? Chop something? Cook something?"

I smile. I'm glad she's staying, and I almost want to kiss her for asking to help. "How about entertaining a nine-month-old so he doesn't destroy the apartment?" I ask, hopeful.

"Done," she says excitedly, holding out her hands for William to climb over to her. He takes to her immediately, and it puts a smile on my face. "I can really see you in him, you know," she says.

"Really? All I see is his father. I knew he always reminded me of him. I just thought I was going crazy."

"I guess that's understandable. Most likely you'd be looking for signs of him, surrounding yourself with familiarity."

I chuckle. "Now you've been hanging around Jayce for too long. He said the same thing once."

I start towards the kitchen, and Jenna follows me with William still in her arms. He's reaching up and twisting her hair in his fingers. I don't have the heart to tell her he's about to pull on it. She'll find out soon enough.

"I'm sorry I ever told Jayce to stay away from you. I realise I haven't apologised for that yet."

I wave her off as I start getting what I need out of the fridge and cupboard. "Your brother was crushing on one of your investigative targets. I get it. I didn't at first, but that was when I thought you were a journalist."

"Well, I'm sorry anyway. And I'm sorry for lying to you, and I'm—"

"Seriously, no need to apologise. The fact you've lied to me only makes you like the rest of my family."

Her eyebrows fly up at this. "Referring to me as family already, huh? You and Jayce must be pretty serious."

I try to hide it, but I can feel myself blush. "We're taking things slow because of the kids."

"I probably shouldn't say this, he'll kill me, but I don't know how taking it slow is really going to work for Jayce. He's head over heels in love with you. Kids or no kids, it doesn't make a difference to him."

"Really? He seemed pretty eager to take a step back."

"Well, he was a little freaked out, but to be fair, so were you by the sound of it. Do you know what he told me after he first met you?"

I shake my head at her.

"He said that there was this inexplicable thing, something inside of him that was yelling at him to ask you out, to get close to you. He'd never had that with anyone before. I was actually shocked when he told me he *did* ask you out. And that he was rejected." She chuckles. "He's usually the one getting asked, not doing the asking. At first he thought it was his hormones just wanting to screw you—"

"Charming," I interrupt.

"That's my brother for you." She smiles. "And even though he found out through me who you were, he still volunteered at the clinic anyway. He told me he couldn't help himself, even though he was under the impression you were taken. He never planned on making a move, he said he just wanted to spend time with you. I think his head nearly exploded when he found out you and Paxton weren't real. He kept his promise to you, though—he always kept everything you ever told him to himself. It drove me nuts, especially because of the case I was building against Paxton."

I bite my lip to prevent myself from grinning like an idiot. "I felt the same way. I knew I shouldn't have gotten involved with him, but I found myself wanting to spend time with him anyway."

"I'm glad he's found you," she says quietly, matching my shyness.

* * *

The sound of sizzling meat makes my mouth water. It's real meat that Dad trekked out to the Eminent Falls farmers markets to buy, not the laboratory-manufactured fake stuff. The charred barbeque smell only fuels my hunger.

"Smells good, Dad," I say, as I walk past him to check on Nuka and William playing in the corner of the rooftop courtyard.

People are scattered around. Jamie and Ebb are talking to Jenna, Jayce is talking to Shilah, and Mum is chasing after Tate, fussing over him and making sure he's comfortable.

Aunt Kenna has brought Vic along, but they're downstairs in the apartment getting drinks. They announced they're officially "dating" upon arrival. Ebb threw up her hands at the news, screaming "Finally!" It made me feel guilty for not picking up on their feelings earlier. I asked them how they could even date when their schedules had them working opposite shifts. My mind briefly flashed to what Jayce and I got up to in the supply closet not all that long ago and shudder to think Aunt Kenna and Vic had done the same. They reassured me, though, when they told me that it's all a recent development.

The clinic has been doing so well with donations and support from the medical industry that they've been able to reopen twenty-four-seven and take on a third doctor so their workload is a lot lighter now. Vic suggested they go for dinner on their first day off together, so they did, and now they're a couple. Simple as that. I couldn't be happier for my aunt. She put her entire life on hold to work for the Resistance and the Institute, to protect Shilah and me. She deserves happiness.

"Got yourself a nice entertaining area up here," Drew says from behind me.

I turn and give him a hug. "Thanks. It's a shame we won't be here for much longer."

"Oh?"

"Can't afford to stay here." You can't miss the disappointment in my tone. I really do love it here. I never thought I'd feel so comfortable in the city.

"I heard about that, and I've had some thoughts on the matter. You know I can afford to buy out your mortgage, right?"

"You what?" I practically shout. Everyone stops to look at us. I wave them off and turn back to Drew. "You what?" I whisper.

He lets out a single laugh. "My parents are rich. I have a trust in my name that's been gaining money since before I was sent to the Institute."

"Since when are your parents rich?"

"Since always."

"But your dad's working as a janitor," I say, confused.

"Because he and Mum feel terrible about turning me over to the Institute when I was a teenager. They said they wanted to make it up to me, that they wanted to spend time getting to know me again. So I told them they could work for me." He grins.

"That's horrible!" I say, laughing. "You make your parents

clean toilets as punishment?"

He shrugs. "Yup. Wouldn't it have made you feel better if I spent the rest of my life scrubbing your toilets?"

"Actually, yeah … that would be pretty good."

"But anyway, as I was saying. I want to buy out your mortgage."

"You want to buy the apartment?"

"Not the apartment, just the half the bank owns. You can pay me a small amount of rent each week to pay me back, or you can live here rent-free and give me half if, or when, you sell the place. We can work something out that works for both of us."

My excitement skyrockets before I realise the gravity of the gesture. "I can't accept that. It's too much."

"You can, and you will," he says, hugging me again. "Besides, real estate is a smart investment, you know. If it makes you feel any better, we'll have contracts and all that legal crap drawn up. So much paperwork will be coming out of your ears. In a few years, if one of us wants out, we can sell the place together or buy the other out. It'll be a partnership—fifty-fifty."

"You don't want to move in or anything, do you? Because I was only your roommate for three months, and that was long enough," I say with a smile.

He shakes his head. "I want to do this for you. I meant it when I said you've saved my life more than once—literally and figuratively. If it weren't for you, I'd still be that arrogant, confused jerk. I'd still be at the Institute as a prisoner, not the director. Actually, if it weren't for you, I would've died alongside Jax in that car accident two years ago. You say this is too big, I say it's not enough."

"Thank you," I whisper as I wrap my arms around him once again.

Jayce clears his throat behind us. He raises an eyebrow at Drew as we pull out of the embrace. "Not trying to steal my woman, are you?" he says playfully.

"Not likely. She's too much drama for me." Drew looks down at me. "You know, you really should try settling down."

I laugh as I push him away from me and wrap my arm around Jayce's waist. "I plan to," I say, smiling up at Jayce. "Speaking of drama"—I nod towards Jenna, who's trying not to stare at us—"go talk to her."

Drew runs his hand through his hair. "Okay, I will," he says, inhaling deeply as if the air can give him courage. He begins to walk over to her, and Ebbodine and Jamie retreat as they see him approach.

Jayce kisses the side of my head. "Everything okay?"

That's such a heavy question, but as I look around at my family, my friends, I realise that everything is more than okay. I'm finally free. I'm finally *home*. I turn to Jayce and kiss him with everything that I have. When I pull away, I look into his bright, shimmering blue eyes and nod. "Everything is perfect."

EPILOGUE
THREE YEARS LATER

Sweating, breathing deep, arms heavy. Actually, my whole body feels heavy under the weight of my protective gear. We've been outside this abandoned warehouse for what feels like hours, although it's probably only been twenty minutes. I want so badly to get in there and get this over with.

"Okay, team, hold your positions," the voice in my earpiece says. I can't help letting out an exasperated groan.

They've brought out everyone for this. We have two special response teams on site, all of us with one goal—*Take Brookfield out.* I'm on the east side of the building with Jenna, and the rest of our team's spread out over the area. The only other officers we can see are across from us, taking cover behind the next warehouse.

"Psst," Jenna says beside me. I tilt my head in her direction. "Look at the newbie over there sweating bullets." She laughs, nodding towards a new recruit. He looks as if he's about to throw up.

"Hey, no teasing. I'm sure you didn't look much better on your first raid," I whisper.

"You didn't look like that," she says to me.

"It helps that my first raid was a Brookfield residence. It was personal for me. Still is."

"We'll get him today," Jenna assures me.

"You've been saying that for the last three years, Sergeant."

She rolls her eyes at me.

"Three years, Jenna. We've been playing this cat-and-mouse game for three years. I'm ready for it to be over. It needs to be over."

"It will be."

"Okay, team, move in," the voice in our earpieces instructs.

"Finally," I say, relieved but with a hint of excitement.

"After you." Jenna nudges me.

I go first, kicking open the rusting door. Brookfield has made a habit of finding abandoned places like this to hole up in. Thus far, every time we've managed to track him down, it's been right after he's fled.

We charge in, guns poised, swiftly moving from one

partitioned off area to another, gracefully moving in between old furniture, storage crates full of God knows what, and around random obstacles like brooms, food cans, and broken glass. We make our way through one end of the warehouse to the other, coming up trumps.

"There's nothing here," I say, my shoulders slumping in disappointment even though I was kind of expecting it. "I friggin' knew we were too late. We're always too late."

Jenna comes up beside me and sighs. "I'm sorry, Allira."

"Yeah, yeah, heard it all before."

"How about you go home?"

"No thanks, boss. I'd rather help with the sweep here. See what we can find."

"The rest of the team can handle that. You need rest. You haven't rested since you joined the force. You've been busy busting your ass on cases and doing the Defective advocate-slash-public figure thing. You need a break. Everyone deserves a break now and then."

"But—"

"No buts. That's an order. Go home, relax, and spend some time with those beautiful kids and that stupid brother of mine." She smiles. "Actually, I'm ordering you to take the annual leave you've been building up. Take the next two weeks off, and come back refreshed."

"But—"

"Stop butting me! Go, now!"

I grimace at her.

"I'll let you know if we find anything," she says, forcing me out of the warehouse.

* * *

It's been hard not being in contact with HQ every day, but after the first few days, I think Jenna ordered Jayce to take my work tablet away from me. I haven't seen it for almost two weeks.

It's funny that the small piece of technology I was clueless about when I started on the force has become a necessity to me. I feel naked without it. It's probably with my anniversary present that I know Jayce has bought but is hiding from me. He has to give me my tablet back today, though, I'm officially back on duty and on call.

"Babe?" Jayce calls out from the entryway.

"In the kitchen. And don't be starting that war with me again!" I yell back at him.

"What war?" he asks innocently, coming up behind me and kissing me on the cheek.

"The cutesy nickname war. Nice try sneaking it in there. How was the shooting range with Drew?"

"Fun as always. Where are the kids?"

"Nuka's at a friend's house, and William's in his room," I reply, going back to chopping tomatoes.

"I guess I better start getting ready for the family barbecue, hey, muffin?" he says elbowing me.

"Yes, you should. And no pet names."

"Why not?" he asks persistently.

"I don't do nicknames. You should know that after being with me for three years. Why do you so badly want to give me a sickly, demeaning nickname anyway?"

"It's not demeaning, bae," he says. The smile drops from his face when I turn and scowl at him. He stands closer to me, whispering in my ear. "Fine then, what about killa, because you're so damn vicious?"

I sink into him. "No."

"You're no fun. Maybe I should call you buzzkill."

"Definitely no."

He lets go of me and turns to walk away as I go back to making a salad. I think he's left when I hear him right behind me.

"What about wifey?"

I drop the knife on the counter, barely missing cutting my finger open. "W-what?" I stutter, slowly turning to see him on one knee, in our kitchen.

He reaches for my hand and holds it in both of his. "I did plan a big speech, you know, with lots of cutesy pet names thrown in there, but seeing as you don't like that, I'll cut to the chase. Will you ma—"

"Yes." I accidently cut him off, but it's too hard not to.

He jumps up off his knee and takes me in a big hug, only pulling back to kiss me. This would be totally romantic, too, if it weren't for the fact that I get a whiff of his aftershave when his lips touch mine, sending my stomach into a frenzy—and not the good kind. I barely make it to the sink before I'm vomiting for the millionth time today.

"Still vomiting? It's been a few days now, maybe you should go see your aunt. Unless it's the idea of marrying me that's making you sick?" he jokes, rubbing my back as I continue to vomit.

"Maybe the baby doesn't want us to get married," I counter, my head still in the sink. Not exactly the best way to break it to him, but it's done now.

His hand immediately stops rubbing my back. "Baby?"

"Are you calling me another stupid nickname, or are you actually asking if that's what I said?" I turn back around to face him, my stomach empty once again.

"Baby?" he repeats himself. His eyes are hopeful, not at all fearful like they were when he found out about Nuka and William.

"I just found out. You're going to be a daddy—a real one." I cringe as soon as the words leave my mouth, realising how it sounds.

His shoulders slouch as he tilts his head to the side disappointedly. "You know I hate it when you say stuff like that. Nuka and William are my children, just as much as that baby in there is," he points to my stomach.

"I know. I'm sorry." Jayce is an excellent father. He treats Nuka and William as if they were his own, and William even calls him Daddy. "I didn't mean it that way. I know how you feel about the kids—I feel the same way about Nuka as I do about William, and I wouldn't trade them in for the world. But this"—I grab his hand and put it on my belly—"is made of *us*."

He wraps his arms around me and buries his face in my hair. He kisses my neck, making his way to my lips before he remembers what I was just doing.

"Clean your teeth, then I'll kiss you," he says. "You know I love you, but eww, vomit breath."

"It's like we're married already," I mutter, walking towards the bathroom.

Jayce takes over from me in the kitchen as I go clean my teeth. When I come back out, I see a ring box sitting on the kitchen bench.

"Is this … is …" I can't find words.

Jayce puts the salad in the fridge and comes over to me, smirking. He grabs the box and lifts the lid, slowly—painfully slowly. The nerves in my gut flutter ...or is that nausea again?

I can't be sure.

"I had this designed for you," he says, taking out the ring. It's an oval lab-diamond, not overpoweringly big, but still bigger than what I know we can afford. Surrounding the diamond are smaller diamonds, except for two near the top of the oval. One is an opal, and the other is a peridot. "Nuka's and William's birthstones. I guess we will be adding another stone in nine months."

"I love it," I say, hesitating a fraction of a second. Tears threaten to fill my eyes at how beautiful it is.

"You sound like you're unsure of that." He sounds deflated.

"I really do love it ... but ... how much did it cost? We're not exactly rolling in money right now. I know it'll be different when you get a job, but things are kind of tight at the moment."

"Today must be the day for good news," he says, his smile back on his face. "I've been recruited. I start the minute I finish my doctorate. Pretty decent pay, Monday to Friday, health benefits—everything."

I throw my arms around him.

"Yeah, then you had to go and show me up with this," he says, rubbing my belly again.

"Sorry. How about we only tell your news today?"

"And the engagement," he says, ceremoniously sliding the ring on my finger and then placing his hands back on my stomach.

"Okay. We'll keep the baby a secret. Although, Tate's going to know the minute he sees you. I can't believe after all this time you still can't block him out." I smirk at him. "I'll have to bribe him to keep his mouth shut. But you know, if you don't stop touching my belly, everyone's going to figure it out."

"Sorry," he says, moving his hands to my hips. "I'll try to stop."

He leans in and kisses me with the same intense need he's always had for me. We don't allow ourselves to kiss like this often because we know what it always leads to, and it's hard to control ourselves once we start.

"We don't have time," I say, pulling away breathless and frustrated.

"Sure we do," he says, lifting me up onto the kitchen bench.

As if on cue, security buzzes from downstairs, and William comes running out of his room yelling, "They're here!"

I let out a laugh as Jayce groans, putting his forehead on my shoulder. "Damn it," he complains.

"I told you we didn't have time," I say, pulling myself off the kitchen counter.

We try to have these family meet-ups once a month. It's usually always here because we have the biggest place. With everyone being so busy, it's really the only time we can get everyone in a room together.

We decide to wait until everyone has arrived to make our announcement. We're only waiting on Ebb, Jamie, and

Annalynne, their three-month-old.

"Any word from Jamie?" I ask Jayce, who's sitting in the living room with his parents, Jenna, and Drew. They're still together. They live together, even though he isn't there during the week. He still stays at the Institute Monday to Friday and comes home on weekends. They aren't married and have no future plans to wed—as far as I know anyway. Jenna's always telling me how she doesn't understand the need to get married.

I agree with her in some ways. It really is just a piece of paper to me. Jayce and I have been committed for the last three years. I don't need to make it official to know I belong to him and him to me. But I *want* to stand in front of our families and friends, and promise myself to our little family, forever.

"Yeah, I called him earlier. Apparently they were fighting again. And then they had to make up—twice," Jayce replies with a roll of his eyes.

We were right when we concluded that Jamie and Ebb were perfect for each other because they're so much alike. The only problem with two high-spirited, independent people getting married? They always have something to fight about … and then to make up for. All. The. Time. It can get exhausting, not to mention awkward. Watching them fight is like watching foreplay. Hopefully it'll all be out of their system by the time they arrive today. I do not want to walk in on them *again*.

They were reluctant at first to realise what they had. They dated for about two months before their first split, Ebbodine saying she was too young for such a serious relationship. And yet at every family barbecue for the next few months, Ebb and

Jamie were drawn back to each other once again. Ebb finally realised her true feelings when Jamie turned up one month with a date. *That* was an eventful barbecue.

She told me when they got engaged that she finally understood how I felt when Chad died. She couldn't imagine having to live life without Jamie. I almost fell off my chair when she admitted she was wrong. I only wish I could've recorded it some way, had proof of the once in a lifetime event occurring.

"They'll be here soon," Jayce assures, putting his arm around my waist.

"I'm going to go get a beer, you guys want anything?" Jayce's dad, Carey, asks.

I love Jayce's parents. I know it's usual for people to dislike their in-laws, but they are genuinely the nicest and sweetest people. They welcomed Ebb, Drew, and me with open arms. Surely it would've been a shock to have all three of their "normal" children bring home a Defective partner all within a few weeks of each other, but they handled it with grace, and from what I could sense, even a little pride; they raised their kids right. They even treat Nuka and William as if they were their own grandkids.

Luckily, I have work as an excuse to not drink today, keeping our little secret a secret. I look at Jenna. "I don't think the sergeant over here would be too happy if I were to drink while I was on call."

"Good move, Rook," Jenna says.

"How do I *still* have that nickname?"

"You'll always be Rookie to me," she replies with a wry smile.

"I'll grab a beer, Dad," Jayce says. Just as they get up to go to the kitchen where Tate and Shilah are talking to Mum and Dad, Ebb and Jamie arrive.

"Geez, what was so important that Jayce had to call us three times to hurry up?" Ebb exclaims, getting everyone's attention. "Did he finally pop the question or something?"

My eyes go wide as I instinctively hide my hand behind my back.

"Oh my God, he actually did it?" she screams.

I look over at Jayce. "Aren't you glad we decided to wait for them to turn up to announce it?"

Suddenly, I'm being hugged from every direction, from everyone, and so is Jayce. Shilah's the last to get to me.

"Getting married, hey?"

"Yup. Going backwards. Meet, raise kids, then get married." I shrug. "But when have I ever done anything conventionally?"

"I'm so happy for you," he says, leaning in and kissing my cheek. With his contact it's impossible to not get a vision. His ability is still growing and evolving, long after the rest of ours have plateaued.

Jayce stands over me as I hold our baby girl in my arms. He looks down at his daughter with a look of love, adoration, and astonishment. Yup, she has him wrapped around her finger and is only minutes old. He touches her cheek with his forefinger. "Illyana," he whispers.

"I know that look," Tate says from beside us. "You just had a vision. It's the same stupid look Shilah has all the time. So out with it—what did you see to make you all gushy like that?" He's grinning, devil-like.

I smile. "I'm keeping this one." It's all I have to say. Tate knows I'm pregnant thanks to Jayce and his damn open mind. *Thank you for keeping it a secret.* He smiles and nods at me in return.

After flashing the ring around, countless taunts over how hard it will be at work being the sergeant's sister-in-law, and getting bombarded with wedding detail questions—all of which have the same answer of "I don't know, he only asked me two hours ago!"—I sneak Jayce away to our bedroom to tell him what I saw.

"Want to know what your daughter's name will be?"

"Daughter?" He stumbles back, sitting on the edge of the bed, clearly overwhelmed. "I guess there wasn't any chance of it being a surprise with you and your brother around."

My mouth opens in shock. "I'm sorry! Did you not want to know the sex?"

"To be honest, I'd only just visualised the baby part of it—not the sex or the name, what they … sorry, she, will look like …" He pauses. "A girl?" He smiles, looking up at me.

"I can keep her name a secret if you like. Then you'll have a surprise when she's here."

"There's only one name I've ever considered if I was to have

DEFECTIVE

a girl. It was my grandmother's name. Illyana."

My smile says it all.

"Really? That's the name?" He matches my smile, pulling me towards the bed. I stand between his legs as he hugs me, putting his head on my stomach. He turns his head to kiss my belly and whispers, the sound coming out just like it did in my vision, "Illyana."

A continuous buzzing noise starts up from somewhere. I follow it to Jayce's bedside table, tilting my head towards the noise.

"Ah. I'll get that," Jayce says, sinking onto the floor and reaching under the bed. He pulls duct tape from underneath it, attached to my work tablet.

"You taped it to the bottom of the bed?" I exclaim.

He shrugs. "Jenna told me to confiscate it."

I narrow my eyes. "I knew she did that," I mumble.

 Grabbing the tablet from Jayce, I rush out into the living room. I try to download the data that tells us about the job, but Jenna is already on the phone with HQ. I look between her and my tablet which is still trying to load the data. It seems to be taking forever. Technology is slowly advancing back to what it was before the pandemic broke out. Our tablets work off satellites which orbit the planet, same as our trackers.

Before the pandemic, the country had access to up to six of our own satellites, plus the satellites of ally countries. Being cut off from the rest of the world means that currently we have access to two satellites which is only enough for government officials and employees—such as cops—to have access. We can send wireless messages, have phone conversations, and input and download any type of data into our tablets. It took a long time for me to get used to such a device, having grown up on the run without so much as a TV.

Jenna stares at me wide-eyed, while nodding to whoever's on the phone. When she gets off the phone, the whole room is silent.

"Well?" I ask. "Have we been called in?"

She lets out a deep breath. "We've been more than called in. Allira, it's really him this time. They've found Brookfield."

"Are they sure?" I try not to scoff, I really want to believe her, but it's hard to when I've heard this so many times.

She nods. "Turns out he's been living under the pseudonym Branson Tyler. Those warehouse raids? He set them all up. He's been playing us. We've found his permanent residence. We're raiding it, like right now."

"Now?"

"Yup. You coming, Rook?"

I turn to Jayce and kiss him quickly before turning away to rush out the door with Jenna when he pulls me back. "Be careful out there. Take good care of her," he whispers, brushing his hand against my stomach.

"I won't let anything hurt her," I reassure him.

* * *

"Are you ready for this?" Jenna asks. We're in our tactical response van, on our way to our target's location.

I raise my eyebrow at her. "Of course, I'm ready. I'm always ready."

"I just figured you might be a little rusty after your vacation," she says, smiling.

"This is the whole reason I joined the force. A few weeks off isn't going to change me."

She gives me a stern look.

"Okay, not the whole reason I joined, but it was one of the main ones. I've been waiting for this moment for five years—ever since he escaped the Institute."

"I know, I know," she says, giving in.

How Brookfield has eluded us for this long is beyond me. He's one resourceful man.

It doesn't take us long to reach his residence, and a wave of nausea hits me as the van rolls to a stop.

"Come on, baby, not now," I mutter to Illyana, taking a few deep breaths.

"Are you sure you're okay?" Jenna asks, concerned. "You're looking a little pale."

"I'm fine," I lie.

"Allira, I know this means a lot to you, but you're not looking too well. You look like that newbie from a few weeks ago. Get it together or I'll have to pull you out. I'm running this op, I don't need any screw-ups."

"I can do this," I say sternly. I want so much to tell her it's because I'm pregnant, not nervous. I'm just worried if I tell her about the baby, she'll pull me out anyway—not as my sergeant, but as my soon-to-be sister and Illyana's aunt.

"Okay. Let's go." She opens the van door and we move swiftly towards the house … more like a demountable trailer, really. There are three small steps leading to a narrow porch with weeds and vines growing over the banister and lattice work that surrounds the small patio. This will be our entry point.

We're all armed and in head-to-toe black protective gear which is making me hot. I'm sweating, and it's not from the nerves. We spread out and position ourselves strategically around the perimeter and then wait for Jenna's orders to go in. Nothing happens, and it's quiet for quite a few minutes, the radio silence making me nervous.

After a few more minutes, my pulse is skyrocketing, and my heart is frantically trying to beat out of my chest. I love this part of the job. I feel alive; I feel wired. But today, it's just making me feel off. Something's not right. Maybe I can sense that this is really it this time. He's in there, I just know it. I feel it in my bones.

Jenna's voice finally comes over the earpiece. "Our negotiator has been in contact with him. He has no hostages and is willing to cooperate." *That's good news.* "On one condition," she continues. *That's not good news.* "He wants to talk to Daniels."

I press my finger to my ear, pushing the tiny button on my earpiece to talk. "He knows I'm here?"

"He does, somehow. Stay where you are, I'm coming to you." She approaches me moments later with a fellow officer. "You don't have to go in. We can still treat this as a hostile situation and ambush him."

"And risk other lives when he's agreed to come out peacefully?" I shake my head. "I can go in."

"He might not be planning to come out of this alive," Officer Cooper says. "He says he'll cooperate, but you've been in situations like this before. He could be planning ..."

"Suicide by cop," I realise. "Okay, if that's the case, send me in unarmed so I can contain him instead."

Jenna scoffs. "That is the most absurd idea you've ever had, Rook. You're going in armed, and you're going in prepared to shoot him if he tries anything."

"Fine, so it's agreed—I'm going in."

Jenna grunts at me in frustration. It's not the first time I've manipulated the sergeant's words to get what I want. It pisses her off, but I think she's also a little proud. I'm her protégé; she's trained me well.

"If we're going to do this, we're going to do it right. You'll have us stationed right outside. You'll open your earpiece so we'll be receiving you the whole time. You *will* be armed, and you *will* have your gun in hand at all times. If he makes one move to harm you, you shoot him. Got it?"

"I've got it." I nod.

"Jayce is going to kill me," she mutters.

"I'll be fine, I promise. He won't even have to know."

"A few hours into your engagement and already planning to lie to him?" she says lightly.

"Whoa, you're engaged, Daniels?" Officer Cooper interjects. "Congrats."

"Thanks. And I'm not lying to him. You know how he can worry, Jenn—Sergeant." I look between Jenna and Officer Cooper. I don't know what to call her when we're working but talking about our family. It's an odd feeling I've never gotten used to, especially around co-workers. "It's just best if work stays at work."

"Uh … Umm … I'm going to go fill the others in on the plan," Cooper says, backing away from our now personal conversation.

"I can do this, Jenna. We both know I can do this. I have a history with him, and I know how he thinks. If any of us is going to be able to get him to come out voluntarily, you know it's going to be me."

She nods in agreement. "Let's just do this."

Once we're all ready and in position, I stand by his front door, gun in hand, preparing myself to go in. I let out three quick breaths before calling out to him.

"It's me, Allira."

"Ah, come in, Miss Daniels." His voice is calm. That worries me.

Opening the door, I check for anything out of the normal—like rigged wires or explosives—in the doorway. It's all clear. Making my way through the entrance to the small dwelling, I don't need to search far to find him. He's sitting in a recliner in the corner of what I guess is his living room. He's nursing a shotgun, but his hands aren't near the trigger. He's looking old, older than I remember. Then again, it has been five years since I last saw him.

I aim my gun at him. "You know, this will go a lot smoother if you put the gun on the ground and slide it over to me," I say casually to let the others know he's armed.

He smiles. "Who said I'm going to make this smooth for you?"

"It's words like those that will cause the officers outside to want to come inside. That won't end well for you." I want to mentally high-five myself for sounding calmer than I actually am. The adrenaline is surging.

Now he laughs. "This isn't going to end well for me no matter how this goes. You know that, right?"

I'm silent. This *is* a planned suicide, and he wants me to be the one to kill him. "You know, we didn't expect you to stay hidden so long. I have to give you credit where it's due," I say, trying to turn the conversation to something positive. "We've all had bets on how long it'd take for you to come out of hiding once your funding source died, and I have to tell you, you've surprised me."

He half-smiles. "And how long did you think I would last?"

"A month."

He scoffs. "You underestimated me. I'm sure you won't do that again, will you, Miss Daniels?"

"Of course not," I say, still pointing my gun at him.

"I've been following your career, as you could imagine. What with your very public rallies and campaigns, your charity work, school visits, your speeches on equality. One would think you were *trying* to make yourself a target." He raises an eyebrow at me. "I was very tempted, you know. Three years ago, that speech you made. It was almost too good to resist. You're the girl who got away, after all."

"Aww, you make it sound so romantic." The bile threatens to creep up my throat.

"Both you and Jacobs are lucky to be alive. You know that, right? And isn't he like your brother now? That's a tad bit weird, isn't it?"

I hear Jenna in my ear. "*Bastard.*"

"Technically no, he's not my brother. But he is dating my future sister-in-law."

We've laughed numerous times over the fact that if Jayce and I were to marry, which we now are, and Jenna and Drew were to marry, that Drew and I would become brother and sister in-laws. But hearing it from Brookfield's mouth somehow makes it less funny.

"Ah yes, Sergeant Harrison. She was on my tail long before you were."

It's creepy how much about our lives he knows. It's starting to scare me. This needs to end, now. Any reservations I had about killing the man in front of me are gone. I just need to bide my time until it's justifiable homicide.

Sweat is dripping off my brow but my hands remain steady on my gun.

"How did you last so long?" I ask him. "Why didn't you come back after Paxton died? There wouldn't have been anyone to dispute your claims then. No non-Defectives anyway."

"Do you understand the charges I would've been tried for? Kidnapping, torture, attempted murder. I wasn't going to face that. I used the money Paxton gave me to live, to start a new life. And I'm not going to sit by and let you bully me again, like you did when you took everything away from me. I'm giving you the chance to do what you should've done five years ago."

"I'm not here to kill you. I'm not like you," I say, while in my head I beg him to reach for his gun.

He shakes his head. "And I thought you were smart. You do remember what happened the last time you let me get away, right? You think your co-workers out there will be quick enough to save you?"

My eyes widen as he goes for his gun. This is the moment. He's giving me what I want. He's giving me no choice. A simple moment of hesitation finds me hearing a gunshot going off, but the strangest thing follows. The bullet from his gun moves towards me at an impossibly slow speed. It's as if time has stopped, but not quite. The bullet flies by my head as I easily step aside to avoid it. It pierces the wall behind me.

I race towards Brookfield as fast as I can, his face not even registering that I've moved. *What is going on?* Without thinking it through, I holster my gun and go for his. When my hand touches his, he quickly snaps his head around and sees me, surprised I'm suddenly by his side.

"How did you …" He stops himself when he realises I've got a hold of his gun. He goes to grab it back and we struggle for it.

The intensity in which he fights me grows as the seconds tick by. My breathing becomes stilted. If I let him overpower me, I'm dead.

He lets go of the gun, pushing me, and sending me flying backwards into a glass coffee table that shatters under my weight. He reaches behind him for a second gun, but I'm quicker. I ignore the stinging pain in my arm and back, grab my own gun back out of its holster, and give him what we both want. I shoot him dead.

It's over.

That can't be it, right? Everything happened so fast, so quickly. *It's really over?* My gun is still poised, pointing at his lifeless body slumped in the chair. My head falls back, glass crunching underneath it as I rest it on the floor. Trying to catch my breath, I stare up at the roof, still trying to process what just happened. It's not the first time I've taken a life, but it is the first time I haven't felt guilty.

My team rushes in, Jenna and Officer Cooper helping me off the ground while the others ensure Brookfield is permanently down.

"You're hurt," Jenna says, looking at my arm.

Still breathing deep and heavy from adrenaline, I look down to find a shard of glass from the table sticking out of my arm. "Shit, hey."

Jenna's on her handheld radio, asking for an ambulance. I'm looking at the blood oozing out, trying to assess how to get the glass out.

"Touch that arm and I will kill you," Jenna calls out to me. I roll my eyes at her. "We're going to get you to the hospital, and then you can explain exactly what happened in here."

"What do you mean? Couldn't you hear everything?"

"Up until the gunshots. We rushed in as soon as we heard them, but I don't understand how you ended up over here." She points to the glassy mess on the ground. "Or how you avoided being shot when he was aiming directly at you." She points to the hole in the wall on the other side. She leans in and quietly asks, "Were you borrowing an ability of sorts?"

I shake my head. "If I was, it was unintentional. No one here is Defective, so I wouldn't know who or how to borrow their ability. I've borrowed abilities in the past without realising though, so it's possible if someone Defective is nearby. A neighbour or something."

"We'll talk about this later. We need to get you to the hospital. I'll call Jayce when we get there."

Ah, crap.

* * *

I'm sitting in triage at the hospital as the doctor assesses the glass in my arm. The skin is starting to feel really tight around the glass, and I don't think that's a good thing. Is it swelling? Why haven't they just taken the glass out yet?

Before I know it, Jayce is running into my room looking terrified. He's followed by Drew, Shilah, Tate, Mum, and Dad. Jenna tries to sneak in behind them.

"What are you all doing here? Where are the kids? Didn't Jenna tell you I'm fine?"

"The kids are with my parents," Jayce answers. "I was so worried." He's approaching me with caution. I can tell he wants to touch me but is scared I'll break.

I grunt. "I'm fine. They're just going to take the glass out and stitch me up. Easy. Even I could do it with my six months of nursing school," I joke.

The doctor who has been silent for a while now looks at me. "We might have to get a CT on this. I'm worried the glass is in too deep, and we might have tendon damage."

"For Pete's sake. It's fine. Just take it out," I say exasperatedly.

"I'd feel much more comfortable if we sent you for a CT."

Jayce and I give each other a look. "I can't go for a CT," I say, looking around the room before looking down at my hands. "I'm pregnant."

"You're what?" Jenna yells.

Yeah, she's reacting how I thought she would after what I did today. I didn't really realise just how close I came to dying until I got to the hospital. That bullet should've hit me.

"Look, I just want to get this thing out of my arm and go home to my kids, okay? And Jenna, don't give me that pissed-off look. I did my job today, I did it well, and we got the bad guy in the end. I didn't tell you I was pregnant because I knew you'd act like this and wouldn't have let me go in."

"You went in by yourself?" Jayce asks me while glaring at Jenna. "You allowed her to do that?" he scolds her.

I use my good arm to raise my hand and rub it over my face. "It was my decision to go in by myself. You can't blame Jenna for what I did. This is my job, you have always supported it. Why is it different now that I'm pregnant?" I let out a sigh. "You know what? Now is not the time for this conversation."

Drew steps forward. "Where's Brookfield now?"

"He's dead," I say flatly.

"You did it?" His eyes light up. Out of everyone, he's the only person who understands. We're both truly free now. That whole life is behind us.

"She almost got herself killed in the process," Jenna says.

Drew and I simultaneously roll our eyes at her and then laugh. Jenna and Jayce are not amused.

The doctor finally comes to my rescue when he says, "There are scans that are safe to have whilst pregnant. I really must insist we get it done as soon as possible. I'm really sorry, but all of you are going to have to wait in the waiting room. Even you, Sergeant."

They all reluctantly leave after the doctor ushers them out. I look up at him through my lashes. "Thank you."

"I kind of sensed you didn't want to get into all of that here," he says.

I half-smile. "You're right about that. So I'll be getting that scan now?"

"I just said that to get everyone out of the room. Looking at this more carefully, I think you're right. I'll just go ahead and stitch you up."

I let out a sigh of relief. "Thank you."

He gets everything he needs prepared, gives me a local anaesthetic, and begins to pull the glass out. Weirdest. Sensation. Ever. When it's out, he begins the stitches, but he has to stop when he's about halfway through.

"What the?" he says.

I look down at my arm and can't believe the sight. My arm is healing exceedingly fast. The stitches he just put in are no longer even needed. He cuts them out and examines my arm.

You can't even tell where the glass was.

"Why didn't you just tell us your ability is to heal?" the doctor asks, confused.

"Because it's not. Unless … is there another Defective person being treated nearby or who works here? My ability is to borrow. Maybe I'm doing that?"

"I can check, but as far as I'm aware, there are no other Defectives here."

Thinking about it, none of it makes sense. Somehow time slowed down at Brookfield's place, and now my skin is healing itself, all without being close to someone who's Defective.

Dread and realisation course through me.

"Could you please send my family back in? Uh … actually, just my fiancé and sergeant."

The doctor puts down his equipment and goes out to get Jenna and Jayce. When they appear, I don't know what to say— especially when they look down at my arm with complete and utter confusion across their faces.

"I know why today was so confusing for you," I say to Jenna. "And I have some news about the baby." Jayce's eyes go wide in fear and panic. "Don't worry, she's fine, she's safe." He lets out the breath he was clearly holding in. I look at them both, contemplating how to approach this. "Today when Brookfield shot at me—"

"He shot at you?" Jayce exclaims.

"Bigger issues here, Jayce," I say before continuing. "As soon as the gun went off, it was as if time slowed right down—either that or I started moving at super-speed. Anyway, I thought that maybe someone nearby was Defective, but just now when the doctor pulled the glass out of my arm ..." I reach over and grab the doctor's scissors off the tray.

"What the hell are you doing?" Jenna asks frantically.

"Just watch." I use the blade and slice my forearm, only a little, but it still friggin' hurts. It begins to heal immediately. Their shocked faces says it all.

"Two abilities?" Jayce asks.

I nod. "Illyana will definitely take after her mummy."

ABOUT THE AUTHOR

As a writer, I lead an extremely exciting life. When I'm not base jumping, playing my guitar and singing for a sold-out crowd, or having tea with the queen ... Okay, all of these things are lies.

The truth is, I live on the Gold Coast in Queensland, Australia, with my husband and son and you'll most likely find me with my laptop on my lap and a coffee in my hand.

www.kaylahowarth.com

OTHER WORKS BY KAYLA HOWARTH

RESISTANCE

(Book 2 of The Institute Series)

DEFECTIVE

(Book 3 of The Institute Series)

THROUGH HIS EYES: An Institute Novella

(Book 4 of The Institute Series) EBOOK

EXCLUSIVE

THE LITMUS SERIES

(An Institute Spin off)

LOSING NUKA—Available Now

PROTECTING WILLIAM—Available Now

SAVING ILLYANA—Coming 2017

Printed in Great Britain
by Amazon